# LOST AND FOUND

TWIST OF FATE #1

LUCY LENNOX

SLOANE KENNEDY

SKLL BOOKS LLC

ISBN-13:

978-1548557362

ISBN-10:

1548557366

# CONTENTS

# LOST AND FOUND

Lucy Lennox

Sloane Kennedy

# TRADEMARK ACKNOWLEDGEMENTS

The authors acknowledge the trademarked status and trademark owners of the following trademarks mentioned in this work of fiction:

Rugrats
Iphone
Ranger Rick
The Sound of Music
Who Let the Dogs Out
Let it Go
Do you want to build a snowman
Frozen
Cinderella
Sketchers
Big Brothers Big Sisters
Legos
Legoland
Godzilla
Ickis
Aahh Real Monsters

Barney
Transformers
Moon Pie
Chips Ahoy
Band Aid
Flight for Life

# ACKNOWLEDGMENTS

We would like to thank our beta readers, Claudia, Courtney, Karie, Kylee, Leslie and Lori, for giving us quick, valuable feedback on our first collaboration project. You have no idea how much we appreciate your support.

# CHAPTER 1

## XANDER

"No," I said coldly just as the man in front of me smiled wide and stepped forward, clearly intent on embracing me.

"Xander?" he said softly, his voice a mix of confusion and hurt. I ignored him as the sharp pain in my belly threatened to send me to my knees.

*Bennett Fucking Crawford.*

"Xander?" Jake said in surprise.

"No," I simply said again and then I started to walk away, not caring that what I was doing was beyond unprofessional. My only thought was to get the hell out of there. My dog, Bear, quickly came running after me, easily ditching the kids who'd been lavishing him with the belly rubs he assumed were his due.

*Benny, please, I need you...*

I shook my head in the hopes of casting that voice aside.

*My* voice.

My scared, broken, fourteen-year-old voice.

Fire crawled up my spine as I remembered how Bennett had looked at me that night... right before he'd turned his back on me. It had been the last night I'd seen him.

"You okay?" Jake asked with a confused look on his face.

I should have been relieved at the sound of my good friend's concern, but it just made me want to stride off into the woods.

Alone.

I did *alone* well. I knew *alone*. *Alone* never let me the fuck down.

"I'm fine," I snapped. He was smart enough not to touch me, but his expression drew into a frown. Gary, the head of the wilderness expedition company I worked for, strode over to us from across the trailhead parking lot. Both he and Jake looked at me like I'd grown a second head.

"What's going on?" Gary asked.

I couldn't help but glance back at the bus where over a dozen kids were mingling, along with several adults. But my eyes automatically sought out just one of those people. Dark hair, warm brown eyes, lean body…

Fuck.

"I know one of them," I motioned with my head towards the bus. "We grew up together."

Both men looked that way.

"Which one?" Gary asked. "Aiden—"

"No," I interjected. "Bennett Crawford."

"Bennett," Jake said in surprise. "*The* Bennett?"

I nodded. I'd never told Jake everything about Bennett and me, but he knew enough. "Fuck," he whispered.

"What? What am I missing?" Gary asked.

"Look, I'm sorry," I said. "I can't do this."

"Xander, they're here. They've paid… the kids are looking forward to this trip," Gary began. He shook his head. "Come on, man, I'm counting on you."

Guilt went through me as I studied Gary's face. Yeah, he was technically my boss, but I worked freelance as a wilderness guide and was in high demand. I didn't need the money from this group of inner-city kids, and I could easily find another company to guide for. But I also wasn't the type of guy who just left people in the lurch. I looked back at the kids who were completely unaware of what was happening as they talked excitedly amongst themselves and went through their gear.

"I'll take the Five Lake Loop," Jake offered. My eyes snapped to his and he sent me a smile. I'd been friends with Jake for several years, ever since we'd met on an adventure expedition to Patagonia. When he'd moved to Haven, Colorado a year ago, I'd suggested Gary hire him as a guide. While I appreciated what he was trying to do, I knew it would never work. There was a reason I'd been selected to guide the group of older kids. I just hadn't realized who the chaperones would be for those kids until I'd seen the names on the roster just moments before the group had gotten off the bus.

"Jake, you don't know the Five Lake Loop and you're not equipped to teach rock climbing or high-water river crossings yet," Gary said kindly, voicing my own concerns. "Xander—"

"I'll do it," I murmured, cutting him off. As much as I wanted to just take off and disappear for a few days, I couldn't let Gary down... or the kids I automatically dropped my fingers to search out Bear's head. The Newfoundland mix had become my shadow in the three years since I'd found him abandoned as a puppy in one of the campgrounds at the end of the summer camping season. I'd felt an immediate kinship with the dog as I'd watched him sitting among the remnants of a deserted campsite, staring in the direction of the narrow dirt road leading out of the campground.

Waiting for his loved ones to come find him, no doubt.

I'd known that feeling.

All too well.

I turned and began striding back towards the group of kids who were starting to look a little bored. My hiking boots made crunching sounds on the sparse pebbles scattered across the unpaved lot. The late afternoon sun slanted through several tall pine trees just beyond the bus, and shadows danced along the overgrown tufts of grass at the edges of the clearing where the kids stood talking.

I felt, rather than saw, Bennett's eyes on me as I approached, but I ignored him and went to the tall, arrogant-looking man standing next to him. "I'm Xander Reed; I'll be your guide. We'll be leaving in fifteen minutes, so if any of the kids need to make use of the facilities one last time," I motioned to the building opposite the bus, "they should do it now."

The man with Bennett was a good-looking guy who should have had all my cylinders firing. He had a rangy, muscular body and sharp blue eyes. His chestnut hair was thick and his little bit of beard scruff was usually my kind of thing. But I felt nothing. Well, not true… I felt *something*. But it wasn't directed at the tall stranger.

"Aiden Vale," the man returned as he shook my hand. He glanced uncertainly at Bennett, but I didn't follow his gaze.

"Xander…" Bennett said, but I didn't look at him.

Aiden spoke up. "Mr. Reed, this is my associate, Bennett Crawford—"

"Fifteen minutes," I said and then I was moving again.

"Xander, wait!" I heard Bennett call, but I ignored him. I wasn't surprised when he followed and darted around me so he could step into my path. I'd gotten a glimpse of his tenacity on the very first day we'd met as polar opposite five-year-olds. Bennett hadn't remembered the exact details of our first meeting, but I remembered that day as if it were etched into every brain cell. My parents had spent all of breakfast arguing about the fact that my mother had to work on a Sunday, and after she'd stormed off, my dad had taken me to the park to play.

Though he hadn't been interested in playing with me like he usually did.

He'd merely sat on the park bench by the small playground and stared off into the distance after telling me to go swing by myself for a while. I'd sat on the swings watching him, wondering how to make it so he wouldn't seem so sad all the time. I hadn't even noticed the short, dark-haired kid plop down on the swing next to mine at first. It wasn't until he'd started talking a mile a minute that I'd turned my attention on him.

"You like rats?" he'd asked me.

I'd immediately laughed at him. "Rats?"

"*Rugrats*, I mean. You know, the cartoon."

*What a weirdo,* I remembered thinking.

I'd tried ignoring him at first, but Bennett had been hard to ignore.

He still was.

I forced myself to stop walking so I wouldn't bowl him over, because unlike when we were kids, I was now considerably larger than he was. He was only a few inches shorter than me, but my active lifestyle had given me the kind of body you couldn't get in a gym. And while Bennett looked fit, I probably had a good thirty pounds or more on him.

"God, Xander," he whispered. His eyes raked over me. I inwardly cursed myself as the effect of his perusal went straight to my dick, though I knew he couldn't be looking at me that way. Jesus, what the fuck did it matter how he was looking at me?

"What?" I snapped.

Bear whined, but before I could put my hand down to reassure him I was fine despite my raging anxiety, Bennett dropped his fingers to the animal's muzzle. My dog sniffed him a few times and then he pressed his big body up against Bennett's legs. Stupid fucking traitorous dog.

"I just… I thought we could talk," Bennett said.

"About what?"

"About what?" he repeated dumbly. "About… everything. About that night, about your dad—"

I didn't even consider who might be watching as I fisted my hands in Bennett's shirt and forced him backwards until his shoulders hit a tree. "You don't get to talk about my dad ever again, you hear me, Bennett?" I practically snarled at him. "You gave up that right. You gave up everything when you turned your back on me."

Bear began barking frantically and I remembered where we were and that we weren't alone. I jerked away from Bennett and tried to get control of myself. "Stay the fuck away from me," I warned quietly as I reached down to settle Bear.

"Xander…"

I ignored the plea in his voice and turned my back on him.

And I did it without regret… just like he'd done to me fifteen years earlier.

## CHAPTER 2

### BENNETT

I was embarrassed to admit that despite the tension simmering between us, not to mention the agonizing guilt weighing down on my chest, I couldn't stop staring at his goddamned ass. It had only been a few hours since reuniting, and I was already so tuned in to Xander's body, I could barely spare a single moment's thought for anything else. Namely, the kids.

And I loved these kids. I'd already spent time with many of them in one of the after-school programs my father's company sponsored, and I knew what a wilderness adventure like this one could do for them. Broaden their horizons, provide them time and space to think, show them the expansive beauty of their world, and give them the opportunity to learn leadership skills. It was a once-in-a-lifetime trip for most of these guys. And I was lucky enough to be there for it.

I glanced around the darkening campsite as the boys settled down from the excitement of setting up their tents and sleeping bags. We'd only hiked an hour or so down the trail from the drop-off when Xander had stopped and declared a nearby clearing as our campsite for the night

The eight teenage boys in our group were the ones who were old enough to learn more advanced skills like navigation, rock climbing, and river crossings. The younger group had gone with two other volunteers and a guide. They would focus more on the easy stuff like basic hiking and camping. Since I was a city guy myself, I was more nervous about being with the so-called "advanced" group than I cared to admit, but Aiden had reminded me that my rapport with the older kids was an important asset, since they weren't quick to trust just anyone.

A boy named Toby came up to sit next to me on the large rock where I'd perched after dinner. The breeze had picked up, and I noticed several kids slipping on warmer clothes. Dark clouds cast black shadows across the inky blue sky, and I was surprised I didn't hear more animal noises. Owl hoots or bear growls or something.

Toby handed me a pile full of wide elastic straps and loose plastic pieces. I stared at the collection of items in my palms.

"What am I supposed to do with this?" I asked.

"Fix it for me," he said.

I stared some more. "What's it supposed to be?"

"Headlamp. I don't know how to work it."

"And you think I do?" I asked with a raised brow. "You're talking to the guy whose lights at home are all controlled by his iPhone. I don't know how to work an actual, physical light source."

I turned to face him, moving to sit cross-legged so I could drop the pieces between my legs to keep them from rolling away. Apparently, this was a teaching moment I had to figure out. "Okay, first— parts identification. If it's a headlamp, we know we need straps to go around the head. Any clue which of these pieces are the straps?" I gave Toby a blank look.

He rolled his eyes. "Don't fuck with me. You're not that stupid." He grabbed the elastic straps and set them aside. That left several plastic pieces and a battery.

"Now, there should also be some kind of lighting apparatus," I said in my best dorky voice. "A bulb, a lamp of sorts. An illumination station, if you will."

"Jesus, you're weird," he muttered, grabbing the light-up portion of the device from the pile along with the battery.

"Hmm, finally, we need a way of connecting the light dealie to those complex wrappings—"

"I got it. Thanks for nothing, Einstein," he said in a huff, grabbing the final clip left on the rock and wandering off.

"Huzzah! You knew how to do it yourself after all. Imagine that," I called after him. "You're welcome."

He shot me a rude gesture over his shoulder and I smirked as I stood up to find my own sleeping bag. I stopped short.

Xander stood only a few feet away, staring at me. The electricity between us crackled ten times louder than any campfire. It was an unexpected, but not entirely unwelcome, surprise to the dynamic between us, since we hadn't had the opportunity to explore that aspect of our friendship before we'd gone our separate ways as teenagers. Hell, I didn't even know if he was gay. Probably not.

Not that it mattered, since the guy would just as soon beat my ass as do anything more pleasurable to it.

I wanted to say something. To tell him how much I missed him and how sorry I was for every bad decision I'd ever made that hurt him, but the words froze on my lips. By the time I could even take a breath, he'd turned away with a shake of his head.

I stared after him with a mixture of regret and resignation. His rejection stung just as much as it had several hours earlier in the parking lot.

He hated me.

And I didn't blame him one bit. Not after turning him away fifteen years ago.

After standing there for a beat, I moved forward to find my sleeping bag so I could get it set up in my tent. I approached my large pack and began unbuckling the sleeping bag from the outside of it. I tossed it on the ground next to me and reached deep inside my frame pack for something warmer to change into.

Under Xander's direction, the kids had split up into two groups of four people to form tent groups. I wasn't sure if I was expected to join one of the small groups or form some kind of leader tent group with Xander. Just the thought of that made my dick twitch.

*Simmer down, you lonely bastard,* I thought. *There's nothing good for you here, so just do me a favor and hibernate for about seven days.*

I glanced around to see where the object of my thoughts was, and caught him leaning over his own pack several yards away. It was almost fully dark by now, but there was enough ambient light from lanterns and head lamps to make him out. He'd taken off his boots and hiking shorts and was standing in just boxer briefs and a T-shirt.

*Ohdeargod.* He was standing there in his underwear.

The muscles of his thighs flexed as he shifted his weight, obviously looking for something in his pack. Xander's long hair was loose from its tie and hung in thick waves over his shoulders. He was barefooted, which he'd told the rest of us to never be in the backcountry.

*"Your feet are your only mode of transportation out here. Treat them like the invaluable resource they are. We can't risk foot injuries, so remember: never go barefoot. Ever."*

It was so hard to get used to his deep masculine voice. The sound both surprised and comforted me because it still held such familiar notes. It was the sound of my childhood, of happy adventures on my parents' huge property, of late nights spent lying side-by-side in his bed or mine when one of us snuck out to be with the other. Nothing ever happened, of course. We'd been too young and hadn't spared much time for thoughts of serious things like sex. And honestly, we hadn't needed to.

We'd had each other, after all, and that was all we'd needed.

"Would you like me to ask Toby for one of his straps to maybe rig your jaw up with?" Aiden's voice cut through the quiet space around me, causing me to jump.

"What? What are you talking about?" I sputtered.

"You haven't stopped drooling over him since we got to the trailhead. This is a fucking problem, Bennett."

I took a deep breath and looked at my best friend. My current best friend. Fuck, why did that feel like a betrayal to Xander— who currently wanted nothing to do with me?

"Am not," I said stupidly.

"Oh god," Aiden muttered, throwing out his sleeping bag and

reaching for mine, presumably so he could put it into my tent for me. "Just go hump his leg and get it over with, for fuck's sake."

I smacked his shoulder and cracked open my water bottle to wash away all evidence of the drool he may or may not have been correct about. "Shut up. You're imagining things. But you have to admit it's a shock."

"That's an understatement," he said dryly. "Should I go tell him I know what your cum tastes like and see what he says?"

I choked on my water, spilling it down my neck and onto my boots.

"Jackass! Seriously?" I gaped at him. "You're such a fucking ass," I hissed.

Aiden glanced behind me, presumably toward Xander, and raised his voice just loud enough for the man to hear. "Speaking of ass, I could describe how it feels to be buried so deep inside—"

I dropped my water bottle and lunged forward to clap a hand over his mouth.

"Shut. The. Fuck. Up," I ground out between clenched teeth. "I don't know what I ever saw in you to begin with."

"C'mon. You were in love with me. Admit it," Aiden said with a grin.

"I was young and stupid," I muttered.

"You had excellent taste," he corrected with a wink. His eyes slid to my ass again. "And the whole bossy bottom thing you've got going on is hot as fuck."

"Jesus," I muttered, as I bent forward slightly so I could pull my wet shirt away from my skin.

"Can't wait to tap this ass while I've got you bent over some boulder or up against a tree," Aiden purred, and I jumped when his hand slid over my ass.

"What the fuck?" I said. Aiden was a handsy guy, but we still had boundaries.

"You two about done?" Xander's low voice grumbled from somewhere behind us as he approached and glared from a few feet away. The light formed shadows along his jaw and I noticed Bear trailing close behind him. I wondered if he had anyone else in his life who loved him as much as that dog appeared to.

I sent Aiden a death glare. I knew he'd grabbed me and said all that shit because he'd seen Xander heading our way.

"I'm not sharing a tent with you if you're going to be an ass," I said to Aiden.

"You two can't sleep together. I mean near each other. You need to move your tents so each of you is near one of the kids' group tents. Spread out," Xander said.

Aiden's mouth quirked up around the edges, but before he had a chance to make a snarky comment, Xander added, "Get some sleep. Sunrise comes early in the wild."

And with that, Xander turned around and took his gorgeous goddamned ass to the farthest edge of the camp, leaving me alone to think about the time in my life when I truly *had* been young and stupid.

# CHAPTER 3

## XANDER

*Bennett's gay.*

What were the fucking odds?

The late morning sun soothed my skin as I realized that not only was I trapped with the asshole for seven unbearably long days and nights, now I had to deal with the fact that he played for my team. And if that wasn't bad enough, he'd apparently brought his own teammate along for the ride.

No wonder I'd hated Aiden Vale on sight. Of course, I'd thought it was because he fit the profile of the rich Wall Street banker type guy to a T and I hated those kinds of guys with a passion. Not that it had always been that way. No, it hadn't been until I'd walked through the doors of Knollwood Academy on the first day of high school that I'd been reminded that, despite having been golden boy Bennett Crawford's best friend for almost ten years, I was still just a loser from the wrong side of the tracks.

Though in my case, there'd been no tracks… just the expansive, pristine acres of perfectly manicured green lawn that had separated Bennett's family's palatial home from the small caretaker's cottage my father and I had shared on the edge of the estate's property line. I recalled the first day in my new high school. I'd had to ignore the hushed whispers of the other kids as they'd marveled over the arrival of "that scholarship kid." I'd searched for Bennett, who'd had to get to school early for crew practice, but by the time I'd found him, he'd already had his books in hand and had been among a large group of boys I'd never met before. I'd expected him to stay behind to wait for me to get my locker open, but he'd merely cast me a nod and said he'd catch up with me later.

I hadn't seen him for the rest of the day.

I should have recognized the moment for what it was.

The beginning of the end of our close friendship.

I'd lost Bennett to guys like Aiden that very day, though I hadn't realized it until later. And I hadn't actually accepted it until one terrible night in late September when my life had been changed forever.

*Bennett is gay... and he's fucking Aiden.*

I shook my head as I increased my pace on the rocky trail. Poor Bear had to run to keep up with me. I'd spent the better part of the morning avoiding Bennett and his asshole of a boyfriend. I'd sounded like a goddamn drill sergeant when I'd told the kids they had thirty minutes to eat their breakfast and get their tents broken down, but even their grumbling about what a tightass I was hadn't been enough to deter me. I'd left the group alone as I'd gone ahead to scout the trail, a move that had been wholly unnecessary and had served only to get me away from Bennett's worried glances and Aiden's smug smirks. I hadn't returned until it had been time to get everybody going.

The fact Bennett was gay or that he had a boyfriend shouldn't have changed anything, but somehow it made things even worse— something I wouldn't have thought possible. And I refused to examine why it mattered so damn much. It wasn't like I'd spent all these years pining for something I couldn't have.

I'd left Bennett behind the second he'd turned his back on me.

As a friend.

As a future lover.

Didn't matter.

He might as well have been dead and buried six feet under for all I cared.

*Bullshit*

Damn! Since when had my fourteen-year-old self decided he was going to be the voice of reason in my head?

"Xander!"

At the sound of Bennett's voice behind me, I increased my stride. I just needed a few more moments to myself. To steel myself from grabbing the man and shaking him and asking him why the hell he'd ditched me fifteen years ago. What had I done to drive him away? Why hadn't I been good enough anymore?

"Xander, hold up."

I flinched as Bennett's fingers closed around my upper arm. I yanked it free of his hold, but when the motion unbalanced him and he stumbled, I quickly grabbed him by the elbow to steady him. We both froze as sparks danced along the points where we touched. Before I even realized what I was doing, I moved closer to him so our chests were touching. Bennett's pretty lips separated as he tilted his head just enough so he could look me in the eye. The open desire I saw there had me pulling him even closer. It wasn't until he let out a breathy sigh that I remembered myself and quickly ripped my hand away before stepping back.

Bennett blinked slowly and then swallowed as he struggled to collect himself. "Thanks," he finally muttered.

"What do you need?" I asked.

"The kids," he said between heavy breaths. I turned to look and realized what had happened. I'd been so distracted, I'd ended up leaving the entire group dozens of yards behind.

"Sorry," I said and then cursed myself. I didn't owe this man any apologies. But I did need to get my shit together. I was known as one of the best guides in Colorado for a reason, and it certainly didn't include leaving my charges in my wake where they could easily step off the trail and twist an ankle, or wander off to check something out and get lost in the process.

"S'okay," Bennett managed to rasp out and then he smiled. "Guess we're the worst of the worst."

I had no clue what he was talking about, but when I didn't respond, he continued on his own. "You know, city slickers."

One of the things I'd always loved about Bennett as a kid had been his ability to find the humor in just about anything. He'd always been what I needed. But now, his very presence was like rubbing salt into an open wound. Of course, anything he did stung. The way he'd helped the kid assemble his headlamp the night before, the subtle glances he'd sent my way when he'd thought I hadn't been looking... hell, even when I'd sensed his eyes on my ass as I'd changed. It was like everything I'd ever wanted in a partner, but in the body of the wrong man. The man I couldn't, or rather, wouldn't ever have.

"You should head back to the group," I said. "I'll slow down."

"Or I could just walk with you," Bennett suggested. "You can tell me what you've been up to these past few years."

*I've been trying to get over your betrayal.*

"Not a good idea," I said as I forced my gaze to the kids who were slowly inching their way closer to us, Aiden bringing up the tail end of the group. I absolutely did not notice the way a sheen of sweat clung to Bennett's skin, making it glow, or the way his pulse thrummed against the corded muscles of his neck as he took a few sips of water from his bottle.

To my disappointment, Bennett fell into step next to me as soon as I began moving again. I'd allowed the kids to catch up enough so that I could keep an eye on them and be available for questions. Over breakfast, I'd gone over basic map skills and navigation with the kids, and I'd taken several opportunities throughout the day to stop and show them how to determine where we were on the map. The day's hike was a several-mile stretch that had begun in the wildflower meadows on the edge of the Woodland Rise Wilderness area and headed west toward Drummond Lake. I had plans not to push it too hard today so there wouldn't be many sore muscles around camp tonight.

The trail we were currently on was wide enough for two people to walk comfortably side by side and would remain that way for a while, so unless I outright told Bennett not to walk next to me, I was stuck with him for the time being. My plan was to let the kids take turns leading the group since we were still on obvious marked trails, but by the following day, the trails would become less obvious and we'd be navigating by map across unmarked terrain. The sun was high in the sky and the morning clouds were burning off to leave just a few fat, puffy clouds suspended in a sea of deep blue.

Since we still had at least half a mile to go before I could hand the leadership duties off to the first kid, it meant I had to play nice with Bennett until then, especially since young ears were within listening range.

"How long have you been doing this?" Bennett asked a few minutes later, his breath much less labored. As fit as he looked, I suspected his lean muscles had come from a gym because the terrain, though not overly challenging yet, was clearly wreaking havoc on him.

"Guiding? I've been hiking these woods pretty much from the day Aunt Lolly and I arrived here. I've been getting paid to do it for about ten years now."

Bennett's forehead crinkled in thought. "Lolly? Is that who you went to live with after your dad—"

At my sharp look, Bennett wisely didn't finish the statement. "I wasn't sure what happened to you after… afterwards," he murmured.

"Why would you?" I asked. "You sure as shit didn't care that night."

Fuck, why had I brought up that night? It was done, dead, in the past.

Except it really wasn't because pain slashed through my chest. I was once again that desperate kid reaching out for his best friend.

"I asked my parents if they knew where you'd gone—"

"I don't care if you prayed to the Virgin Mary about me, Bennett. I don't give a fuck."

I managed to keep my voice low enough so the kids wouldn't hear me.

Bennett, blessedly, fell silent for a few minutes. When the trail opened up into a large clearing, I used the opportunity to let the kids take a break so they could drink something and munch on protein bars while I explained that the screechy chatter splitting the air above us was a pair of American Kestrels. I told them about how the bird was North America's littlest falcon and still able to snatch up rodents from the ground mid-flight. The kids took turns looking at the birds through a few shared pairs of binoculars and then we were on the move again. Bennett, thankfully, returned to Aiden's side as I began explaining to the first kid, a boy called Lucky, what to expect as he took over leading the group.

I tried to ignore the look of anguish on Bennett's face as he and Aiden chatted, but when Aiden put his arm around Bennett's shoulders, I saw red. I barely refrained from going back there and telling him to get his fucking hands off of Bennett.

Jesus, I was never going to last seven days at this rate.

I spent the rest of the afternoon supervising the kids who were leading, and when we finally reached Drummond Lake, I smiled to myself as I heard one of the kids in front of the group stop and gasp. Within seconds, Bennett was there.

"What's wrong? Is everyone okay?" Bennett asked, looking ahead to see what had made the kid react so strongly.

His entire body language changed, and I felt like I was seeing the Drummond Lake vista laid out before me for the first time— only now, I saw it through his eyes. The long trail cutting through the grass, the deep blue of the water sparkling in the summer sun, the verdant greens of the trees stacked on the hills beyond, and the giant snowy peaks of Woodland Rise shooting skyward in the distance.

Bennett just stood there, staring. And a stupid part of me wanted to sneak up beside him and take his hand in mine. To put my lips against his ear and say, *See? This. This is me. This is where I've been. And now you're here with me.*

When he looked at me with a huge smile on his face, my need to show him that part of me disintegrated as all the years of hurt and resentment came back.

"Xander, it's amazing—"

I didn't even let him finish his statement before turning away. "I'm going to set up camp."

I let the kids explore the rocky shoreline as I headed for the spot I typically chose as the best camping site. I was glad for the few moments of privacy as I started getting the site set up.

But of course, it didn't last.

I tried to ignore Bennett as he appeared a few feet away and set his pack against one of the three large logs surrounding the campfire area. I caught him sneaking glances in my direction, but surprisingly, he didn't say anything. I watched him take a small camera from his pack and when he saw me looking at him, he said, "For the kids' parents."

I didn't acknowledge the comment, nor did I watch him walk away. When I sensed a presence again, I was in the process of laying out the poles for my tent.

But it wasn't Bennett whose foot suddenly stepped down on the pole I'd been about to reach for.

"You're a real prick, you know that?" Aiden said when I looked up at him.

I was tempted to tell him to fuck off, but I tempered my anger. He was the client, after all. Didn't matter that he was also fucking Bennett... or that he'd become that person in Bennett's life that I should have been. Even if they weren't sleeping together, I would have known they were best friends just by looking at them. The fact that Aiden was prepared to go to battle with me on Bennett's behalf was just further proof of that.

"What I know is that you should stay out of it," I said calmly. "Your dick belongs in his business, not mine," I added.

"That's the part that's really pissing you off, isn't it, Ranger Rick? That I have a part of him you never did."

I managed to quell my response to knock him on his ass, but barely. As it was, I had to take a few steps away from him, so I pretended to get something out of my pack just so I had something to do with my hands. Otherwise I was afraid they'd end up wrapped around his throat.

"Yeah, he told me about you guys when you were kids," Aiden continued. "He told me what he did to you, too."

I couldn't hide my reaction to that. Mostly because it felt like just another betrayal in a long line of many. What else had he told this asshole about me? How I was just the caretaker's son? How Bennett had deigned to let me live in his shadow until he'd no longer had any use for me? Did he tell this man about all the plans we'd made as kids? Did the fucker know *he* was everything *I* should have been to Bennett?

"You should walk away now," I said coolly.

"Or what? You gonna grab me like you did him?" Aiden said snippily. "Yeah, I saw you yesterday, big man."

I assumed he was talking about the moment I'd slammed Bennett against that tree when he'd mentioned my dad. My hands fisted on their own and then I stepped over the log. Aiden was about my size, though not quite as heavily built. But he'd still be a worthy opponent, especially since he didn't back down once we were pressed chest to chest.

And just like that, Bennett was there, pressing between us. "Don't," he said quietly, though his voice was flustered and tense. He forced Aiden back a few steps. "Leave it alone, Aiden."

"You were kids, Bennett," Aiden bit out. "You made mistakes, but you were still just a kid."

Aiden's declaration set off something inside of me that I was helpless to control.

"He wasn't a kid, asshole," I barked. My eyes fell to Bennett's wide ones. *"He was my entire fucking world!"* I yelled, my voice cracking as the wound inside my chest that had scabbed over so long ago ripped open and bled for all the world to see.

Aiden had the grace to look surprised, but I didn't give a shit. Because my eyes were on Bennett, who was looking at me with so much pain and regret that it had tears stinging the backs of my eyes. Had he never really understood what he'd done to me? God, that made everything so much worse. I ignored Bear who'd begun whining at my side, and I turned and stumbled over the log, knocking my pack aside in my desperation to escape. I barely noticed that all the kids were standing shell-shocked just behind us, their mouths open wide.

I didn't care.

All I cared about was doing what I'd done that night fifteen years ago when Bennett had taken away the one remaining good thing in my life.

I ran.

# CHAPTER 4

## BENNETT

I wanted to go after him. In fact, my feet had carried me clear across the campsite before Aiden's large arms grabbed me around the waist and spun me around.

"Don't," he said. "He's not worth it."

"Shut the fuck up," I hissed. "You don't know shit. You saw him! He's hurting."

"Let him hurt, Bennett. If he can't forgive you for something you did when you were a child, he doesn't deserve your comfort or your friendship. It wasn't your fucking fault."

I felt a stinging in my throat and my entire body ached to follow Xander into the forest. After a moment of internal struggle, I sagged in Aiden's arms.

"He hates me. I mean, I knew he hated me, but I had no idea how affected he was by this." I extricated myself from my friend's arms and straightened my clothes. "I didn't know it was... *fuck*. I didn't know it was this bad."

"Why don't you go sit by the lake for a little while and calm down? I was going to do one of the ice breaker games with the kids before dinner anyway."

"Yeah, okay," I said, stepping away from him and retrieving my water bottle from my pack. "Thanks."

As I made my way past the edge of the trees toward the lake, I was overwhelmed by the beauty of our surroundings. The late afternoon sun glinted off the surface of the water and cast shadows on the eastern side of the Woodland peaks in the distance beyond.

I thought about what Xander had said about hiking these woods since he'd moved to Colorado with his aunt. I'd never known where he was, where he'd ended up. There had been no way to even picture him in his new life. One minute he'd lived within a three-minute walk from my bedroom window and the next he'd been gone without a trace. I'd never even gotten to say goodbye.

After hearing a splash, I noticed a bird take off from the surface of the water. It pumped its wings to take it high into the fir trees to my left. I made my way to the edge of the lake and settled on a large boulder, reaching out to unlace my boots so I could test the temperature of the water.

When Xander and I had been eight years old, his dad had taken us camping in the Poconos. I remembered Mr. Reed teaching us how to fish and the look on Xander's face the first time he'd gotten a bite on his line. I was pretty sure the fish had been less than two inches in length, but Xander had been proud as a fucking peacock about that thing. He'd danced around so long bragging about his big catch, that by the time he'd been ready to release it back into the water, the fish had been on its last legs. The poor little thing hadn't made it, and Xander had been gutted.

He'd cried his fucking ass off, and later that night after Mr. Reed had gone to sleep, I'd snuck into Xander's sleeping bag, wrapped my arms around him, and told him the little guy was in a better place. By the time I'd finished describing my idea of fishie heaven, Xander had been laughing so hard I'd had to cover his mouth with my hand so he wouldn't wake up his father. We'd woken up the next morning in a tangle of limbs and it had just felt so normal and right. He'd been my best friend. Touching him hadn't been weird, it had just been... natural.

At least I'd thought so. Until several years later when *my* dad had caught us curled up together on the sofa in the movie room watching Lord of the Rings. And then everything had changed. I'd thought I'd been protecting Xander, but now…

I still remembered Dad's warning about me needing to keep my distance from Xander. To remember we were "just friends." I'd laughed at first. Surely he'd been joking. Xander and I hadn't just been friends, we'd been joined at the hip— we'd done everything together.

But that had been the beginning of things going bad for Xander and me. When I thought back on it now, I figured maybe my dad must have seen something even I hadn't been able to at the time. I'd always thought my father's issue with how close Xander and I had been had had to do with our difference in station. I'd only realized later on in life that it likely hadn't had anything to do with Xander's dad being a gardener and everything to do with the fact that I would eventually commit the ultimate transgression against my powerful, high-profile family by proving to be solely attracted only to members of my own sex.

Heat and pain warred inside my belly as I remembered the stricken way Xander had looked right before he'd said those terrible words.

*He was my entire fucking world!*

Regret seared my insides like acid as I considered the damage I'd done. It didn't matter that I'd thought I'd been doing the right thing at the time… that I'd done what I'd done with a child's naive understanding of the world. I'd hurt him beyond words. My big, strong, quiet Xander who'd always felt more deeply than he let on…

I dashed at the tears that began to pool in my eyes and leaned down to find the right kind of smooth rock from the ones scattered at the edge of the lake. When I found the perfect one, I flung it as hard as I could and watched it skip once, twice, four times across the glassy surface of the water.

"Holy shit, dude," I heard from behind me. I turned around and saw a couple of the boys approaching and I quickly forced back the tears that were still threatening to fall. "That's totally sick. Can you show us how to do that?"

I forced a smile to my lips and nodded. Regardless of how things were going with Xander, I needed to focus on why I was there— to show these kids some love and attention while allowing them to see how amazing their world was. They sure as hell didn't need to know that all I wanted in this moment was to go find Xander and beg him to forgive me. To wrap my arms around him like I had when we were kids, and let the entire world around us disappear.

I spent the next thirty minutes teaching anyone who wanted to learn how to skip rocks. By the time we'd exhausted all the prime skipping rocks in our small section of the lake's edge, Aiden had joined us to ask if I wanted to collect wood for the fire.

"Sure. Why don't you remind the kids to fill up their water bottles and change into warmer clothes before the sun sets?" I suggested.

"No problem. If you run into Ranger Rick out there, tell him to get over himself and come help," Aiden said.

I bit back a snarky retort, since I knew Aiden was just expressing his anger on my behalf. As I wandered into the woods, the fact that I chose to go in the direction Xander had earlier was a coincidence. Regardless, a few minutes later I heard rustling and cracking sounds and came upon Xander stomping on some fallen branches to break them apart. There was a tidy stack of firewood a few feet away. He'd obviously been busy while he'd been avoiding us… no, not us, *me*.

"Hey," I said quietly.

His movements stopped, but he didn't turn around.

"I didn't know," I began.

Silence.

"I didn't know how badly I'd hurt you," I tried again. "Xander, I'm so—"

"I don't care." His voice was low and rough and he still didn't turn around. "Keep your meaningless apologies to yourself. It was a long time ago, Bennett. I'm over it."

*Yeah, right.*

"You never said goodbye," I said, hating how needy I sounded. "I came to find you that night and you were gone. The cottage was completely empty. I didn't even know where you'd gone."

He finally turned around and narrowed his eyes at me. "Did it matter? It's not like you gave a shit at that point anyway. You'd made that perfectly clear during your little pool party with your friends."

Pain shot through my gut at the mention of the night when everything had changed between us forever. The last time I'd seen him for almost fifteen years. I'd literally had seconds to choose between losing Xander for that night or losing him forever. I'd chosen that night, but it had ended up being forever anyway. I still didn't understand how it had happened.

"I made a mistake," I whispered.

Xander stepped forward, so close I could see the sunny streaks of blond in his long brown hair. Then he got into my face, and I could see the whiskers on his jaw and the brightness of eyes I'd looked into a thousand times before.

"I. Don't. Care," he repeated. His words were said with a coldness I'd never heard before and it chilled me to the bone. He wasn't the Xander I'd known as a child. He was different. Harsher, more defensive and belligerent. I wanted *my* Xander back— the one who'd sung "Who Let the Dogs Out" every single time I'd accidentally left the door to his dad's cottage open and his dog, Sputnik, had gotten out. I'd always worried he'd get mad at me. Since we hadn't had a dog in the main house, I'd always forgotten to look out for Sput.

But Xander never *had* gotten mad at me. He'd just sung the song at full volume to punish me until we'd either found the dog or dissolved into fits of laughter and Mr. Reed had been forced to take over the search. And then the song would be on my mind for days after. So, I'd done my best to pay him back with an ear worm of my own. The more annoying, the better.

Frustration and a keen sense of helplessness went through me, and I reverted to the same self-defense mechanism that had served me well when we'd been children. I spun on my heel and grabbed some of the wood from the pile he'd created before walking back toward camp, singing the song from *Frozen* at the top of my lungs.

*"Do you wanna build a snowman?"*

"Bastard," I heard him mutter from behind me, though I could sense the tiniest hint of amusement in his voice too. At least it was better than the dreaded silence or the hate-filled anger.

"Oh, don't like that one? Hmm... how about this? *Let it go, let it gooooooo...*"

# CHAPTER 5

## XANDER

If I could have tuned out Bennett's voice, I would have. As it stood, I'd already spent enough time away from the campsite that the kids had to be wondering what the hell kind of a wilderness guide I was, since I spent more time on the wilderness part and less time on the guide part. After Bennett had left me alone so I could finish collecting the firewood, I'd had to force myself to return to the campsite before darkness fell so I could help get the fire going and make sure everyone had gotten their tents set up. To my surprise, the fire had been started and the kids had been working on some kind of team-building activity that Bennett and Aiden had been directing. I hadn't stuck around long enough to see what it was, because as soon as my eyes had met Bennett's across the small space, I'd felt trapped, and all the humiliation from our earlier encounter had come rushing back to me.

I hadn't meant to admit what Bennett's defection had done to me, and I most certainly hadn't wanted Bennett's boyfriend to have that kind of ammunition to use against me. It was clear as day that the guy hated me, a feeling that was very, very mutual. I'd ended up taking Bear down to the water so he could have a quick swim. I'd sat on one of the logs near the shoreline and waited for that normal peace that being out in the wilderness so often brought me, but the chatter and laughter drifting down from the small rise of the campsite had proven to be too much of a distraction.

Just like it was now.

I'd chosen a spot closer to the fire while we'd eaten dinner and begun sorting through my pack for the umpteenth time, though it hadn't been necessary. I'd just been going through the motions so I wouldn't keep checking to see what Bennett was up to. I'd seen Aiden approach him several times out of my peripheral vision, but every time he'd touched Bennett, I'd had to force myself to look the opposite direction so I wouldn't be tempted to get up and go knock the man on his ass. I mean, for Christ's sake, we were on a fucking wilderness expedition, not in some nightclub. I wouldn't have been surprised if the assholes snuck off into the darkness to have a go at each other.

The thought of Aiden bending Bennett over some rock just like he'd talked about doing the day before, along with the words he'd thrown in my face tonight, had my anger building all over again.

*I have a part of him you never did.*

I'd figured out I was gay the summer just before things had fallen apart with Bennett. I hadn't understood at first why my heart had suddenly started racing every time I saw my friend, or why my palms would get so sweaty and it would be hard to breathe whenever he touched me. Not to mention the constant boners I'd started to experience around him. It had gotten so bad near the end that I'd been afraid to go swimming with him in the pool in case he could spot my predicament in the clear water. Which meant we'd had to limit our swimming to the small pond on his parents' property, and since his father would yell at us every time we'd done it, we'd resorted to only swimming in there at night after everyone had gone to bed.

Once I'd realized that what I was feeling for Bennett went beyond the bounds of friendship— and this only after I'd rubbed one out in the darkened woods as I'd walked back to my house after a particularly handsy swimming session— I'd worried about what it would mean for our friendship. I'd never gotten any kind of hint that Bennett was experiencing the same feelings I was, and he'd often talked about girls in his class he'd thought were cute. So, I'd done my best just to pretend that the feelings didn't exist. By the time I'd been close to finding the courage to tell Bennett the truth, he'd started to pull away from me, and I'd been afraid that telling him I was gay would widen that divide between us even further.

After the chance meeting at the playground when we were five, we'd become inseparable. Despite the fact that Bennett came from Greenwich's upper crust and my parents had been firmly rooted in the middle class, Bennett had always been a pushy little shit. He'd pestered his parents to keep taking him back to that particular park every day until they'd finally given in. The park had been within walking distance of my house, but for Bennett's family, it had been a good ten-minute drive. The only reason he'd even been at that playground that first day had been because he'd made his nanny stop there on the way home from a doctor's appointment.

All because he'd spied me through the car window sitting on that swing and had decided I looked like I needed a friend.

I smiled to myself at the memory and involuntarily glanced up to search Bennett out. Electricity fired through me as I saw him watching me, and I couldn't help but wonder if he'd somehow known I was thinking about him. He was still telling the kids the horror story he'd loved scaring me with when we were kids about the boy on the antique roller coaster.

"CRACK!" Bennett boomed, and the kids all jumped where they sat around the fire.

Several of them cursed under their breaths and one of them blurted, "Seriously, B? Shit!"

Bennett just started laughing the way he always did when he got to the part about the boy finding the skeleton in the coaster right as the coaster begins to break apart.

"Then the skeleton grabbed the boy to keep him safe, but when the boy looked down, it was nothing but twigs wrapped around his arm," he continued. The firelight glinted off his amused eyes, and I couldn't hold back a smile.

He'd fucking loved telling me that story because he'd known it scared the shit out of me every single time.

The first time he'd told it to me had been when we'd convinced our fathers to let us sleep under the stars down by the pond on the Crawford's estate. We'd rolled out our sleeping bags next to each other and had started a little fire after making a fire ring with some rocks.

As the firewood had popped and snapped, Bennett had begun to tell me about this kid, Damien, he'd met at one of the fancy summer camps his parents had sent him to. I had always hated when he'd gone off to camp because it'd meant I'd be stuck at home without him. We'd written letters back and forth, but it hadn't been the same. When he'd returned home, we'd spent hours catching up and making up for missed adventures.

The story about Damien had scared the fuck out of me. According to Bennett, the kid had gone to the shore to visit his grandmother and had found this haunted roller coaster. As the story had continued, it had gotten more and more farfetched until I'd finally realized it was all made up.

But the kicker about that damned story? It didn't matter if you knew it was bullshit, and it didn't matter how many times you heard it. It was still scary as all fuck. Because the sounds he used to tell the story were the sounds you heard sleeping outside at night. Cracks of the roller coaster were cracks of branches. Pops of the coaster struts were pops from the firewood. The wind itself was the cold breath of death, and so help me fucking god, Bennett was an expert at making the old woman's voice sound like the hoot of an owl.

The first time he'd told it to me and I'd realized it wasn't true, I'd smacked him on the back of the head and called him something ridiculous like buttwipe. He'd laughed so hard, he'd fallen over backwards off the log we'd been sitting on. I'd yelled at him that it served him right to fall on his ass, and then I'd tried like hell to pretend the story hadn't scared me. I'd lied and told him I was over it, but he'd known the truth. He'd always known when I was bullshitting.

So, that night when it had been time to slide into our sleeping bags, Bennett had pretended like he was the scared one, afraid of being alone. He'd asked me if we could zip our bags together so he'd know if I left him during the night. As if I'd ever, ever leave him alone in the dark.

Of course I'd agreed, and we'd ended up falling asleep telling each other as many jokes as we'd been able to think of in order to keep from getting scared. I still remembered what had happened right as we'd been about to finally drift off to sleep.

First a log had cracked somewhere off to our right, and then a giant boom of thunder had split the air about ten seconds before the skies had opened up.

I wasn't sure our feet had even hit the ground before we'd been safely back inside Bennett's bedroom in the big house.

We'd dried off, re-settled ourselves in his double bed under the covers and laughed at being such scaredy cats. When our laughter had died down, Bennett had turned to me with his trademark goofy grin on his face.

"Dude, I'm totally telling that story like a million more times in my life. That was *the best*."

I chuckled as I recalled that moment.

Bennett's goal in life had always been to make me laugh.

And I'd sure as hell needed that, especially as I'd been forced to watch my parent's marriage implode. I'd never really understood what had brought my parents together, because they'd never actually seemed happy.

In love? Maybe.

Happy? Most certainly not.

Not if their constant fights had been anything to go by.

My parents had met in college, though they'd been an unlikely couple even then. My father had been an art history major with dreams of teaching someday. My mother had been an energetic business student with the lofty ambition of someday running her own Fortune 500 company. I'd heard enough stories to know my arrival hadn't been planned, and while neither of my parents had ever said I'd been the reason they'd gotten married, I had always wondered if that was the reason I'd never seen any pictures of my mother in her wedding dress from the neck down.

As a child, I hadn't thought it unusual that my father had been the one to stay home with me all day. I'd learned later on that my mother hadn't even needed to take time off of school to actually have me, since I'd been born a week before the fall term of their junior year. My mother had been there for the start of class, my father hadn't. When graduation day had rolled around, my mother had accepted all sorts of scholastic awards and accolades while my father and I had sat in the crowd. I'd asked my father once why he hadn't gone back to school when my mother had completed her degree, but he'd never really answered my question other than to say, "It is what it is, Son."

Once my mother had graduated, she'd gone on to get a Master's degree and my father had been left to continue caring for me during the day and working as the night janitor for the college my mother had attended. I'd spent the nights with my father's parents, since my mother had been preoccupied with studying. I'd heard my parents argue often enough as a child to know that had always been the plan—for my mother to establish herself in a career that paid the bills, with the promise that my father would be able to finish his own education once they had more money to go around, as long as he took care of me until that happened.

That promise had been one in a long line of many that she had broken.

A mere two years after graduating with her MBA, my mother had accepted a prestigious job with a hoity-toity marketing firm overseas. When my father had expressed his worry about uprooting me to move to Europe, my mother had come up with a simple solution. The divorce had been finalized the day before she'd left the country, and neither my father nor I had ever seen her again. I'd learned later from Aunt Lolly that my mother had agreed not to seek sole custody of me if my father agreed not to ask for child support. It wasn't that my mother had actually wanted me, she'd just used the threat of taking me thousands of miles away from my father to get out of any parental obligation the courts might have enforced upon her.

My father had done his best to insulate me from the fact that my mother hadn't wanted me, but even before I'd known about the custody arrangement, I'd still felt left behind. Luckily, I'd had Bennett in my corner at that point, and on the days he hadn't been able to draw me out of my sadness at being unloveable, even by my own mother, he'd held me and promised me he'd always want me.

Just like with my mother, it was a broken promise I hadn't seen coming.

"Here."

I glanced up to see a hand thrusting some gooey, chocolatey marshmallow goodness my way. While I should have berated whoever it was who'd wasted space in their pack for the ingredients necessary to make s'mores, I couldn't begrudge the kids the fun of toasting marshmallows on sticks over an open flame and slapping them onto a perfectly-shaped chocolate bar between two crispy graham crackers.

"Thanks," I said as I took the treat. I expected the kid to return to his spot by the fire, but to my surprise, he sat down next to me. Bear immediately began nuzzling the kid's chocolate-covered fingers.

"It's okay?" he asked as he motioned to Bear.

I nodded, since the amount of chocolate was so insignificant that it wouldn't cause the dog any harm. The boy smiled when Bear's big tongue came out to lap at his fingers.

I guessed the boy to be around fifteen or sixteen. Gary had told me that all the boys in the group were between the ages of fifteen and seventeen, while the group Jake had taken charge of had younger boys between twelve and fourteen. The kid next to me was on the short side and pretty scrawny. His short black hair was spiky, like he was constantly running his fingers through it. His darker skin tone had me thinking he was at least part Hispanic.

"You don't want to listen?" I asked as I motioned to where the rest of the group was sitting.

He shook his head. "Heard it before. B tells it good, but…"

"He tells it too good," I ventured.

The kid smiled slightly. "They're gonna be pissing themselves all night in this place," he said as he nodded towards the kids. True enough, each boy was completely fixated on the story, which was the point. In mere minutes, Bennett would be performing his signature shock and awe move that would have the kids falling all over themselves to get away. I'd at least had Bennett to hold onto when he'd been scaring the ever-loving hell out of me.

"You're Lucky, right?" I asked. Bennett had had the kids introduce themselves one by one yesterday morning, but truth be told, I'd still been reeling from seeing Bennett again, so I'd only half-listened.

The boy nodded.

"I'm Xander," I said as I reached over to shake his hand. I knew the introduction wasn't really necessary, but it still felt like the right thing to do.

Lucky shook my hand and then put his hands back on Bear.

"You got a dog back home?" I asked as I finished the s'more.

"Nah," he murmured. "Had a cat once when I was little, but Jerry got pissed that it kept scratching his good chair so he let the neighborhood dogs have it."

The food I'd just eaten threatened to come back up as what he was saying sank in.

"Jerry?" I asked, simply because I had no idea what else to say.

"My mom's, ah, boyfriend… well, at the time anyway. Not sure if she's still with him."

"You don't live with your mom?"

Lucky shook his head, but didn't say anything more. I fully expected that the conversation was over when the boy remained silent for several minutes, but he surprised me by saying, "It's cool out here."

"Yes, it is," I acknowledged.

"Did you… did you like, go to school or something?"

It dawned on me what he was asking. "You mean college?"

He nodded.

"I did. But not specifically because it was a requirement for this job."

Lucky glanced at me, his confusion clear as day in the firelight. "You went to school because you… *wanted* to?"

I chuckled and said, "Yeah, I did." I let my eyes drift off into the darkness. There was enough moonlight filtering through the clouds that I could see the outline of the trees and the shimmering lake. My heart swelled at the sight. “I went to Colorado State University and got a degree in Fish, Wildlife and Conservation Biology.”

“Oh,” Lucky murmured, his eyes downcast. “I do okay in school, but I don’t get straight A’s or nothin.”

“Lucky,” I said and I waited until he looked up at me. “I belong in these woods,” I murmured as I motioned around us. “Degree or no degree. I went to school because I wanted to learn more about the wilderness I loved. I can’t say I was always the best student when I was your age, but if you want something bad enough, you’re willing to work as hard as you have to for it.” My eyes automatically drifted to Bennett.

I hadn’t been lying when I’d said I hadn’t been a great student… not like Bennett. I’d been fortunate to get a scholarship to Bennett’s private high school, but I’d had to work hard to keep up with the intense private institution’s curriculum. While I’d wanted to make my dad proud by maintaining the scholarship, I’d been more afraid that losing it would have also meant losing that last connection to Bennett. Sensation shot up and down my spine as Bennett’s eyes once again met mine over the fire. I immediately returned my attention to Lucky so I wouldn’t get caught up in Bennett or his damn story and the memories that came along with it.

“You have to fight for what you want, Lucky,” I said softly. I didn’t add that you also needed to know when to walk away. The kid needed to keep his dreams for as long as he could, after all.

Lucky nodded and fell silent again. Bear began prodding my hands, and I knew he could sense my anxiety building. I let my fingers sift through his thick fur.

“You and B, you were friends, huh?”

Lucky’s question had me sucking in my breath. I didn’t want to answer him. “A long time ago, yes,” I finally acknowledged.

“But not anymore?”

Pain exploded in my chest and I was sure I was going to have a heart attack. “People change, Lucky. They go their separate ways,” I forced myself to say. I was so on edge by the shift in conversation, I jumped when I heard the kids scream and shout at Bennett when his story hit its crescendo. I leapt to my feet and said, "I should go check things out." There was absolutely nothing that needed to get checked out, but hopefully Lucky didn't know that.

"Yeah, sure man," I heard him mumble and I felt like a shit for just ditching him. But as I listened to the kids giving Bennett a hard time about the story at the same time that they were saying how cool it was and they couldn't wait to hear it again, I wanted to throw up. Because memories of lying huddled with Bennett under a blanket, his head tucked against my shoulder, our hands linked between us… it was all just too much. I forced myself not to look at Bennett as I hurried from the fire into the darkness, Bear at my side.

I didn't look at him, but I felt Bennett's eyes on me just the same.

# CHAPTER 6

## BENNETT

"Can't sleep?"

I shook my head as Aiden came around behind me and stepped over the log. He sat close enough that his hip was brushing mine, and I automatically laid my head on his shoulder. It was a move I'd done countless times in the years since we'd ended our brief and very one-sided relationship. I wasn't sure why Aiden still allowed the contact… maybe because he knew I was a tactile person, or maybe because he just felt sorry for me when I got like this.

The fire hadn't completely died out when I'd crawled out of my tent an hour earlier, so I'd built it back up and had been staring into the burning embers ever since, as if they could somehow tell me how I'd managed to mess things up so badly.

"I don't suppose it's because you're feeling guilty for scaring the shit out of everyone, is it?" he asked.

I smiled. My story had gone off without a hitch… well, depending on how you looked at it, anyway. The kids had cursed me to hell and back afterward, and I'd seen more than one take a buddy with them when they'd gone to answer nature's last call before bedtime. If they hadn't been so worn out from today's hike, I suspected at least two or three of them would have been sitting with me around the fire, too rattled to go to sleep.

Unfortunately, my insomnia came from a whole different place.

My eyes automatically drifted to Xander's tent.

He hadn't spoken even one word to me since our run-in in the woods. I'd caught him shooting looks my way now and again, but his expression had been unreadable. I'd been surprised to see Lucky approach him and even more surprised when Xander hadn't chased the young man off. I was tempted to ask Lucky what topic had had them in such deep discussion, but I'd managed to hold back. I'd known how hard it was for the troubled teen to open up to anyone, so I hadn't wanted to make a big deal about it or make him feel self-conscious. And whatever Xander had said to him hadn't seemed to upset him, nor had he dismissed the teenager outright.

"I don't like seeing you like this," I heard Aiden mutter. I could tell by his inflection whose shoulders he was placing the blame for my mood on, and that didn't sit well with me. Yeah, I knew Aiden wanted to protect me— it was in his nature, after all. But I didn't like that Xander was the target of his fury.

I lifted my head and glanced at him. "You don't know him, Aid… he has a reason to feel this way."

"So do you, B."

I shook my head and turned my attention back to the fire. "It was different for me."

"Why? Because you were the one with all the advantages? Because you had money and his family didn't?"

"It was more than that. He never saw me as Bennett Crawford, son and only heir to the Crawford fortune. He didn't care who my dad was or that people were making all these plans for me from the moment I was born. To him I was just… Benny. It wasn't until high school that he started to look at me differently," I murmured. "Not that he didn't have a reason to."

"You didn't have a say in the matter, remember?"

"I never told you about his family and mine, did I?" I asked.

"No."

"After my parents realized I wasn't going to stop asking to see him, they began arranging play dates. Sometimes I'd go over to his house, sometimes he'd come to mine. When we were seven or so, our parents finally started hanging out… I guess they figured it just made sense. My parents actually liked Xander's mom a lot… it took them a little longer to warm up to Mr. Reed because he was pretty quiet… like Xander," I said with a smile. Xander had definitely inherited his mother's dirty brown-blond hair and cool blue eyes, but he'd had his father's quiet nature and stoic attitude… something I'd worked my damnedest to overcome.

"Mr. Reed eventually came out of his shell… we even vacationed together once."

"Let me guess, Daddy's yacht, the South of France," Aiden drawled.

I elbowed him. "Greek islands."

Aiden rolled his eyes. "So what happened?"

I shook my head. "His mom just up and left one day. Filed for divorce and moved to Europe to become some marketing bigwig. Kicker is, she didn't even fight for custody of him. I don't think he ever saw her again… not even after his dad died, not if he went to live with his Aunt Lolly." I reached down and grabbed a small rock off the ground and began rolling it between my fingers. It was a nervous habit I'd tried to break, especially since it pissed my dad off to no end, but Aiden knew all about my weird quirks.

"He was devastated. Kept asking me what he'd done wrong… why his own mother hadn't loved him. I didn't know what to tell him," I whispered.

I felt Aiden's hand settle on the back of my neck. It was a testament to how upset I must have seemed, because he rarely touched me when emotions were involved. Aiden didn't do emotions well— not showing them and most definitely not being on the receiving end of them.

"Xander's mom leaving was hard on his dad, but for a lot of reasons." I glanced at Aiden and said, "She was the breadwinner in the family and Mr. Reed stayed home to take care of Xander. I guess he was planning on going back to school, but then Mrs. Reed left…

anyway, he didn't have a job and things were tough. So, my dad offered him a job."

Aiden nodded. "In his investment firm?"

I shook my head. I'd told Aiden about how close Xander and I had been as kids and that he'd lived in the guest house on my parents' property, but I'd never gotten into the details of how that had come about or that the guest house had actually been the caretaker's cottage. "He hired Mr. Reed to be the estate's caretaker. In exchange, he got a small salary and he and Xander lived in the little cottage on the property."

"Fuck," Aiden muttered as he realized what I was saying.

I fell silent as my thoughts drifted to the day Xander had realized what his father working for mine had really meant. At first, all we'd both seen had been the benefits in that we'd be living within minutes of one another. At eight years old, we hadn't cared about the semantics of it all. As far as we'd been concerned, we were neighbors and that had been the extent of it.

But when Xander and I had witnessed my father berating Mr. Reed for some oversight with how he'd mowed the grass in the wrong direction or something equally ridiculous, there'd been a subtle shift in our friendship that I'd spent years trying to overcome. But I'd managed it. I'd had to fight like hell to prove to Xander that I never saw him as anything other than my best friend, but I'd done it.

Until the day I'd had to walk past him on the first day of high school and pretend he was just some guy.

It had been the beginning of the end.

"And I thought my dad was a prick," Aiden murmured.

I chuckled. Aiden's dad was an asshole, but for a whole slew of other reasons.

"I think I told myself Xander was okay after I discovered he was gone because I needed to believe that to make it through each day, you know?" I said softly. I rubbed the smooth stone between my fingers.

"He was your world too, wasn't he?" Aiden asked gently.

I cursed the tears that threatened to fall. "Yeah, he was," I said. "I thought if I could just keep us together long enough until we got to college or something..."

I snorted as I realized how ridiculous my lofty dream had been back then. I'd thought that once I'd turned eighteen, I'd somehow find the balls to stand up to my father. It hadn't even been about wanting a different kind of relationship with Xander at that point, though the seed had been planted for sure the summer just before we'd started high school. No, I'd just wanted to get to that magic age where I was supposedly allowed to say no to my parents. But even at nearly thirty years old, I still hadn't figured out how to get that word to actually mean anything with them. My father just had me over too many barrels at this point.

Just like he had the night Xander had begged me not to do what I'd promised I never would.

Leave him.

I felt Aiden's fingers close over mine, which had started to frantically rub back and forth over the stone.

"So what are you going to do about it?" Aiden asked.

"About what?"

He nodded his head towards Xander's tent. "Ranger Rick," he said with a smirk.

"In case you missed it, he's not talking to me," I muttered.

"Who said anything about talking?" Aiden's eyes danced with mischief as he took the stone from my hand and tossed it on the ground. "I say you go in there, unzip that sleeping bag of his and hoover his dick before he even knows what hit him."

"Ass," I said as I punched him in the arm.

"You can hoover that too," Aiden chuckled.

"We don't even know if he's gay," I said, as if *that* were the only thing stopping me from doing what Aiden had suggested.

"I've been on the receiving end of that mouth, B. If he isn't gay already, he will be by morning."

I shook my head and laughed, though inside my gut was stirring with excitement at even the prospect of getting my mouth on Xander. No, it was way too risky, not to mention highly inappropriate with the kids around… even if Xander's tent was on the outskirts of the camp site. Jesus, was I even considering this?

Yeah, fuck it, I was. Because maybe Aiden was right and I'd never get the chance to tell him with words what I was feeling. Maybe nothing in my current arsenal of weapons would get my foot in the door with Xander— to give me the chance to explain why I'd done what I'd done that night. Even if he shut me down, maybe I'd get the few seconds I needed to prove to him that I hadn't ever left him.

Not really.

"I can't," I whispered, more to myself than Aiden. But I had to wonder what was really stopping me. The fact that it was something so outside of my wheelhouse, or the fact that it might not make any difference?

I felt Aiden's lips skim my temple. "Just think. If it doesn't work out, this time you can be the one to walk away. Go get 'em, babe." And then he was gone, leaving me alone to stare at Xander's tent, which was suddenly luring me to it like a goddamn Siren's call.

"What the hell," I murmured as I climbed to my feet. I literally had nothing else to lose.

# CHAPTER 7

## XANDER

After the stress of the day, I slept hard. I hadn't expected to, really. I'd expected to toss and turn with thoughts of Bennett plaguing me like they had the night before, but the cold air of the mountain night and the familiar sounds of the surrounding wilderness worked their magic. Soon I was in the midst of the kind of dream that was so delicious, I wanted to hold on to it and savor it all night long.

In the dream, Bennett snuck into my tent the way he used to sneak into my room when we were younger, only this time we were no longer kids. He was full-grown— a man who exuded strength and masculinity. I didn't see him enter the tent, but a part of me just knew he was there. His scent, maybe, or the little hairs all over my body that seemed to prickle whenever he was near.

"Benny?" I whispered in the dream. "You scared?" Normally I was the one who was scared, but maybe this time was different. My eyes were only half-open, but he seemed terrified as he crawled closer.

I automatically opened my sleeping bag the way I'd done for him a thousand times before and he slid in alongside my body.

"Xander," he whispered, and it was a sound of longing— hesitation and want all rolled into one. He said something else, but I was still focused on how he'd said my name.

"C'mere," I said, holding out my arm so he could snuggle closer. He was watching me with big eyes and still seemed spooked. "You okay?" I mumbled, pulling him tight against me and almost groaning at the feel of his body against mine.

I saw Bennett's mouth move, but I couldn't make sense of what he said, a clear sign I was exhausted. But I didn't really care what he was saying, either. I was just so glad he was finally here… where he belonged. His hand felt cool against my heated skin and my body involuntarily shivered as his fingers danced over my side, my back, my belly. Everywhere he touched, he left delicious pulses of energy behind.

I was about to beg him to finally let me get a taste of him, but before I could open my mouth, his lips were on mine. My whole body shook with the impact of that first touch of his mouth.

It wasn't anything like I'd imagined. It was so much fucking better.

I could barely breathe, think. I could only feel as his mouth worshiped mine and I knew, just *knew*, he was finally mine. I didn't care that it wasn't real. I didn't care that it was the best fucking dream I'd ever had. It was everything I'd ever wanted but knew I'd never have. Bennett Crawford, full-grown and in bed with me.

Fuck.

If I was going to dream about being in bed with Bennett, I was going to go for it.

"Want you," I growled against his ear.

A deep groan escaped him before he sprawled his body half-on, half-off mine. "I want you so badly, Xander. *Please*."

I stretched my neck up to brush my lips across his and it set off an explosion of action. Bennett's mouth chased mine and latched onto it, and I grabbed the back of his head with both hands to keep him there — our tongues fighting each other and breaths coming fast and hard. Bennett's cock pressed into my belly and I grunted, arching my hips up to press mine into him as much as I could.

Bennett's hands were on my face and the kissing was fevered. It seemed like our hands and mouths were everywhere, trying to release years of pent-up desire for each other. I wanted him so desperately, I was afraid I was going to burst into tears with the frustration of needing to get inside him.

My hands managed to get underneath his clothes and I felt miles of warm Bennett skin under my palms. It was too good. That was when a wisp of reality blew across my consciousness with warning bells.

No dream was this good.

No dream handed me my biggest wish on a silver platter.

# CHAPTER 8

## BENNETT

I was terrified. What if Xander hated me even more after I snuck into his tent? Was that even possible? Maybe not. Maybe that only meant I had nothing left to lose.

After unzipping his tent flap as silently as I could, I crawled in. Bear lifted his head up from where he lay curled in a ball at Xander's side and then stood and stretched before sauntering past me out the tent flap, as if he knew what I was going to do and didn't want to stick around to watch me humiliate myself. I could hardly blame him.

I looked back toward Xander to see if he was still asleep. Sure enough, he was dead to the world. There was enough ambient moonlight coming through the mesh panel over his head to show me just how peaceful he looked.

God, he was beautiful. Even more now than he'd been as a kid. The planes of his face were a combination of familiar and strange. Thick eyelashes rested on his cheeks and I was desperate to reach out and stroke his face.

His sleeping bag was completely unzipped, and he was lying half in and half out of it in nothing but boxer briefs, despite the cold night. I had to stifle a smile as I remembered how hot of a sleeper he was.

He'd been like my very own furnace during cold nights spent sleeping out under the stars when we were kids.

I wasn't able to peel my eyes off the miles of exposed skin laid out before me. He was fit and tanned, presumably from living a life outdoors, and it seemed like every muscle was lean and defined. I reached my hand out instinctively, as if to run fingers over the bumps of his abdominal muscles, but I stopped myself before making contact.

*Fuck*. I was a creeper. I needed to turn around and leave. What the hell had I been thinking? But just as I started to turn and make my escape, I heard his sleepy mumble.

"Benny?" He paused before adding, "You scared?"

My throat tightened at the same words he'd asked me so many times when we were kids, and I squeezed my eyes closed for a moment. I turned to look at him and felt the stupid-ass prickly feeling behind my eyes as I whispered his name longingly. I forced myself not to move any closer to him, though my body screamed for me to do it. "Shhh, I'm not here. Go back to sleep."

"C'mere," he said as he pushed the sleeping bag off the rest of his body and opened his arms invitingly. I knew I shouldn't. I knew that. But I didn't care. The chance to feel his arms around me one more time…

I stifled the tears that threatened to fall, shoved away the shame of what I was doing, and crawled into his open arms.

"You okay?" he murmured, reminding me he was still clearly half-asleep.

"No," I whispered to myself. "I want to kiss you so badly, it's tearing me up inside." I couldn't stop myself from letting my hand slide all over his side, chest, and belly.

Xander's eyes dipped to my mouth as his tongue came out to wet his own lips. The combination sent blood straight to my dick and I groaned. Fuck it. I was, at most, five seconds away from being kicked out of his tent when he came fully awake, and I was sure as shit going to take advantage of those five seconds before that happened.

Before I could reconsider, I leaned forward, landing my mouth on his as softly as I could. *Just a taste,* I told myself. *One fucking taste to last me the rest of my life.*

My hand slid gently along the side of his face as the first feel of his mouth hit my senses and I sucked in a breath. That's all it was supposed to be— just a goodnight kiss before I left him to fall back asleep. With any luck, he wouldn't even remember I'd been there.

But before I could pull away, Xander's hand came up to hold the back of my head and bring my lips close again.

"Fuck," he growled before latching his mouth onto mine. This time there was nothing soft about it. The kiss was fevered and frenzied. Within seconds, it was all seeking tongues and nipping teeth, roaming hands and arching cocks. My brain short-circuited, and I lost all remnants of rational thought.

Xander Reed was making out with me and the entire fucking world ceased to exist. The only things left were our heated breaths, thundering hearts, and seeking fingers. His body was on fire, and I tried my best to run my hands over every inch of skin available to me. His own hands had finally settled on my ass and were pulling me in tight so we could grind our dicks together.

"Want you," he said, his voice low and rumbly against my ear.

They were the words I'd been waiting a lifetime to hear. Words I'd heard many times from all sorts of men, but never like this. Never from the only man I'd wanted to hear them from.

"I want you so badly, Xander. *Please,*" I begged without shame as I pressed him onto his back and covered his upper body with mine.

My cock was hard and pulsing, making me wonder if his was leaking too. I had to touch him. What I really wanted was to put my mouth on him, but I'd settle for sneaking a hand into his underwear and copping a feel.

While Xander sucked on the edge of my earlobe and whispered unintelligible words, I ran my palm across the sparse trail of hair leading from his navel to his waistband and dipped below to find the head of his cock pushing out of the top of his boxer briefs. I slid my hand inside to grasp his length, but instead of feeling him arch up into my touch the way I would have expected, I felt his entire body stiffen.

I lifted my head up and locked eyes with him. His were wide with shock and everything that followed seemed to happen in slow motion.

"What the fuck are you doing here?" he growled, scrambling back away from me until running into the side of the tent and almost capsizing it. The poles snapped back into their proper position when he stopped moving, and he had to put his hand up to support the nylon shell above him.

His eyes were crazy, and his free hand flew up to cover his mouth.

"I-I...," I stammered. "We... we were kissing, and you—"

"Out," he demanded in a low voice dripping with hatred. "Get the fuck out of my tent."

"But Xander—"

"Fine, then I'll go," he bit out, moving toward the tent flap.

"No, I'll go," I said quickly, not wanting to kick him out of his own tent in the middle of the night. My hands were shaking so hard I could barely manage the zipper. When I looked back at Xander, I saw him run his hands through his hair, reminding me that I'd had my own fingers in his gorgeous long hair only moments before. Would I ever get to touch it again? Not likely.

His eyes narrowed as he glared at me, and I felt my face burn with humiliation.

"I'm sorry," I whispered before turning to leave. And fuck if I wasn't sorry for those being the only words I seemed able to say to him anymore.

# CHAPTER 9

## XANDER

*I'm sorry.*

Bennett's words from the night before kept echoing in my brain. Words I thought I'd heard him mumble when he'd turned away from me the night my dad had died. Words I wasn't sure I'd ever believe coming out of his goddamned mouth again.

I tightened the top rope anchors, making them secure around a giant tree trunk at the top of the crag for the rock climbing workshop I was giving in a few minutes. Aiden and Bennett were doing another one of their team-building exercises with the boys several hundred yards away while I secured our climb and prepped the harnesses.

We'd spent the morning hiking over Fury Pass to Merry Flats. The wildflower-filled meadow between Mt. Fury and Woodland Rise was one of my favorite places to camp. When we'd come over the pass to the meadow, several of the boys had burst out singing, skipping and twirling like the von Trapp kids from *The Sound of Music*. By the time we'd reached the campsite on the far side of the meadow, there'd been more songs stuck in my head than I could count.

Bennett must have read my mind because he'd looked over at me with a nervous smile when one kid in particular had belted out Do-Re-Mi, a song Bennett knew drove me up the fucking wall.

I'd bit my tongue to keep from smiling back at him. God, I missed our inside jokes— having someone who could read my mind and know exactly what I was thinking sometimes. The entire time we'd been on the trail that morning, I'd recalled the feel of his hands on my skin the night before, his mouth on mine, and the hot puffs of breath against my neck.

After I'd kicked him out of the tent, my dick had been rock hard— a granite spike that had refused to go down, regardless of how pissed I'd been at Bennett for sneaking into my tent while I was asleep.

Finally, after cursing at myself for ten minutes, I hadn't been able to stop myself from jacking off to the memory of that fucking kiss. Bennett's taste, his tongue sliding against mine, and my desire to flip him over and pound into him had kept me from being able to fall asleep peacefully. Just once— *just once* I wanted to feel what it would be like to slide my cock into his tight body and fucking own him.

I shuddered at the thought and wanted to kick myself again. Jesus, why couldn't I stop obsessing over him?

I finished tying the knots and triple-checking the top ropes before climbing back down the small rock face to the ground below. Bennett and Aiden brought the group over to the base of the wall and began helping the first few kids get on helmets as I landed softly beside them.

One kid, a tall, dark-skinned boy named Calvin, who I guessed to be around seventeen with several tattoos on his arms, and black gauges in his ears, looked at me with a smirk on his face. "Aww, man. We were hoping you'd fall and bust your ass."

Before I had a chance to respond to the snide remark, Lucky spoke up. "Dude, seriously? You just climbed down that thing without falling. How'd you do that?"

"Lots of practice," I said with a smile. "Plus, I had a rope attached to my harness to make sure if I did fall, I wouldn't hit the ground. It's called a top rope. I climbed up to attach anchors so we have safety mechanisms in place before I teach you how to climb today. I'm going to go over the top rope and belay while the first couple of climbers get their harnesses on."

I got all of the boys' attention and began to teach them about the ropes and harnesses they'd be using for their first climb. When it was time for someone to go first, Calvin stepped forward immediately. "Me. I totally got this."

Forcing myself to smile instead of roll my eyes at his cocky attitude, I showed Calvin how to clip in to the belay set-up and attach the top rope to his harness with a carabiner.

"Stay there while I get Lucky squared away. I can't have both of you start until there are two adults on belay, okay?"

I ignored his muttered complaint and helped Lucky get connected. As I worked, I looked over at Aiden and Bennett who were standing shoulder to shoulder, watching me. I tried not to imagine the two of them naked together, and wondered what Aiden would think about his little boyfriend's midnight visit to my tent. Never in a million years would I have pegged Bennett as the cheating type. It was just further proof he wasn't the guy I'd once known.

"I need one of you to help belay," I said, unable to decide which man was the lesser of two evils.

"I'll do it," Aiden said quickly, before Bennett even had a chance to speak. "I've done it before."

As he approached and grabbed a harness from the pile of supplies at our feet, I couldn't help but look at him in surprise. "You have?" I asked. "When?"

He narrowed his eyes at me. "Do you really care? Just believe me when I say I know how to do it. I'll take Lucky."

Okay, so the man was being an ass as usual. I wondered if he knew what had happened between me and Bennett in my tent. Surely not. Knowing Aiden's type, he would have confronted me by now. Hell, if the roles had been reversed and I'd discovered Bennett had cheated on me, I'd kick Aiden's ass so hard…

I watched him get situated with the belay device before asking Lucky if he was ready. The kid looked at Aiden with a huge grin and said, "On belay?"

Aiden nodded and smiled back. "Belay on."

Okay, maybe he did know what he was doing.

As the two kids climbed up the rock side-by-side, I heard them talking to each other. At first, it sounded like regular smack-talk between friends, but then I realized there was an edge to it.

I quickly looked over at Aiden to see if he'd noticed. He was concentrating on the ropes and watching Lucky's feet.

Calvin's voice drifted down, just loudly enough for me to make it out. "What the hell kinda shoes are those? I thought you couldn't afford anything decent like that."

"B got them for me. Not that it's any of your damned business," Lucky snapped.

"Aww, how sweet. Lucky has a Sugar Daddy. At least yours is better than the one your mom had, huh?" Calvin chuckled before pulling himself up with another foothold in the rock.

Lucky stared after him. "What the fuck is that supposed to mean?" The response came out in a low growl, and I could barely make it out over the sound of the kids joking around behind Aiden and me.

"Lucky, Calvin—" I shouted up at them. "Less talking, more focusing. Bennett, can you back the kids up a bit so we can hear the climbers' instructions please?" I asked over my shoulder, not taking my eyes off the boys as they climbed higher, with Lucky slightly ahead of Calvin.

"Sure," Bennett said. I knew he was upset with me, but he did as I asked and got the other boys to back way up into the meadow behind us.

"What is it?" Aiden asked in a low voice.

"What's what?"

"They're not having any problems with this climb, so why are you worried about us not being able to hear them?"

I didn't bother telling him I didn't want the other kids hearing the shit Calvin was giving Lucky. I knew exactly what it was like to be on the receiving end of that crap. A guy like Aiden just wouldn't get it. I shrugged as I let out more rope. "Just good form, that's all."

"Whatever," I heard him mutter.

"What's Lucky's story?" I asked, just loudly enough for Aiden to hear.

He answered in the same low voice. "His mom's a prostitute. They lived with her pimp for a long time until the guy kicked Lucky out. Bennett found him on the streets and helped him find a good foster family."

"You're kidding?" I asked, not taking my eyes off the boys who were close to the top by now. I heard Aiden shift his weight.

"I wish I was. The kid hadn't had a proper meal in weeks. He'd been scavenging and was on the verge of having to pick up the same profession as his mom if B hadn't found him when he did. Makes me sick just thinking about it, and I know at least for a while it gave Bennett nightmares."

My eyes briefly drifted to Lucky. He was so small and scrawny... I couldn't even imagine what a life on the streets would have done to him. I'd already grown fond of the kid and even the idea of him having to sell himself to men...

I had to force myself not to look at Bennett. Despite all the shit between us I felt a spark of pride knowing what he'd done for the boy.

"Did Lucky stay at the same school?" I asked, wondering if maybe part of the problem included Calvin and other guys at his same school.

"Yeah, that was one of the benefits of the foster family he ended up with. It was the least impact to his life. Same friends, same teachers."

"That's not always a good thing," I suggested.

"On rappel," Lucky called out from above.

I glanced at the kid, noticing the huge smile of accomplishment on his face from reaching the top of the small climb first. Calvin, on the other hand, was frowning. Typical bully. Couldn't even enjoy the pleasure of his own accomplishment because he was too busy being all pissy about a kid he perceived as lesser beating him.

"Great job, guys," I called out.

"Rappel when ready," Aiden called to Lucky.

With the way Calvin was eyeing Lucky before he called out "On rappel," I decided I would keep an eye out for Lucky as the week went by, especially when he was hanging around the larger boy. While I hadn't faced any acts of violence from the kids at Bennett's and my private high school, their cruel taunts had left wounds just the same.

When the next two climbers were roped in and on their ascent, I felt Aiden's eyes on me.

"What?" I huffed. God, the guy just rubbed me wrong, and not just because he was fucking the man I wanted… the man who should've been mine.

"Jesus, you're an ass," he said.

"Seems to be a popular opinion around here," I muttered, thinking of Bennett who'd taken some of the boys to a nearby creek to wash their hands and collect water for dinner prep.

"I don't know what Bennett ever saw in you."

I felt my jaw tighten and tried to concentrate on the kids above me. "Well, I sure as hell don't get what he sees in you."

Aiden barked out a laugh. "Really? C'mon, man. What's not to love? I'm a catch. Tall, gorgeous, and rich as hell."

If my teeth ground together any more, they might just break apart.

He continued. "Plus, my dick is fucking huuuu—"

"I get it," I bit out. "Good for you."

"And, god, he knows exactly what to do with it too," Aiden drawled. "The man's mouth is like—"

"Stop talking," I spat. "Right fucking now."

The asshole just laughed. "My, my, aren't we touchy today? What's the matter, Xander? Wish you could have a little taste of him too?"

It was on the tip of my tongue to tell him that I'd had my tongue down his lover's throat the night before, but I held back.

*Just focus on the climbers, Xander. The kids.*

I watched the boys and tried to enjoy the feeling of the warm sun on my back and the sound of the cool breeze teasing through the trees nearby. My head was spinning with thoughts, and all I wanted to do was take off into the mountains. Remove the climbing gear and walk away. Hike toward the cool blue water of Elk Lake and up the switch-back trail to Fractured Pass.

But I knew I couldn't. I owed it to Gary. His business depended on clients like Bennett and Aiden's foundation, and he worked hard all winter to make sure those coveted summer spots were filled. I also owed it to these kids who obviously needed this trip out of the city they'd been stuck in their whole lives. And I owed it to myself to prove I was strong enough to handle all of the Bennett shit without breaking down. Guys like Bennett and Aiden had no control over me anymore.

I took a deep breath and let out more rope.

"So," Aiden said in a cheerful tone, as if he hadn't been deliberately baiting me a moment earlier. "Tell me about your friend Jake. Is he single?"

I felt my jaw drop open. Was he kidding? Surely this was more of his bullshit meant to rile me up. "What? Why?"

Aiden shrugged. "He's hot. Is he gay? Please tell me he's not the dominant top he appears to be, because I haven't been able to stop myself from fantasizing about getting in that ass ever since I laid eyes on him at the trailhead."

"You are the cockiest asshole I've ever met," I said. "Are you for real? I hope you're kidding right now, at least for Bennett's sake."

He laughed. "Oh, *now* you're worried about Bennett's frail heart? That's cute."

"Does Bennett know you're making plans to fuck some stranger when we get back to the lodge?" I asked.

Aiden just laughed and shrugged again. "I don't need his permission. But, no, I haven't mentioned my infatuation with Jake's ass to him. Maybe I could get Jake *and* Bennett together for a—"

Luckily, the sound of one of the kids reaching the top and asking permission to rappel down kept me from dropping the ropes and beating the fuck out of the asshole. The next hour was spent in virtual silence as the rest of the kids took their turns. Fortunately, Aiden seemed to have gotten a clue and the only times he spoke to me were in relation to the kids and the climb. Once the last kids were down, we spent a few minutes detaching ropes and removing harnesses before I told the group they could go back and start dinner while I removed the anchor ropes up top.

"Want me on belay?" Aiden asked with a giant grin after the last kid walked off.

"Go to hell," I growled.

Thankfully, Aiden took off to join the rest of the group, but not before shouting to me from the edge of the trees one last time. "Bennett Crawford is one of the best men I know, Xander. And for some strange reason he thinks you hung the fucking moon. Hurt him again and you'll answer to me."

I ignored him as I began my climb, but of course it didn't work because he yelled, "Xander, did you hear what I said?" There was no humor in his voice this time and I knew the warning was just that. Despite all the shit he'd said about pursuing Jake, the edge in his voice told me he'd just as soon beat the shit out of me if I didn't heed the warning. I wondered why the hell he wasn't warning me to stay away from his boyfriend instead.

I glanced at him only long enough to see him shoot me one last glare before taking off down the path, but his last question echoed in my head, bringing back memories from so many years ago. The night that changed everything.

*"Xander, did you hear what I said?"*

*"Where's Bennett?" I asked. Mr. Crawford dropped a heavy hand on my shoulder. I automatically stopped rocking back and forth because he'd already told me twice to stop doing it. My butt hurt from sitting in the hard plastic chair for so long, but I was afraid to leave it.*

*Because I knew what leaving it would mean.*

*It would mean everything the weird-smelling guy in the white jacket had said about my dad was true. And it couldn't be true.*

*I began rocking again, mostly to stave off the bile that was crawling up my throat. If Mr. Crawford didn't like the rocking, that was just too bad because I figured he'd like me throwing up on his fancy shoes even less.*

*"Xander, did you hear what I said?" he repeated.*

*"Where's Bennett?" I asked again. Bennett would know what to do. He'd tell me it wasn't true and then we'd go home and he'd tell me good night and then he'd wink at me... that wink that said I'd be seeing him again just as soon as he was able to sneak out of the house.*

*I hadn't seen that wink in a long time.*

*But I'd see it today.*

*I had to.*

*Because my dad was dead and Bennett would know I needed that wink and I needed his arms around me and I needed his stupid jokes.*

*"Bennett isn't here," Mr. Crawford said. I could tell he was getting impatient with me, so I tried to focus.*

*"Xander—"*

*"I heard you," I cut in. "You said Aunt Lolly is on her way from Florida. She's going to come stay with me."*

*"Right," Mr. Crawford said and I could hear the relief in his voice. Man, did he think I was too stupid to remember the few words he'd said after I'd watched the paramedics load my dad into the ambulance?*

*I barely noticed as Bennett's father wandered off to talk some more on his cell phone. I heard only enough to know that my dad's death was proving to be an inconvenience for him.*

*"Xander, honey, do you want a soda?"*

*I looked up at the round-faced nurse who'd introduced herself as Sarah-Anne. "Where's my dad?" I asked.*

*Her gentle smile faded and she glanced down the busy corridor. It had been two hours since I'd followed Mr. Crawford into the bustling ER. Even now, we were surrounded by people doing everything from coughing to crying to laughing, and ranting, but I barely noticed them.*

*"They're just finishing up with him," she said.*

*Finishing up? What did you have to finish up when it came to a dead man?*

*Part of me didn't want to know. "Can I see him?"*

*The woman straightened and then began looking around the room. "Um, why don't I look into that for you?" she said awkwardly and I knew my question hadn't been the right one. I didn't bother saying anything else as she made a comment about coming right back. I knew she wouldn't.*

*I winced. I didn't always say the right thing.*

*Except to Bennett. Bennett always got what I was saying... or what I wasn't.*

*I debated calling him, but I didn't remember his new cell phone number. I looked around the crowded waiting room and then got to my feet. I needed to see my dad.*

*Because I still didn't believe it.*

*Dad had been talking to me. Even as he'd been holding onto his arm and telling me to call for help, he'd been talking. He'd been warm. He'd told me how much he loved me and that everything was going to be okay.*

*Someone had just messed up. They'd gotten it wrong.*

*I began walking towards the electronic doors all the doctors and nurses kept disappearing through. I saw Mr. Crawford in a corner of the waiting room, still on his phone. Even though he was facing me, he didn't notice me. But that was nothing new.*

*Bennett's parents were pretty good at not seeing the help.*

*No one stopped me when I walked through the doors. The smell of blood and some kind of strong chemical hit me at the same time, threatening to send my already rolling stomach into overdrive. As I made my way down the hallway, I began peeking through the edges of the curtains that blocked off the different treatment rooms. I numbed myself to the sight of people covered in blood and bandages. I didn't hear the sobs or cries of pain. I didn't wonder about what was wrong with them. In truth, I didn't care. I couldn't... not while my dad was lying in a room somewhere worried about me.*

*That's what he would be, too. Worried about me. No matter how much pain he was in or how concerned he was about how we were going to pay for however much all this hospital shit cost, he'd be thinking of me first and foremost. And the sooner he saw I was okay, he'd get better and then we'd go home.*

*But when I finally found him in the last room at the end of the hallway, I knew that weird-smelling doctor guy hadn't messed up. Neither had Mr. Crawford when he'd called my Aunt Lolly and told her that her brother was dead. I placed my fingers on my father's too-cold skin and all I could think was this was wrong, this was wrong,* this was wrong. *And my last coherent thought was that only Bennett could fix it.*

The sound of Bear barking ripped me from my thoughts and I realized I'd reached the top of the small rock face and had just been hanging there, lost in the memory. The pain was as raw now as it had been then, as I'd waited for Bennett to show up at the hospital that day.

He never did.

# CHAPTER 10

## BENNETT

After spending the entire afternoon watching Xander's arm muscles flex as he worked the climbing ropes, I was about ready to come out of my skin. He'd avoided me like the plague on the morning's hike, which was nothing new, but then he'd seemed even weirder after the afternoon's climbing lesson.

Every time he spoke to me, he spat the words. And god forbid Xander needed to speak to Aiden. Then he'd just ignore the guy like Aiden didn't even exist. For some reason, it just made Aiden laugh. It had taken me a while to realize what was happening between Xander and Aiden, but it had finally dawned on me that Aiden was deliberately baiting Xander, and as soon as Aiden reached camp after leaving Xander to clean up the remnants of the rock climbing, I pulled him aside.

"What the hell are you doing?" I asked.

"What do you mean?" Aiden asked with mock innocence.

"You're egging him on. Every time Xander says anything, you've got some smartass response that's meant to get a rise out of him. I want to know what the hell you're up to."

Aiden's blue eyes studied me as his smirk faded. "Bennett, just trust me, okay?"

"No, not okay. What does that even mean?" I was so tired of feeling like I was a kid stuck between two schoolyard bullies.

"The man clearly still has a thing for you. I'm just helping him figure it out."

I stared at him. "Are you fucking crazy?" I hissed. "First of all, no he doesn't. He hates me. Secondly, I need your help patching things up with Xander like I need a hole in the head. Stop helping." I ran my hands through my hair before muttering, "Jesus."

Aiden laughed. "This actually reminds me of how we got together."

The remark had something inside of me suddenly releasing and my breath came out in a whoosh of laughter so loud, several of the kids looked over to see what was going on.

"Oh my god. Please don't remind me," I said with a grin. It was too late, of course. I was already running the memories of that night through my head.

Aiden snorted. "Joey and… what was that guy's name? The one you roomed with freshman year."

"Gus," I said.

He chuckled. "Right, Gus. Why can't I ever remember that guy's name? You roomed with him that whole year. I always want to call him Mouse for some reason."

"Maybe you're thinking of the mouse from *Cinderella*," I suggested. "Gus Gus."

"I'm not going to ask how you know that. Anyway, Gus was sobbing on your shoulder and Joey was in tears on mine, and you and I spent two hours trying to broker the peace deal of the century to help our roommates patch things up."

I laughed again. "It didn't work."

"That's an understatement. But something good came out of it anyway," he said with a sweet smile.

"Yeah. I guess. Not like you and I lasted any longer than Joey and Gus did, though. You dumped my ass."

Aiden's hand came out to tip my chin up. "I'm still here, aren't I?" he asked quietly.

For some reason, his touch was exactly what I needed, and I

stepped into his embrace and put my arms around his waist. Aiden was still there for me, just like he had been for the past ten years. Even though the dating portion of our relationship had been one-sided, we'd still managed to stay friends somehow.

He gave me a tight squeeze before releasing me and pointing to a fallen log for us to sit on.

"Do you know why I really broke things off with you, Bennett?" he asked in a low voice— his serious voice. Serious Aiden was always a sight to behold, but I didn't necessarily like when it was directed at me. Maybe because I knew he only saved that voice for when he was going to tell me something we both knew I wouldn't want to hear.

"Because you're a commitment-phobe who's terrified of letting anyone get close enough to tear down the steel walls around your wounded heart?" I asked, hoping to keep that lightness between us for another few seconds.

Aiden blinked at me before shaking his head. "Ah, no… but thanks for that."

"No prob," I said. "Continue."

"I always felt like I was a placeholder for you."

"What do you mean?" I asked, trying not to feel a pinch of hurt from his words.

Aiden blew out a breath and stretched his legs before crossing them at the ankles. "Bennett, you've been in love with that guy over there since the dawn of time. Your first wet dream was probably Xander walking across the playground with his light-up Sketchers."

I felt my face heat up. "He couldn't afford Sketchers," I mumbled. I didn't add in the fact that I'd given Xander my new Sketchers for his birthday that year and told my father I'd lost them at school. Luckily, he'd been too preoccupied to notice how my best friend's new, expensive sneakers had looked so very familiar.

Aiden's warm hand landed on my shoulder and I turned to look at him. "He's the reason you do all of this, isn't he?"

"Do all of what?" I asked.

"Your dad is desperate for you to take the helm of The Crawford Group, but you insist on running the foundation instead."

I bristled at his words and opened my mouth to respond. Aiden held up a hand before I had a chance.

"I know, I know. You love working with the kids. You'd rather help people in need than help rich assholes get richer. Save it. You've told me all that before. I was just wondering why. Is it because of Xander?"

My eyes snuck a glance back toward the campfire where the man in question was busy demonstrating some climbing knots the kids had asked about earlier in the day. I hadn't even noticed his return or that darkness had started to fall.

"No," I said softly. "I never saw him like that, you know? I actually envied his life in a lot of ways… what he had with his dad." My thoughts drifted to all the fun Xander, Mr. Reed and I had always had when I'd gone to their house for dinner or they'd taken me on one of their excursions to the beach or hiking. Yes, I'd had more money, but Xander had seemed rich in so many other ways.

"I don't want to be like them," I whispered. It was a truth I'd never even admitted to myself.

"The kids?" Aiden asked in confusion.

I shook my head. "My parents. It's always been about money and status and privilege. I keep thinking there'll be a point where something inside of me will switch and I'll look at a guy like Xander and see someone… lesser. Like how my dad saw Xander's dad." I glanced at Aiden and said, "They were friends once, did you know that?"

"Xander's dad and yours?"

I nodded. "Well, friends might have been a stretch, but when Xander's mom was around, their whole family would come over and Mr. Reed and my dad would sneak off to the study for a drink. He only ever did that with his friends. But when Mr. Reed started working for him…" My heart clenched and my throat felt tight. "He had to use the employee entrance if he wanted to come into the house."

"The employee entrance?"

I nodded. "All the people who worked at the house could only enter through this side door in the laundry room. If they wanted to talk to my parents, they actually had to use this phone on the wall…

they weren't even allowed to come all the way into the house. Only the maid had free roam of the house, but even she had rules. They just became... non-people to my parents."

"You're nothing like that, Bennett," Aiden said firmly. "You *couldn't* be like that if you tried."

I wasn't so sure, so I didn't respond. I let my eyes settle on the kids who were all completely engrossed in what Xander was saying to them. I dropped my eyes as soon as Xander glanced my way, because I was too messed up to deal with yet another look of hatred or disgust.

"I don't want those kids to ever feel like that... like they don't matter. Like they have to use a certain door. I know that doesn't make any sense—"

"It does," Aiden interjected and I felt his fingers brush the back of my hands where I had them clasped between my legs. "It makes perfect sense, B. But I think there's more there, too."

There was, but I was too wrung out to try to explain it. Fortunately, Aiden didn't press me on it.

"So if running the foundation is what you want to do with your life, when are you going to tell your dad?" Aiden asked.

I felt a familiar bolt of nerves shoot through my gut. "I've already tried. He refuses to accept it. When he offered me the position with the foundation, he made me agree that it was temporary. He's already talking about having me shadow the VP when I get back because the guy's retiring next year. My dad wants to retire early too, which means I'll only have a couple of years as VP before I take over as CEO." Even saying the words out loud had weight pressing down on my chest and I couldn't stop my breathing from ticking up.

Aiden put a reassuring hand on my knee and my eyes automatically sought out Xander. Predictably, he was glaring at me, and I quickly pulled my knee out from under Aiden's hand.

After watching Xander turn away to continue speaking to the kids, I heard Aiden chuckle softly. I turned and narrowed my eyes at him. "What?"

He stood up and brushed off the seat of his pants. "The pair of you are so blind. It actually hurts to watch."

Aiden wandered back toward the campfire, deliberately stepping in Xander's line of sight as he walked past. I noticed Xander's jaw tighten by the shadows from the firelight and wondered if Aiden realized how close Xander was to losing his self-control. I could tell it wouldn't take much to set my old friend off.

As I got up to make my own way back, I remembered a time in middle school when some kids at a nearby lunch table had made fun of Xander after they'd seen his dad pick us up in his old pickup truck from school one day.

"Hey Bennett," one kid had called out. "You getting rides from your parents' gardener these days or is Xander's dad doing double-duty as your chauffeur?" The rest of the kids at the table had cracked up and slapped the first guy on the back for his comment.

I'd looked over at Xander to see his reaction and had seen the familiar tight set of his jaw that had usually meant the timer on the bomb had been set and detonation was imminent.

"Don't do it," I'd warned my best friend under my breath. "They're not worth it."

"Benny," he'd growled softly.

"I know. Just wait, okay? We'll eat outside and then I'll let you beat the shit out of me on the basketball court."

"You're not the one I want to beat up," he'd muttered with clenched fists. He'd never actually gotten into any physical altercations with the kids who'd considered it their duty to endlessly needle him about his place on the socio-economic totem pole, but I'd known it was just a matter of time, since the kids' taunts had become bolder and bolder.

"Hey, Norwood," I'd called to the instigator in a voice that had reached all corners of the lunchroom. "Mrs. Franklin wanted me to tell you she finally got her period, so you don't have anything to worry about."

There'd been a beat of complete silence before the entire cafeteria had erupted in laughter and Simon Norwood's face had turned the color of the school's cardinal mascot.

Once Xander and I had slipped safely outside to a picnic table,

Xander had looked at me with wide eyes and a huge grin. Bingo. The reason I'd done almost everything in those days. That fucking smile.

"Mrs. Franklin?" he'd giggled. "She's like a thousand years old. Why'd you pick her of all the teachers?"

I'd shrugged. "I figured she was the least likely to hear about it since she always forgets to put in her hearing aids," I'd said, finally allowing myself to laugh too.

I hid the smile the memory evoked as I approached the campfire and sat down next to Lucky and snuck one last glance at my old friend on the other side of the flickering orange flames. His jaw had loosened, but his face remained unsmiling.

Goddammit. Why did that cut me so deeply?

I began to wonder if there would ever be a time I could once again put that smile back on his face.

# CHAPTER 11

## XANDER

The following day was a long hike, but it was one of my favorites. We spent the morning traveling past Elk Lake and across Fractured Pass. The plan was to continue down from Fractured Pass to Woodland Basin and camp at Basin Lake. Once settled there, we'd have time to teach the boys how to fish before dinner.

When we stopped for the kids to take photos at the top of the pass, they took advantage of some late-thawing snow and threw snowballs at each other. Once the excitement of the pure white snow died down, I explained what a hydrological divide was and how the Continental Divide ran through the Rocky Mountains.

"If you poured a bucket of water over the top of the Continental Divide," I explained, "the water running down one side would eventually drain into the Atlantic Ocean and the water on the other side would end up in the Pacific."

"No shit?" one kid asked.

"No kidding," I said. "And in the Canadian Rockies, there's the world's only confirmed triple hydrological divide. Can anyone guess what the third body of water involved in that triple divide is? Remember, we're talking about water draining in Canada."

The most popular guess was the Bering Sea and I realized several of our guessers were fans of a certain crabbing program on television.

"Nope. The third ocean reached by the triple divide on Snow Dome mountain in Canada is the Arctic Ocean," I said.

I saw Lucky staring north across the tops of several snow-covered peaks in the distance. "Wow, that's so cool," he murmured to himself.

"It is very cool," I said, walking up and standing next to him. "How'd you know which way to look for the Canadian Rockies?" I asked.

"Simple geography. They're north of us in Alberta, and that way's north… right?" he asked, turning to look at me with a raised brow.

I smiled. "Yep. That way's north. Good job. Seems like someone I know was paying attention to the map skills I taught on the first day," I suggested with a wink. I loved how Lucky straightened a little more at the compliment.

"Well, if you don't know which way's which out here, you're kinda screwed, right?"

I couldn't help but laugh. "You are, indeed. Now, which direction is tonight's camp at Basin Lake? Can you find it from here?"

He turned around in a slow three-hundred-and-sixty-degree circle before narrowing his eyes on a nearby landmark that stood out. "Do you have the map?" he asked.

I handed him the folded paper map without speaking and watched as he oriented it with the marks of the compass.

"Basin Lake is that way," he said, reaching out an arm to point in the correct direction. "Right?"

"Right you are," I said with a pat on his shoulder. "Lead on, navigator. You're in charge of getting us there."

"No way," he said, shoving the map back at me. I didn't take it.

"No take-backs," I said, indicating the folded paper. "That damned thing is too heavy for me anyway. I'm already carrying all the climbing equipment, and I'm an old man."

He rolled his eyes at me, but I could see a hint of pride in his step as he walked to the front of the group.

"Okay, everyone. Apparently, I'm leading the hike this afternoon.

The quicker we find Basin Lake, the sooner Bennett will have to prove those stellar fishing skills he keeps bragging about," Lucky announced.

I followed him up to lead the pack, laughing under my breath at the idea of Bennett as an expert fisherman.

"What?" Lucky asked as we began hiking down the far side of the pass. "Is B bullshitting us or something?"

I shrugged and said, "For all I know, he's an expert now."

"But when you were kids?" he asked with a grin.

"When we were kids, it was a whole different story. One time we watched a movie where a guy caught fish with his bare hands. So, Bennett and I decided to try it out in his parent's koi pond."

"Koi? What's that?" Lucky asked, his brow furrowed.

"Those are those big-ass goldfish with the fancy tails, right?" Calvin asked as he sidled up next to us.

"That's right," I responded.

"So what happened?" Calvin prodded. He was walking next to Lucky, so I kept an eye on him just to make sure he didn't try to mess with the younger guy.

"So we went to the pond and plonked right in there in these ridiculous rain boots we'd stolen from my dad's work shed. Of course, as soon as the water level reached over the edges of the boots, they became swamped and came off with our next step. But we didn't care. Just kept wading out to the middle like the guy in the movie had done."

Lucky watched me with bright eyes and I noticed two more boys had appeared on the other side of me to listen.

"What happened next?" one of the boys asked.

"Well, your fearless leader found what he proclaimed was the perfect fish-catching spot. He made a big deal about getting in position so he wouldn't accidentally tip over, and then he held up his hands like a surgeon waiting for gloves. 'Watch and learn,' he said and stupid me believed he could do it," I continued, as a laugh bubbled up my throat. It felt foreign to me at first, but one look at the kids and I hurried on. "So, he lurched in with both arms when he saw one of the big goldfish swim past. Missed. Then tried again. Another miss."

The boys had started chuckling as I described Bennett getting wetter and wetter with every attempt.

"Finally, he wiggled his ass to get ready for the ultimate attempt before giving up. Only this time I could tell by the look in his eyes, he was prepared to go all in." I actually had to stop for a second because another round of laughter hit me unexpectedly.

"Then what happened?" Lucky asked, laughing since I was laughing.

"He… he saw one of the biggest koi swim toward him and took off in a giant flying leap just as his dad walked out of his office onto the back patio and saw us. Right when Mr. Crawford yelled, Bennett turned his head and landed in a giant belly flop on the water. I swear I saw three big koi splash up into the air." I barely managed to get out the words as an image of Bennett's startled expression hit me. "One of them landed on the stone surrounding the patio right in front of Mr. Crawford. He stood there gaping at it, and then just turned and walked back into his office. As if the whole thing was just par for the course with the two of us."

The boys turned to call back to Bennett, who was presumably hiking in the back of the pack.

"B? Is it true you once captured a koi fish with your bare hands?" the kid called out.

I didn't look back, but could imagine the mischievous grin sliding across Bennett's lips.

"Who wants to know?" he called up to us. "Has someone up there been telling stories about me?"

The warmth in Bennett's voice stroked over my entire body. Fuck. Why had I told this story in the first place?

"Yeah. Xander makes it sound like your technique involves cannonballing into the water and splashing poor unsuspecting fish onto shore," Lucky called back over his shoulder. "That doesn't sound like expertise as much as dumb luck."

"I never promised I was an expert at it. Just that I was good at it," he teased back. "We had that poor koi for dinner that night, didn't we, Xander?"

I bit my tongue to keep from laughing. What we'd had for dinner that night had been exactly nothing. We'd been sent to Bennett's room without dinner for fucking up the Crawford's pristine decorative whatever.

"Xander?" Lucky asked when I didn't respond to Bennett's tease.

"Best damned koi dinner I've ever had," I replied with a small smile, and I couldn't resist the urge to look over my shoulder at Bennett. His warm brown eyes were on mine, and for the first time since he'd stepped off that bus, I let myself enjoy that memory with him. It felt so good to just laugh. I hadn't even really realized until this very moment how long it had been since I'd done just that.

Because of Bennett… because of all the things he'd done and said when we were kids to make sure I'd always had something to laugh about.

Lucky turned back to his map to double-check our direction as we continued making our way forward.

I forced myself to focus on Lucky and the trail, but for the rest of the hike down to Basin Lake, I couldn't stop my damned brain from replaying scenes from my childhood. Of course, the one I didn't want to remember was the scene I kept coming back to. The last time I'd seen Bennett— when he'd fucking ripped my heart out.

*"Can I see Bennett?" I whispered as I tried to hold back the tears that were threatening to fall. I'd hoped and prayed Bennett would be the one to answer the door, but since life had decided today should be my worst nightmare come to life, it had also figured giving Mr. Crawford a starring role would be more amusing. After a nurse had found me passed out on the floor next to the gurney that had held my father's sheet-draped body, Mr. Crawford had explained that he had things to see to and that my aunt would be arriving soon to take care of me.*

*I'd only met my Aunt Lolly a few times, though it hadn't been because my father and she had been on the outs. No, my aunt was what my father had labeled a free spirit, and he'd explained that Lolly only got seen when she wanted to. I'd never really understood what that meant, but after meeting her a couple times, I'd learned enough to know that although she was an odd duck, she was a loving one. When she'd arrived to pick me up from the hospi-*

*tal, she'd held me for a really long time, and while it had felt good to have someone warm touching me after feeling my father's icy skin, Aunt Lolly hadn't been the one I'd needed.*

*No, the only one I needed was currently tucked away in the too-big mansion somewhere, and to see him, I had to get through Mr. Crawford first.*

*When I'd escaped the cottage for the big house and asked to see Bennett, I could hear music blaring from the back of the house. I could only assume the Crawfords were having yet another party, but that would be good for me because Bennett could easily sneak out when his parents were preoccupied with entertaining their fancy friends.*

*"Please, can I see him?" I asked again when Mr. Crawford made no move to get Bennett.*

*"Now isn't the time," he said blandly.*

*I could feel the tears threatening to spill over my eyelids, so I quickly looked away from him and said, "I'll just be a minute. Promise."*

*I didn't even need the full minute. I just wanted Bennett's arms around me long enough for him to send me that secret message I needed so badly. Whether he gave me his infamous wink or he squeezed me just a little harder than necessary or he whispered something nonsensical into my ear; I just needed something that I could hang onto until he could sneak away to be with me.*

*Mr. Crawford huffed and said, "Just don't keep him." Then he shut the door in my face, and I heard him calling Bennett's name. I used the few seconds to dash madly at my eyes to try and clear them, but nothing I did could stem the tears. God, I just needed Bennett so fucking bad. I thought I could wait for him to come find me, but I knew I couldn't. I felt like I was dying... like it was* my *chest being crushed like a vise. Was this what my father had felt in his final moments? This crushing weight? This uncertainty about whether or not he was dying?*

*When the door opened again, I let out a harsh sob at the sight of my friend and I stepped forward, too impatient to wait for Bennett to come to me. "Benny," I cried out. But before I could reach him, he closed the door a little, leaving just enough room for his body. I stopped mid-stride.*

*"Hey," he said softly, and then he cast a glance over his shoulder. When his eyes returned to me, he murmured, "Sorry to hear about your dad."*

*I nodded because I didn't know what else to do. Why wasn't he letting me in? Or coming out?*

*"Benny, I need—"*

*A voice from somewhere inside the house cut me off and I saw Bennett look over his shoulder again. More voices joined the first and I realized he wasn't alone. And the voices weren't those of the Crawfords' adult friends.*

*"Dude, you coming or what?"*

*Even in my fucked-up state, I knew whose voice that was.*

*Garrett Somersby. Captain of Bennett's crew team and the guy who'd thought it was his personal mission in life to point out that I didn't belong at Knollwood Academy because I was the dreaded scholarship kid.*

*"Bennett?" I whispered, hoping against hope that it wasn't true. That my mind was still playing tricks on me.*

*"Uh," Bennett began, but then the door was being opened, and yes, by Garrett.*

*"Hey, it's the Knollwood freeloader," Garrett said snidely. "You selling girl scout cookies or something to help pay for that scholarship?" he said with a laugh. The door opened wider to reveal several more of Bennett's friends. I saw his father standing several feet away, arms crossed.*

*"I came to talk to Bennett," I murmured, even as an ice-cold chill settled over my body.*

*"What, you want to tell him about some gardening emergency?" Garrett said with a laugh.*

*I shook my head and let my eyes connect with Bennett's.*

Wink, Bennett. Please fucking wink at me.

*More tears fell as I waited, prayed... but there was nothing. Even worse, Bennett looked embarrassed.*

*"Come on, B," Garrett said as he slapped Bennett on the shoulder. Pool's calling our name."*

*He was having a pool party? My dad was dead and Bennett was having a fucking pool party? The boys disappeared back into the house, leaving the two of us alone again.*

*"Xander..." Bennett began, but then his father's cough interrupted him.*

*"You should get back to your friends, Son," Mr. Crawford said. "Xander, you run on home. Your aunt's probably worried about you."*

*I froze for a beat before nodding and turning away. I felt numb. I tried to walk, but I couldn't manage it. I had no pride left. So, I ran and I kept running until I reached the small caretaker's cottage my father and I had called home for so long. But it wasn't home anymore.*

*Not with my father gone. And not if Bennett was no longer the person I thought he was...*

*I didn't even manage to finish my thought before I fell to my knees on the hard cement walkway and finally gave into the rolling in my stomach. When my aunt found me lying beside a pool of my own vomit ten minutes later, I let her believe my tears were only because I'd lost my father.*

*Even if they weren't.*

*Because I'd lost so, so much more than that.*

*I'd lost everything.*

"Xander?"

Lucky's voice caught my attention and I managed to look up to see he'd stopped hiking at some point, which meant the entire group had and everyone was currently staring at me. A quick look at Bennett revealed the concern in his expression.

"Sorry, what?" I asked.

"Is this where we're stopping for the night?" Lucky asked, and I quickly looked around and saw that we'd reached the lake. I nodded and automatically began giving out instructions to the kids. By the time we got the camp set up, I'd gone through all of the emotions of that night over and over, vowing yet again that I wouldn't feel sorry for myself. I wasn't holding a damned pity party. I refused to be sad about it any longer. I refused to be anything. Bennett had no fucking hold on me anymore. He was just some guy.

No, he wasn't even that.

He was no one.

Just like I'd been no one that night when he'd closed the door on me.

Unfortunately, Aiden picked that moment to get in my face about something and I snapped at him, proof that maybe I wasn't as unaffected as I wanted to be.

He stepped back and held his hands up. "Uh, chill, Ranger Rick. I was just trying to find out if you knew where the fillet knife was for the fish."

"Your boyfriend's the fisherman. Ask him," I barked, picking up my water bottle and heading off into the woods so I wouldn't be tempted to ram my fist into Aiden's perfect face.

# CHAPTER 12

## BENNETT

It was getting dark and the kids were settling down in their own tent groups for the night when I finally got Xander far enough away from the other kids to talk to him about what had happened with Aiden earlier. They'd had some kind of blowup before Xander had disappeared for the entire fishing lesson with the kids.

He'd returned to help with dinner but hadn't said a word to anyone the entire time. Now, when I saw him head through the woods to the creek with Bear, I decided to follow him. As soon as he reached the edge of the creek and realized I was behind him, he turned and glared at me.

"Go back to camp, Bennett."

"What the hell is going on between you and Aiden?" I asked.

"He's an asshole. You two deserve each other. Now leave me alone." He spun and continued toward the creek.

His jab hurt, but I pushed down the pain and asked, "Did something happen?"

This time when he turned back, the look in his eyes was a cross between hatred and anguish, and it hit me right in the gut. I wanted to double over with the pain of it, but I stood frozen instead.

"What part aren't you getting, Bennett? I don't want you here. I don't want to talk to you. I don't want to even fucking look at you." Xander squeezed his eyes closed for a moment before pinning me with a hard look. "You know what? Be with him. I thought maybe you deserved better, but I realized I don't know you. Maybe I never really did. Maybe you two are perfect for each other. For all I know, you like guys like that. The one thing I *am* certain about is that I don't want anything to do with you anymore, Bennett Crawford, so just leave me the hell alone."

I stood there staring at him, knowing I'd had a strong hand in changing the sweet, quiet boy I'd known into this angry, bitter man, but I couldn't quell the frustration that went through me, either. I felt like a raw, open wound and my self-preservation instincts kicked in.

"Fine. I've been turning myself inside out to talk to you and apologize for what happened the night your dad died, but if you're so hell-bent on pushing me away, I guess that's it then."

I turned back toward camp before stopping and clenching my fists. As usual, I couldn't stop it there. "Just for the record, I'm not fucking Aiden. We had a thing in college but it's been over for years. We're just friends."

"Whatever," Xander mumbled. "Like I care."

*Seriously?* I whipped back around and stalked closer to him, fighting the tears of anger I could feel building. "What the hell happened to you? When did you become such a jackass?"

Xander stood back up from where he'd been squatting by the stream to fill his bottle. He took two giant strides toward me until his chest was practically pressed up against mine. His familiar cobalt eyes glinted in the dim moonlight streaking through the trees.

"The night you closed the door on me," he said without any kind of hesitation at all.

My chin trembled and I begged the fucking tears to stay put, even if they had to cling to my eyeballs by nothing but a sheer force of will.

"I hate you," I said. It came out as more of a sob than an accusation, and I felt myself wince at the sound of it.

"The feeling is mutual," he rumbled. "Join the fucking club."

I turned again to leave but he grabbed me by the elbow and spun me around, pushing my back up against a nearby tree. "Why do you keep trying to fix this?" he barked in my face, clearly frustrated.

My traitorous dick began to throb at his nearness, even though my self-preservation instinct was telling me to run. "Because… because I want…" My eyes cast downward at the ground. "I want…"

"What do you want, Benny?" It was like a whisper, a caress that I felt all the way into my gut and down into my balls. He stepped forward as he waited for my answer. His chest brushed mine and I felt his fingers stroke my neck before his entire hand came to rest on the side of my throat. I could feel him trembling as he applied just the tiniest bit of pressure. His eyes closed like he was in pain or something and I felt my own lids slide shut because I knew I was the cause of all that hurt and rage.

*You,* I thought. *God, all I ever wanted was you.*

I opened my eyes to see him staring at me and I knew, just knew that not saying the words aloud hadn't mattered. He'd heard them just the same because the next thing I knew his mouth was crushing down on mine. It wasn't a peck or a brush of lips, or even a kiss.

It was a claiming. An owning. An absolute possession of my mouth and my entire focus there in that clearing by the creek.

Gone were the rough scratches of the bark on my back. Gone were the night sounds of animals in the trees around us or the trickling of the water in the creek by our feet. It was just the two of us in some kind of lip fuck unlike anything I'd ever known before.

I couldn't have even said where his mouth left off and mine began. Suddenly, my hands were everywhere— under his shirt, over the warm skin of his back, sneaking around front to find the bumpy ridges of the stomach muscles I'd felt that night in his tent.

Moans escaped his mouth as my hands moved and I suddenly realized that he was holding me up against him by my ass. His large hands squeezed my cheeks as he ground his hard cock against my stomach and pressed me back against the tree.

*Fuck, fuck, fuck.* I wanted to be plastered against him with nothing between us. I wanted his hands everywhere on me and mine on him.

Part of me even wanted to turn and face the tree, shove my bare ass in his face and beg him to fuck me.

"Want inside," he gasped between nibbles along my jaw.

"Huh?" I asked in a daze. "Wha—?"

"Turn around," he growled as he released my ass, causing a whimper of need and desperation to escape me.

Yes, yes, I would turn around and let him do whatever the fuck he wanted. This would likely be my only chance to ever know him this way, and I sure as shit was going to take it. The memory would need to last me a goddamn lifetime. As I began to turn, his hands grabbed my hips and stopped me before deft fingers moved to the fly of my hiking shorts and made quick work of it.

"Oh god," I groaned as the cool night air hit my throbbing dick.

"Turn."

I shuddered at his commanding tone and did exactly as he said. My hands came up to support me against the rough bark and I spared a moment to glance back toward camp and make sure no one was coming.

Were we really doing this? Was this really happening?

"Xander?"

"Quiet," I heard him say as he pressed his lips to my ear and then bit gently down on the lobe. "This ass is mine, Bennett, do you hear me?" he practically snarled as his big hand caressed my globes before giving them a gentle smack. "He might get to have you every fucking night after this one, but tonight, you belong to me."

I knew he was talking about Aiden, but I was too turned on by his possessiveness to even bother trying to tell him *once again* that I wasn't with Aiden.

"Yours," I whispered in acknowledgement. I wasn't foolish enough to think what was about to happen was anything lasting, but I *was* his. I'd always been his. Aiden had been right about that part.

I couldn't stop the moan of desperation that escaped me as I felt his hand begin rubbing all over my ass. His other hand was pushing my shirt up and tucking it under my armpits before smoothing over my back. Both hands disappeared all too soon, but I silenced my protest when I sensed him undoing his own pants and then heard the familiar sound of a condom packet being opened. I'd been fully prepared to offer him the condom and packet of lube I kept in my own wallet, but he was clearly prepared for the moment.

Which had an unwelcome wisp of jealousy curling through my belly as I wondered who that condom and lube were meant for. Not me, because I had no illusions about what this encounter was.

The bark of the tree felt rough beneath my hands and cheek as I waited. I should have used the time to remind myself why this was such a supremely bad idea, but all I could think was, *hurry the fuck up*. I closed my eyes when I felt his latex-covered dick brush my crease as he shifted behind me. He was muttering something to himself and I could have sworn it was words about my tight ass and tiny hole, but my brain was so jumbled by then, I wasn't sure.

Suddenly I felt his free hand grab one of my ass cheeks and squeeze before his lips landed on the back of my neck, sucking and nibbling across my nape before he whispered against my ear.

"Tell me you want this, Benny. I'm about ten seconds from fucking you into this tree. Please god, don't tell me to stop."

The unexpected gentleness after his earlier coldness had me squeezing back the tears. "Please," I whispered. "Please, Xander."

"Please what, baby?"

The endearment finally made the tears slip over and cascade down. "Please. I need you inside me."

# CHAPTER 13

## XANDER

I didn't even know how it happened. One minute we were screaming at each other by the creek and the next I was about to slip lubed fingers inside of my former best friend. It was too late to stop. Hell, I didn't want to stop. I had to have him.

I tried not to think of Aiden or how this would confirm Bennett was a cheater. Or whether the kids could walk up and catch us. It was just the two of us, trying to get inside each other's skin the way I'd always wanted. He was finally going to be mine. Even if it was just for a few fucking minutes, he was *mine*. And I was going to make this moment so good for him that every time he felt Aiden's hands on him, his flesh inside him, it would be me who was there in his mind.

The feel of his smooth skin under my palms was setting every nerve ending on fire, and I felt like I wasn't going to be able to keep my hands still enough to prep him properly. The lube packet almost jumped out of my hands as I brought it to my mouth to tear open with my teeth.

After squeezing some onto my fingers and then my cock, I sent up a prayer that Bennett was somehow naturally pliant and wouldn't require much prep. Because regardless of how much he needed, he was getting about next to zero. I was just too far gone to give him anything more.

I slid a cool, slick finger into his hole and groaned, dropping my forehead onto his shoulder as I felt the tight squeeze of his ass pulsing around my digit. Holy mother of god, Bennett's body was absolute heaven.

*My Bennett.*

"Stop fucking around and get in there," Bennett gasped, reaching around with his hand to grab the wrist of the hand I was currently fucking him with.

"Shhhh," I whispered into his ear. "Don't wanna hurt you."

"You won't. I promise. Please, Xander. *Please.*"

His pleas made my cock jump up against my abdomen and I had to grab the base of it to keep from shooting too soon and wasting the goddamned condom.

"Baby, stop begging me or I'm going to come before I even have a chance to get inside you," I warned in a low voice.

"I'm ready," he said and then he was pulling my fingers from his ass and searching out my cock. The feel of his fingers surrounding me had me ready to blow, so I knocked his hand away and grabbed my dick and put it against his opening. My body was shaking so hard, I could barely breathe.

"Benny," I couldn't help but whisper, though I didn't know why I was saying his name.

"I know," I heard him say just as softly.

And that was it. The thought of giving him one last chance to end this disappeared and I pushed into him, not stopping until my crown was buried inside him.

"Fuck," I growled as his body engulfed mine. "Can't stop," I cried as my body clawed at me for more.

"Don't stop," Bennett ground out and even as I pushed forward, he was pressing back against me. I knew I had to be hurting him, but I couldn't do anything about it.

"Benny..." I said as I pressed against his back and wrapped my arms around his waist.

"Feels so good," he cried out and then his face was turning so he could make eye contact with me. "Kiss me, Xander. Please fucking kiss me."

I sealed my mouth over his as I drove into him and I swallowed his gasp. The angle was awkward as I kissed him, but I didn't care. I didn't want to ever stop kissing him. He was so tight and hot around me, I forgot all about why I'd started this whole thing. I'd meant to fuck him so I could get him out of my system once and for all. But I knew I'd made a terrible, terrible mistake.

Once would never be enough.

A lifetime would never be enough.

I pulled back and pushed into him in one long stroke.

"Yes," he groaned against my mouth.

As desperate as I was just to pound into him, I was reluctant for this to end and I knew that was exactly what would happen as soon as I picked up the pace. But I also knew my body wasn't going to accept the slow fucking, either. Even as my hips rolled slowly against his, wedging me deeper and deeper inside of him, my orgasm was there just beneath the surface.

"Fuck," I bit out as I kissed Bennett one more time. "I have to..." I said with a shake of my head.

"Do it," he urged. "Fuck me hard, Xander. I'm yours."

His words did what nothing else could have. I settled my hands on his hips and slammed into him. Bennett braced his hands on the tree to keep from hitting it as I began pounding into him. His mouth closed over his forearm to keep from crying out as I began fucking him with everything I had. There was enough moonlight to see the gorgeous slope of his lower back and the tight muscles that rippled as he accepted my pummeling. I was holding onto him so hard, I knew he'd have bruises in the morning. That thought propelled me on. He'd carry my mark. Even if I couldn't mark him in the way I really wanted, he'd see those bruises and he'd remember this moment. He'd remember how perfectly we fit together.

Sweat began to roll down my back beneath my shirt and I regretted that I hadn't had the foresight to take it off. The night was quiet around us, so I could hear our heavy pants and the jangling of our clothes as our bodies writhed together in perfect unison.

Bennett released his grip on the tree long enough to drop one hand to his cock. I quickly reached around to knock his hand away. "Mine," I snarled and then I dropped my weight onto his back and gripped his waist hard with one arm while I began jacking him off, all as I continued to slide in and out of him with hard, full strokes. Bennett's whimpers of pleasure erupted into full-on moans and I quickly realized why.

The change in position had me hitting his prostate.

I managed to keep the angle as I lifted my left hand to Bennett's mouth to cover his ever-increasing cries of pleasure. His dick was leaking all over my fingers while his inner muscles worked my cock. I could tell he was purposely clenching around me every time I pulled back and the effect was devastating... in the best way.

"I'm going to come," I warned, barely able to keep my voice from carrying.

Bennett frantically nodded and used both hands on the tree for leverage as he began fucking my dick just as fiercely as I was fucking him. Mere seconds passed before his body locked up tight and he clamped down on me so hard that I was sure he was never going to let my dick go. I shoved into him hard as I felt his scream try to penetrate my fingers. My weight forced him almost flat against the tree as my cock began releasing into the condom. I couldn't stop from humping into him over and over with jerky pumps as my orgasm took over. I bit down on Bennett's shoulder to stifle the shout of pleasure that tore free of my throat as the release consumed every part of me.

It could have been hours or minutes before I finally felt my senses begin to return. I still had Bennett plastered against the tree and my hand continued to cover his mouth while the other massaged his softening, wet dick. I knew I needed to pull out of him, but I knew what it would mean when I did.

It wasn't until the air began to feel cool against my heated skin that I was reminded of where we were and that just a few hundred yards away was the group of kids this trip was supposed to have been about.

And Aiden.

Acid rolled violently in my belly as I released my hold on Bennett and grabbed the edge of the condom so I could pull out of him. I stepped back and removed the condom, tied it off and shoved it in my pocket before rinsing my hands in the cold stream. Bennett didn't move at first. But I knew it wasn't because I'd hurt him, at least not physically, anyway.

I reached for my pants to pull them up and finally saw him do the same with his, but he still didn't turn around. I knew I should say something, but I didn't know what.

"Bennett," I began anyway.

"Don't," he said. "I know what you're going to say."

"What am I going to say?"

"It was a mistake."

He was right, but somehow hearing him say it actually hurt.

Bennett finally turned around, and I cursed the fact that I couldn't see him better. Were his cheeks flushed with color? Was he still breathing hard? Was his body still shaking like mine was?

"We should... we should just stay away from each other for the rest of the trip," I said.

Bennett nodded and I wanted to curse out loud. Again, he was giving me exactly what I wanted.

So why the hell did it hurt so fucking much?

The awkwardness of the moment was broken by the sound of raised voices. When Bear started barking from the direction of camp, I knew something was wrong. I took off running toward camp with Bennett right behind me.

# CHAPTER 14

## BENNETT

It was a bear. I just knew it. A bear had invaded the camp while Xander had been fucking me up against that tree.

All the post-orgasmic bliss along with the rush of emotions that had followed disappeared as I ran as fast as I could back to the camp. The kids. I had to get to the kids.

The sight that greeted me was both a relief and disappointment at the same time. Several of the kids were locked in a heated fight and caught in the middle of the small group was Aiden, who looked like he'd been roughed up a bit. Xander reached them first and stepped between Calvin and Toby. My eyes landed on a small form huddled on the ground just behind Toby and I knew who it was almost immediately. Bear was standing protectively in front of Lucky, but thankfully the dog didn't see me as a threat as I rushed past where Xander was pushing Toby and Calvin apart. Aiden had already managed to break up two of the other older boys who'd been going at it at the same time.

"Sit!" Aiden yelled as he pointed to two separate logs on either side of the fire. "You!" he snapped at Calvin. "Go walk it off!"

"Fuck you!" Calvin retorted. He had blood dripping down from a small cut on the side of his mouth.

"You want to say that to me again?" Aiden asked, his voice low and cold as he approached Calvin. While Aiden was the happy-go-lucky, sarcastic playboy type ninety-nine percent of the time, I'd seen enough to know he was a guy you just didn't fuck with that other one percent of the time. Calvin stepped back at his approach, and then turned on his heel and stalked off towards the lake. I turned my attention to Lucky who was still curled into a ball. I could hear him crying.

"Lucky," I said softly as I carefully put my hand on his shoulder. I knew enough not to grab him, even though I wanted to offer him some comfort. I rubbed soothing circles against his back as Bear came over to snuffle Lucky's face. The dog did what I couldn't and had Lucky's body relaxing enough that he could bury his hand in the dog's fur. The big animal dropped to the ground and began licking Lucky's face. The boy's sobs slowed, but I still didn't hurry him. I tried to be patient, though I was desperate to see his face, to hear him talk. I was dimly aware of Xander and Aiden ordering the kids to bed, but I didn't pay them any attention.

"Lucky, can you talk to me?" I asked as I carefully leaned over him enough to run my fingers through his hair. He finally turned to look at me before sitting up. I managed to stifle a gasp at the sight of a small gash next to his left eye.

"Here," I heard Xander say behind me and I turned enough to see him hand me a dampened piece of cloth. I took it, but instead of handing it to Lucky, I went to work cleaning the blood and dust off his face myself. Bear had plopped his big head down on Lucky's lap.

"What happened?" I asked.

But Lucky just shook his head.

"You know you can tell me anything."

Lucky's eyes darted to a spot just behind me, and I glanced over my shoulder to see Aiden talking to both Calvin and Frankie, a kid who practically worshiped the ground Calvin walked on. The two of them together weren't the best combination.

"He started saying some stuff while we were cleaning the dinner dishes," Lucky murmured.

"What kind of stuff?" I asked. I wanted to get him off the ground, but he seemed more content to have Bear draped across his lap. I let him be and settled myself down into a more comfortable position.

"Nothing," Lucky said with a shake of his head.

I sighed. I'd made a lot of progress with Lucky in the year since I'd found. I'd spotted him outside a club where I'd gone to meet my then-boyfriend. I'd noticed Lucky lingering by the alley next to the club, but it hadn't been until I'd seen an older man approach and try to lure the boy into the alley that I'd realized what was happening. As soon as I'd started walking towards them, the man had taken off, the cash he'd been waving in Lucky's face disappearing back into his pocket. Thankfully, the alley Lucky had darted into had been blocked off on one end because the boy had moved a lot faster than me. It had taken me several long minutes to convince Lucky to let me take him to a nearby restaurant to get something to eat and talk.

The guy I'd gone to meet at the club had dumped me the very next day, despite my explanation that I'd stood him up because of a family emergency. But I'd ended up with something so much better.

"Remember what I told you the night we met?" I asked.

Lucky was silent for a moment before nodding. "Secrets are shit." A small smile tugged at his mouth. "That's when I knew you were a dweeb."

I chuckled and said, "I never claimed to be good with the words." I resisted the urge to ruffle his hair. "Tell me what happened."

He sucked in a breath and said, "He was saying shit all night."

"Calvin?" I asked.

A nod and then, "And Frankie. Started while we were fishing… he kept calling me names and stuff. Like usual."

Yeah, I knew what that meant. I'd had the conversation with Calvin twice already about his treatment of Lucky since we'd arrived in Colorado. I just wished I'd seen the behavior before we'd left New York so I could've pulled Calvin from the trip.

"While we were cleaning the dishes, he started saying you and me… that he knew how I'd paid for the trip."

Since my company's foundation had paid for the trip, I knew Lucky was talking about the things that hadn't been covered. While the cost of the gear had been taken care of, each kid's family had been responsible for making sure they had the right clothes and personal items for the trip. Since Lucky's foster family hadn't been able to afford any of that, I'd paid for it all. I'd even bought him a camera so he could take higher quality pictures than his phone would allow.

"What did he say?" I asked.

Lucky chewed on his lip for a moment and then said, "He asked if you were fucking me or if you preferred taking it."

I sighed because I'd figured it was something that crass. I'd never hidden my sexuality from the kids and I'd sensed Calvin had an issue with sexuality, but hadn't had the balls to say anything to Aiden's or my face.

"I pushed him and told him to shut the fuck up. Then Frankie stepped in and hit me. When I fell, he started kicking me. That's when Toby got involved and then some other guys joined in."

"You know guys like him say that shit because they're afraid, right?"

When Lucky's eyes lifted to mine, I said, "They're afraid of people who aren't like them. And they hide that fear by lashing out... by trying to make others feel like less."

"I couldn't just let him say that about you," he murmured.

I sighed and stifled my need to ruffle his hair. No need in giving Calvin more ammunition to use against Lucky. "I know," I responded. I had no doubt Lucky would have been able to ignore the taunts if they'd just been directed at him. I stood up and held out my hand to help him to his feet. "Why don't you try to get some sleep? We'll talk more in the morning."

Lucky's fingers toyed with Bear's head. "Can... can Bear sleep in my tent?" he asked hesitantly, but I realized he wasn't talking to me.

I looked behind me to see Xander standing less than a dozen feet away. He'd likely heard everything Lucky and I had said.

"Sure," Xander said with a smile. "But be warned, he snores... and farts."

The comment made Lucky smile. He nodded and then he patted

the dog. "Come on, Bear." Thankfully, the dog followed him without any kind of hesitation.

I turned to go toward the fire, but stopped when I saw Aiden standing near the entrance to his tent with his arms crossed. He waited until Lucky disappeared inside the tent he was sharing with Toby and two other kids before he strode across the camp towards Xander and me.

"Lake, now," he snapped. I winced at the sight of the bruise on his jaw. His normally perfect hair was all over the place and his clothes were covered in dust. There was a small tear in his shirt.

Xander and I followed him down to the lake so we'd still be in sight of the camp but out of hearing range. Aiden was fuming, and I didn't blame him in the least.

"You two need to get the fuck over yourselves now. This shit ends, do you hear me?"

"Aiden—"

"Shut the fuck up, Bennett. I'm talking." His eyes shifted back and forth between me and Xander. "No one wants you guys to get past whatever *this*"— he motioned between us with his hand— "is more than I do, but not at the cost of the kids!" He took in a breath as if trying to calm himself.

"I called for you three times when the fight started. The fucking dog heard me and came running," he snapped as he pointed towards Lucky's tent. "Now, I don't need to know what you were doing, because I have a damned good idea. The fact is, this shit between the kids has been brewing for days, but you two have had your heads so far up your own asses, that you either didn't see it or you didn't care. And you're both idiots if you think they haven't noticed that you two can't say one single goddamned nice thing to each other."

Aiden focused his attention on me. "Remember what you told me, B?" he said, his voice softening. "You remember what you wanted this trip to be for them?"

I nodded. "A game changer," I murmured. When I'd asked Aiden to chaperone the trip with me, I'd told him how I wanted each kid to have that one moment in their life where they realized they weren't resigned to the shitty hand life had dealt them. None of them came from big money and most had some kind of trauma in their lives, whether it was abuse or a crappy home life or whatever... I'd wanted them to know there was a whole world waiting for them if they just had the guts to reach for it.

"You have a few days left to make that happen. Both of you," Aiden said as he looked sharply at Xander. "This is your life," he said as he motioned to the wilderness around us. "But most of those kids will never see this place or anything like it ever again. You really want them to remember it as the *Bennett and Xander Ripping Each Other to Shreds* show?"

Xander didn't answer. Neither did I. And Aiden clearly wasn't expecting one because he quietly said, "Work it the fuck out" before calmly walking away.

Leaving Xander and me to figure out how the hell we were supposed to do just that.

# CHAPTER 15

## XANDER

I felt like a complete ass. Because of me and my selfish pity party, Bennett and I hadn't given our full attention to the kids. The trip's entire focus was supposed to be on those kids, but what had I done instead?

Fucked a man I thought was someone else's boyfriend— in the woods. Like a damn animal.

I blew out a breath and sat down on one of the logs around the fire ring. "Have a seat," I said to Bennett. "As much as I hate to admit it— he's right."

"Yeah," he murmured, sitting stiffly next to me.

We faced the fire and I threw a nearby branch into the flames to build it up a bit before speaking.

"I'm sorry," I began.

Bennett's head snapped up in surprise. "What for?"

I took a minute to think about what I wanted to say before speaking. I didn't want to say the wrong thing and accidentally make things weirder between us.

"For giving you so much hell these past few days. For not letting you even talk to me about it." I rubbed my hands over my face and finally had the guts to look him in the eyes. "But,

Bennett… I don't want to talk about that night, okay? I just… I can't."

Bennett studied me for a moment before responding. "Okay. Then we won't talk about it."

We sat together in uncomfortable silence for a few minutes while the campfire popped and the sounds of sleeping bags rustling were fewer and farther between.

Suddenly, Bennett blew out a laugh and shook his head.

"What?" I asked. "What's so funny?"

"This whole thing reminds me of that time your dad was going to take us to a Yankees game, remember?"

He turned to me with a wide grin and twinkling eyes. God, he was so damned cute when he had that look on his face. Like humor and mischief all rolled into one.

"Which one? We went to like a million of them."

"The one with the fight over the jersey," Bennett said with a raised eyebrow.

I snorted. "Oh my god, you're right. Roger Clemens. Jesus, why couldn't my dad have had two Clemens jerseys?"

"He did. That's just it, remember? He was wearing one and he said one of us could wear the other."

"Dude, you totally knew it was my turn with the Clemens one," I accused. "You could have easily worn the Jeter jersey and been fine."

"Fuck you. Take it back," Bennett said, pretending to glare at me until we both burst out laughing.

"What I don't get is why my dad didn't just throw up his hands and offer for us each to wear a Clemens one and he could wear the Jeter one himself. It was his, after all. Not like he didn't support the guy—he loved Jeter."

Bennett shifted to stretch out his legs. I noticed his grin had turned into a nostalgic smile.

"He was trying to teach us a lesson," he said. "About compromise."

I watched the golden glow from the fire dance across his features and felt my stomach flip around. That face I'd seen in the light of a hundred campfires growing up. Eyes I'd looked into more times than I could count. And now lips I'd had the singular pleasure of feeling against my own.

Bennett Crawford was beautiful.

"Well," I said just as softly. "I guess we never learned the lesson, did we?"

He looked up at me, eyes bright with unshed tears. "You must miss him. I know I do, Xander, so I can't imagine how—"

"No," I said swiftly, but firmly. "You agreed. No talking about that night and that includes what happened to my dad."

Bennett sat up straight again and put his hand on my shoulder. The little hairs on my skin seemed to turn toward his touch like flowers to the sun. "You're right," he said. "I'm sorry."

I pretended like he'd never brought it up. "So instead of just handling the jersey thing like adults, we ended up in a fistfight on the fucking lawn," I reminded him.

He chuckled. "And didn't see your dad walk up to intervene until it was too late."

"You gotta admit— you're lucky my right hook landed on him instead of you," I said.

He shoved my shoulder. "Shut up, asshole. I could have taken that punch. You were like twelve years old and scrawny as shit."

"Wanna prove it?" I teased. "Let's go right now."

Bennett laughed and shook his head, but not before eyeballing my body from top to toes. The once-over made my cock fill, and I stifled a groan. No way was I going to consider a repeat of our earlier dalliance.

When he spoke, his voice carried a husky quality. "Maybe tomorrow when we're fresh, big guy. I had a little too much action already for one night."

And there were the twinkling eyes again. I felt my face heat up at his reminder of the action we'd shared earlier.

"So you and Aiden…" I began.

"Me and Aiden…" Bennett said with a small smile.

"You, ah, aren't really together?"

*God, why did I sound like such a freak?*

"Nope. I told you that. In fact, I've tried to tell you several times, but you either wouldn't listen or you refused to believe me." Bennett looked over at me and straightened again before continuing. "Why did you think we were together?"

I rolled my eyes at him, forcing a laugh out of him until he held his hands up. "Okay, okay. He made some personal comments. But really, is that the only reason?" Bennett asked.

"He touches you," I said, feeling my jaw tighten. "I don't like it."

The minute the words were out of my mouth, I wanted to take them back, especially when Bennett's eyes went wide, and he opened his lips to respond.

"Why the kids?" I quickly said before he could say anything.

"What?"

"What got you into working with these kids?"

I watched as he leaned forward for a bit and studied the ground in front of him. He picked up a small stick and began drawing little patterns in the dirt. It was a typical Bennett move. Whenever the focus was put back on him or he had to talk about himself, he would start playing with whatever inanimate object was around. If he couldn't find something to self-soothe himself with, he'd play with his fingers in some way, whether it was tapping them together in a kind of pattern or using them to toy with his hair or another part of his body. The habit had never bothered me when we were kids, but I was surprised he still did it as an adult. I figured it was a coping mechanism brought on by stress.

"Not really sure," Bennett said. "One of my friends in college was part of the Big Brothers Big Sisters program so I got to meet the kid he was mentoring. The kid was real quiet and withdrawn with everyone else, but sometimes I'd see him talking to my roommate while he was helping the kid with his homework or playing video games with him and the kid just... lit up. My friend said the program was always looking for more participants, so I signed up."

"Where did you end up going to college?" I asked.

"Harvard," he said quietly, almost like he was reluctant to tell me.

Maybe it was a reminder of how very different our stations in life were.

"Did you get one… a little brother, I mean?"

Bennett nodded. He'd started drawing an infinity symbol in the dirt. "His name was Colin. He was twelve. He lived in Boston with his mom; his dad had died a few years earlier in Iraq." Bennett's eyes lifted to meet mine. "A soldier."

I nodded in understanding.

"Colin hadn't wanted to be in the program— his mom had signed him up when his teachers had commented that his grades had started slipping after his dad died. He'd already been to therapy, but he was still struggling and pulled away from the kids who used to be his friends. He didn't really have anyone besides his mom, so she thought the program would help."

"That must have been tough," I said.

Bennett was quiet for a long time and then his gaze shifted to mine again. "He reminded me of you."

I stiffened at that.

"I'm sorry, I didn't say that to upset you, Xander," Bennett began, but I shook my head to stop him.

"No, it's okay," I said. "What happened with Colin?"

"It took me a long time to get through to him, and there were a lot of times where I wanted to give up. But I kept remembering that he'd lost everything… that he was… *lost*. It was a year before I finally found something that helped us connect."

"What was it?"

"Legos."

"What?" I asked in surprise.

Bennett smiled. "Legos. He was obsessed with them. Well, not just Legos, but anything he could use to build things."

I laughed at that and wondered how the hell Bennett had managed to figure that out. But he continued before I could ask.

"Anyway, once I had that connection with him, he started talking more. He was a really bright kid, but losing his dad… he'd understood that he was gone, but he hadn't *accepted* it."

I ignored the tension that began running through me as Bennett's story started to hit too close to home. I could tell Bennett knew how his words were affecting me, because he'd stopped playing with the stick and his attention was focused solely on me.

"I'm sorry," he whispered. "Do you want me to stop?"

I shook my head. "No, tell me what happened to him."

"I spent years being his big brother, even after he was too old for the program. I was in my final year of graduate school when he graduated from high school. Guess what I gave him for his graduation present."

Bennett's smile did crazy things to my insides and my earlier tension drained away. "What?" I asked.

"A trip to Legoland in California."

I laughed and shook my head. "God, I've missed you, Bennett," I said softly. I realized my mistake when I heard Bennett let out the tiniest of whimpers. I should have said I'd missed his antics, but in truth, that was just a part of it. My brain had clearly decided this was going to be one of those situations where I was going to say exactly what was on my mind… just like my comment about Aiden touching Bennett so damn much and me not liking it.

I cursed myself, but luckily, Bennett stepped in to pull us back from the quagmire of shit I'd just thrust us both into.

"You would have loved Legoland, Xander," he said with a smile.

"Oh yeah, why?"

"All those tiny cities made out of Legos… you would have felt like Godzilla, short boy."

I chuckled. Bennett had teased me mercilessly as kids when he'd had a growth spurt when he was twelve and had grown a couple of inches taller than me within a matter of months. I hadn't caught up to him until we'd turned fourteen.

"What happened to Colin?" I asked, more to get us back on topic because the thought of our height difference now was reminding me how perfectly we'd fit together against that damn tree.

"I still talk to him every week and try to have dinner with him once a month. He's studying architectural engineering at MIT."

"Wow, that's incredible."

Bennett smiled and began playing with the stick again. "He's an amazing kid."

I wanted to tell Bennett *he* was amazing, but I managed to hold my tongue. "So is that why you're working with these kids?" I asked, motioning to the tents behind me.

He nodded. "After I got my MBA, I began working for my dad's company. They had a foundation that worked with certain charities, but I could tell it was originally only created to help the firm's public image. The foundation basically just threw money at some of the big-name charities and that was it. After I met Lucky, I saw the potential for the foundation to do some real good… for it to help people in an everyday kind of way. Does that make sense?"

"It does," I said. "You wanted to *see* the money doing good."

"Yeah," he responded. "And not just the money. But people helping other people. Hands-on stuff. Kids like Lucky don't just need money handed to them… they need this," he said as he motioned towards the lake with his stick. "Experiences, education— they need to know there's more out there. That the lives they were born into aren't the lives they're stuck in."

I studied him for a moment and said, "Like you?"

He jerked his head up. "What?"

"You know what I'm talking about, Benny," I said softly.

He swallowed hard and then looked away. I moved closer to him and used my hand to force his chin around so he was looking at me. "People always thought I was the one trapped by my circumstances. A gardener's son. The scholarship kid. But none of them really knew, did they, Benny?"

Bennett shook his head. I let my fingers trail along his jaw as I spoke. "You had every toy and gadget a kid could ever dream of having, but all you really wanted was what I had."

He closed his eyes and carefully withdrew from my touch, but he didn't move away from me. "I know we aren't supposed to talk about him, but you weren't the only one who lost him, Xander."

I sighed. "I know."

I saw Bennett wipe at his eyes, but before I could say anything, he bumped my shoulder with his and said, "So tell me more about this not liking Aiden touching me thing."

I knew it was his attempt to both change the subject and lighten the mood, so I shook my head and laughed. "Pass."

But Bennett was Bennett, and I knew he wasn't going to let it go. And for some reason I didn't want to examine too closely, I was okay with that.

# CHAPTER 16

## BENNETT

*Xander Reed is jealous. Xander Reed is jealous of another man touching me.*

It was too good to be true, so I knew it had to be complete bullshit. But I was sure as hell going to tease him for it anyway.

"You like me," I said in a slow singsong voice.

"Shut up. Never mind," he muttered, and then took my stick and did what I'd done— started drawing shapes in the dirt with the tip of it and pretended like I'd ceased to exist.

"You really, really like me," I persisted.

"Goddammit, I take it back. Let the fucker touch you all he wants. I don't care," Xander growled, but there was no real anger in his voice.

I couldn't resist leaning over until my lips were almost against Xander's ear. "Liar," I purred. He was sitting close enough that I could feel his shudder. He glanced at me and then his gaze fell to my mouth, and I was instantly transported back to earlier in the night when he'd kissed me.

Right before he'd fucked me up against that tree.

Even the memory of his cock pushing deep inside of me had me growing hard and I had to tear my eyes from his. I searched out another stick and began to roll it back and forth between my fingers.

To say the sex had been incredible was the understatement of the decade. What Xander had done to me didn't even qualify as sex. I'd been with a decent number of guys after I'd lost my virginity to Aiden at the age of nineteen. But not once had I felt so... *needed*. Not just wanted... needed. Aiden had been a great lover, but there'd always been this sense that he was holding a part of himself back from me. Even after dating for months, he'd kept a piece of himself separate from me, both in and out of bed. But with Xander, it had just seemed like so much... more. Like nothing else had existed in that moment for him but me. That if he could have chosen anywhere to be in that instant, and anyone to be with, he still would have picked me.

I knew I was reading too much into it. He'd said as much after he'd pulled out of me. I'd known it just from the sad way he'd said my name. So, I'd beaten him to the punch and told him it was a mistake.

Even though I didn't think it was, nor did I regret it. And given the chance to have him again like that, I'd take it. Every single time.

But not at the expense of the kids. Aiden had been right. I'd lost focus about why we were here. And I needed to remember that this thing with Xander would come to an end in a matter of days, but the kids... they were forever. Just like with Colin, I wanted to be a part of as many of these kids' lives as I could. As much as I wanted something with Xander, he wasn't my future. He'd made that perfectly clear.

"I think we need to figure out how to make this work for the kids, Bennett," Xander said.

I let my stick play with some of the shapes Xander had drawn with his stick. "I agree. What do you think? Truce?"

Xander was quiet and I smiled when I realized what kind of pattern he was drawing in the dirt. "Yeah. Truce," he said.

I watched him draw an X in the middle square of the Tic Tac Toe board he'd drawn.

"Why are you always X's?" I asked.

He looked at me flatly. "Uh, Xander. X. Duh."

I chuckled and felt my body tighten up when I spied what I'd been working my ass off to see this whole fucking trip.

*The* smile.

The quiet, soft Xander smile that was mine. It was folly to think it was my smile... that he did it just for me, but I chose to believe it anyway.

"You're so predictable," I groused. "You always pick the middle square."

We'd played the game often enough when we were kids that it was burned into my memory.

"Shut up and play," he said.

I picked a square and drew a circle.

"Nice circle," he said snidely. "No wonder you almost failed geometry."

"Shut it," I returned and watched him take his turn. "Can I ask you something?"

He nodded.

"Where did you and Aunt Lolly go?" I asked softly. "I mean... after... you know."

There was just the slightest tensing of his body. I wasn't certain he was going to answer at first. But he kept playing the Tic Tac Toe game so I figured I hadn't pissed him off with the question.

"All over at first. West coast mostly. She had some friends living in a commune in Oregon."

"A commune?"

"Yeah, all these people got together and bought some land and put a bunch of trailers and small houses on it. They shared all the responsibilities, worked the land together, ate what they grew and sold the rest at farmer's markets and stuff."

"What was it like?"

"Not bad," he said. "Just... different. But it's where I realized I wasn't ever going to be that guy." He looked at me and said, "You know, working in a cubicle, staring at a computer all day."

I nodded. Xander had done well in school, but he'd never had any one particular goal in mind when it had come to a potential career. His father had dreamed of him going to college, which Xander had been planning to do, but he'd never been able to answer the age-old question of *what do you want to be when you grow up* like most kids our age had. I'd had the stock answer, the one that had been fed to me since birth. But I'd always dreamed of being able to answer like Xander did.

*No idea, but I'll know it when I see it.*

"We joined a couple of communes for a few years before settling down here in Colorado."

"Does your aunt still live nearby?" I asked.

"Um yeah, she... she lives in a colony in a small town just north of Denver."

"A colony?" I asked. "Like that movie where all the people turned into zombies?"

Xander laughed and bumped me with his body. "No... idiot," he said with a smile. "It's... it's a nudist colony." His face scrunched up slightly.

"Oh my god," I laughed. "A nudist colony in Colorado? Isn't it too cold? I mean... things are probably so shriveled up, you can't tell what they are."

"Shut up— I have to work really hard not to think about that shit."

"Sorry," I said, though we both knew I wasn't.

"They have a lot of indoor activities," he said. "Can we not talk about this? I already have to consider bleaching my eyes every time I visit her there."

I began laughing hysterically and barely managed to keep my voice low so I wouldn't wake up the kids. "You go there?"

Xander pushed me so hard with his hand, I nearly fell backwards off the log. He grabbed me around the waist to stop my fall, but I couldn't stop laughing.

Until I finally realized I was pressed up against his chest and he'd gone deathly quiet. His body was stiff beneath my hand, which had somehow gotten tucked up under his armpit. My other hand was at his back. We both began breathing hard, but I dared not look at him. I knew what would happen if I did.

But god, I really wanted to look. I really wanted what would come after I did. The sweetness of his mouth, the firmness of his lips that were both gentle and demanding at the same time.

"Sorry," I murmured as I untangled myself from his arms.

"S'okay," he said.

After a few moments of tense silence, I asked, "What made you decide to work as a guide?"

"Living in a commune was fine and all, but I knew it wasn't the life I wanted. So, I got a part-time job at a farm supply store. I saved up enough money to buy a car and used it to drive to Denver to get a job that paid better. It was at this really cool adventure outfitter shop. Some guys I worked with asked me if I wanted to go hiking with them one day, and that was it. I was totally hooked. Every second I wasn't working, I was out here. After a couple of years, I started exploring on my own and worked my way up to taking people on guided trips all over Colorado."

I took in what he was saying and thought about it before saying, "But why this?"

He seemed to understand what I was asking, because he studied me for a moment and then looked towards the lake. "You know I was never good with people, Bennett. I never really fit."

I knew that was true. But he'd fit with me. I wanted to tell him that, but knew he didn't want to hear it. It would just stir up things that needed to stay in the past.

"Out here, I don't owe anyone any explanations. I don't have to pretend. I don't have to rely on anyone or anything but myself."

Pain shimmied through my body as I realized what he wasn't saying.

*No one can hurt me again when I'm out here.*

The reminder that our truce wouldn't undo the damage I'd done to this man killed off something inside of me. Maybe I'd hoped, despite Xander's insistence that this truce was for the kids, whatever was between us could have turned into something more.

"It suits you," I said as I tried to mask my inner turmoil. And I meant it. I could tell he loved his world. But I couldn't help but wonder if he still might love it just as much if he could share it with someone special.

Someone like me.

No, not someone *like* me.

*Me.*

Fuck, I needed to stop doing this.

As the silence between us grew, I felt the exhaustion of the day settle over me. Part of me would have loved to stay there all night with him, but being so close to him and not being allowed to touch him was a unique form of torture.

"So, tomorrow is about the kids," I said.

"Yeah," Xander agreed before sending me a smile.

"I should go to bed," I said awkwardly as I stood. Xander stood too and my heart flip-flopped when he didn't immediately step away.

"Yeah, me too," he murmured. Was that reluctance I was hearing?

God, I was terrified of walking away from him. Even with the truce, I was still afraid of losing him again. What if he was cold, angry Xander again tomorrow? What if none of this stuff tonight had mattered? What if what had happened by that tree didn't matter?

*Ask me to fucking come to your tent, Xander.*

I practically screamed the words in my head, but externally I did something much tamer.

But still incredibly stupid.

I reached my hand up to clasp the back of his neck before brushing my mouth over his in the briefest of kisses. "Good night, Xander," I whispered, and then I walked towards my tent.

And another piece of my heart sheared off when he didn't stop me.

# CHAPTER 17

## XANDER

The hike to Gin Lake started with the kids playing a game of I Spy that kept making Bennett laugh so hard, I couldn't help but join in.

"I spy something white and wet," Toby called out as we hiked across Saddle Pass.

Frankie's eyes widened as he stopped and looked around at the snow drifts surrounding us. "Holy moly, Toby," he said with exaggerated goofiness. "Could it be… *snow*?"

"You got it in one, Einstein," Toby responded with a laugh.

"I spy something white and puffy," Frankie shot back.

"Hmmm," Lucky said with a finger to his chin. "The clouds maybe?"

"Bingo," Frankie said.

"Not a lot to choose from, I guess," I suggested. "Maybe you guys need a little help identifying interesting items found above the tree line in the alpine region? I spy something that's a prime example of flagging."

I had taught them about trees growing branches only on one side due to alpine winds at altitude, but I was curious to see how many people remembered that's what flagging meant.

"Bennett's flagging," someone called out. "Does that count?"

I turned back to find Bennett several yards back, hopping on one foot. After handing the map to Toby to keep leading people across the pass, I quickly made my way back to see what was wrong.

When he saw me approach, he tried waving me off. "Just a rock in my boot. Don't worry about it. You go ahead."

I looked around at the snow everywhere. "You can't sit without getting your ass wet and cold. Here, prop yourself against me while you take it off," I said, pulling his pack off before running my arm around his waist to support him. I tried not to lean in and smell his neck. Everyone had recently washed in a lake and I knew he smelled like an intoxicating blend of biodegradable camp soap and his own clean sweat smell. I'd reveled in it the night before when I'd had him pinned up against the tree. God, just the thought of him up against that tree made my blood travel quickly southward.

"Is it hard?" Bennett asked.

"What?" I blurted, looking at him with startled eyes. He tilted his head at me and furrowed his brows.

"Being responsible for everyone out here all the time," he repeated. "I asked if it was hard."

"Uh, yeah. Kind of. I mean, it's easier when it's just me, but I also like showing people how amazing it is out here. So, it's worth it. Being responsible for everyone, I mean."

God, there went my babbling mouth. I felt like I was in middle school all over again. Uncontrollable cock and uncontrollable mouth.

I flushed crimson and glanced down as he shook the rock out of his boot. The curved muscles of his calf flexed as he balanced on one foot, and I couldn't tear my eyes off a familiar scar on the side of his knee.

"Is that the scar you got—"

"Yo, dudes, you coming?" Frankie called out from up ahead. "Aiden said we had to wait for you to catch up before we could keep going."

"Coming," Bennett called out, the word sounding suggestive in light of my current state of extreme arousal this close to him.

I cleared my throat. "Yeah. We're, ah, coming. Be there in a minute."

Bennett looked up at me as he lowered his booted foot back to the ground. "What's gotten into you?"

"Who, me? Nothing... What?"

He laughed. "Yeah, you. And it's obviously something. You're being weird."

I reluctantly pulled my arm away from him, unable to resist grazing his ass with my fingers as I did. His eyes flared and his eyebrows danced at me.

"Is that right?" he murmured. "Got something to say?"

"Nope," I said, handing him his pack before turning around and starting off again down the path the boys had forged across the snow.

As I walked, I argued with myself about Bennett. On the one hand, we had agreed to get along for the sake of the kids. And I wanted to jump his fucking bones— like, all the time, and even more so when I accidentally touched him. But on the other hand, I didn't want him. Not like that. Sure, I wanted to fuck him up against a tree again and find any way of getting him naked and writhing underneath me as soon and as often as I could. But that was just because I was horny and desperate.

I'd gone without sex for too long and clearly my hormones were taking over. That's all it was. Just plain lust for physical release. I'd feel that way about anyone, really. Hell, I'd probably be willing to fuck Aiden if he wasn't such a giant asshole.

But there was a part of me that knew I was bullshitting myself. I wasn't just horny for anyone. I wanted Bennett. And it wasn't just lust. It was the knowledge that Bennett had a piece of me I'd never be able to give to anyone else. A big piece.

Even with him having been out of my life for so long, I knew it hadn't really changed anything deep down in that part of my heart that I never let myself think about anymore. Bennett Crawford was simply *mine*. Had been for a long time now and would be for the rest of our lives. But that didn't mean we could be together. Because he'd pulled the rug out from under me so long ago, I knew I'd never be able to trust him with my heart again.

I set my jaw and reminded myself that it was a truce only. A temporary visit down memory lane with an old friend before he returned to his real life and I went back to mine. I could be friendly without jumping the man, for god's sake.

Couldn't I?

# CHAPTER 18

## BENNETT

I wanted to kick Xander's ass for reminding my body how good it felt to be touched by him. He'd held me up while I'd emptied my boot and then brushed his hand along my ass before stepping away. My balls tightened and I felt my breathing hitch. What the hell was he up to?

Was Xander flirting with me? Surely not. He'd made it more than clear that I would never be anything to him but a reminder of the past he'd just as soon forget.

I followed him across the snowy expanse of the pass and down the ridge past the tree line to the edge of a meadow. Before leaving the shade of the trees, I saw several of the kids had stopped to take a snack break. They'd pulled out bags of nuts and dried fruit and were taking sips from their water bottles.

Just as Xander finished setting down his pack in front of me, he threw his arm out across my chest the way mothers did when they came to a quick stop in the car.

"What's wrong?" I asked.

"Shh. Guys, look," Xander said in a soft voice, raising his other hand to point through the trees. There, on the far side of the meadow, about as far away from us as the length of a football field, was a pair of black bears. One was wandering through the flowers, snuffling at the ground, while the other was sitting straight up, sniffing the air.

"Oh my god," Lucky whispered. The other boys followed suit as they murmured their surprise at seeing the unusual sight.

I stood there in awe of the pair, and all I could think was how amazing it was that this group of inner-city kids was standing in the wilderness of the Rocky Mountains only a hundred yards away from actual bears. I caught movement out of the corner of my eye and glanced over at Aiden.

He was looking at me with a small smile of excited satisfaction and I knew he felt the same way I did. Mission accomplished— after months of planning and hoping, we were finally there, watching these kids experience incredible new things.

I felt a tentative hand on my elbow and looked over to see Calvin, of all people, grasping the sleeve of my fleece.

"You okay?" I asked softly. He looked terrified, and I was almost positive there were tears in his eyes.

He shook his head. "I'm scared, B." It was so quiet, I wouldn't have heard what he said if everyone else hadn't been silent too. As it was, I was the only person who heard his words, and I turned to remove my pack and set it down as quietly as I could.

After catching Xander's eye and tilting my head toward Calvin and the trail behind us, I put an arm around Calvin's shoulder and walked him back into the woods, farther enough away from the bears to give him reassurance we were safe.

When we'd gotten enough distance from the group not to be overheard, I turned to face Calvin. "Do you want to talk about it?"

His bottom teeth came out to scrape across his top lip as he considered my question. A small black and white bird landed on a branch nearby and trilled, causing Calvin to laugh softly. I raised an eyebrow at him, but didn't say a word.

"Even that little bird isn't scared of the bears. I'm a pussy."

"First of all, that bird can fly away at the drop of a hat, so there's nothing for him to be scared of. Secondly, you're not a pussy, and can that please be the last time we use that particular word?"

Calvin blew out a breath but didn't look up at me. "Are you gay?"

The question took me by complete surprise, not so much because it came out of the blue, but because I had thought everyone on the trip knew I was gay. I didn't keep it a secret around the kids because I didn't ever want them to think there was anything wrong with being gay.

Before I had a chance to answer, Calvin went on. "I mean, I'm sorry. I don't know if that was rude or not, and really, it's none of my business. I mean, I think you are. Are you? I think you are. And anyway, it doesn't matter. It's just that I—"

I put my hand on his shoulder to stop his stammering and waited for him to look up at me.

"Yes, Calvin. I'm gay. Why do you ask? Does this have something to do with what you were saying to Lucky last night?"

His face paled and he looked away again. "That was… that was bad."

"Yeah," I agreed. "It really was."

"I'm sorry, B."

"I'm not the only one you should be apologizing to."

"I know, alright? I know that," he said in a huff. "But Lucky… that — that guy drives me fucking crazy, you know? I mean, he's just… and he… well, shit."

Ah, so that's how things were. It was all finally starting to make sense. I was pretty sure I knew what was behind Calvin's behavior now, but I needed to tread carefully if I was going to be of any help to the kid.

"You like him," I said carefully.

"No," he blurted, looking up at me with wide eyes. "I definitely don't like him. Didn't you hear what I just said? He drives me crazy."

"Okayyy. Well, he can't be all that bad. Tell me three things that you *do* like about him," I suggested.

He rolled his eyes at me, and I laughed. "Humor me," I said.

"Fine," he huffed. "He's smart. I guess… I mean, the kid does really good in school, you know? Works hard, I think. Studies a lot."

I nodded. "Go on."

"And he's nice to other people. He holds the door open a few extra seconds, even if the bell has already rung and he'll get in trouble for not being in his seat. If he sees me coming, he waits so the door doesn't close in my face."

"That's thoughtful," I agreed, biting my tongue to keep from smiling. "What else?"

He blew out a breath and looked up through the canopy of the trees above. "He draws pretty good pictures," he said in a small voice. "He doesn't know I know, but I saw his notebook once."

"Hmm," I said. "Sounds like the kind of guy I'd like to be friends with."

Calvin rolled his eyes again, but didn't spout off a snarky remark like I was expecting. I waited for him to say more, but he didn't.

"So why does he seem to bother you so much?" I asked. "Why do you give him such a hard time?"

He thought for a beat before responding. When he finally spoke, his eyes were bright and he looked earnest. "Because the kid needs to learn that being smart and nice and shit is just going to get him beat up. People don't like that. People don't like it when you're artsy-fartsy, you know? So, he needs to keep himself to himself. Grow a thicker skin or he's gonna get hurt again. He's gotta learn sometimes you gotta use your fists to make people listen, you know?"

Nerves skittered in my gut. "What do you mean, again? You mean like last night, or did something else happen?"

Calvin looked off into the woods to avoid meeting my eyes. "Nah, man. I just meant last night."

I wasn't sure I believed him, but knew he wasn't about to tell me whatever else had happened. "Calvin, do you understand that *you're* the one who has a problem with him being the way he is? That last night, the person who was out to get him wasn't some random stranger, but you?"

"Yeah? Well, better me than someone who could do some real damage," he muttered as he turned to walk off, back toward the group.

"Calvin, wait," I said, reaching out to stop him. When he turned back toward me, his eyes were full of unshed tears. "Talk to me. What's this really about?"

"I don't want him to get hurt," he said, one tear slipping over the edge and making its way down his face. He dashed at it, flaring his nostrils in disgust at the show of weakness. Clearly he hadn't intended to get emotional around me.

"You're the one who's hurting him, Calvin. If you stop, he won't be in danger anymore. Don't you see that?" I asked in frustration.

Defiant eyes snapped up to mine and Calvin leaned in toward me. "I'm not the one who wants to hurt him. Last night was an accident! Frankie got between us, and he's the one who hit him. But it was an accident. It ain't me he's gotta worry about! It's his goddamned foster family, you asshole."

And just like that, he took off through the trees to rejoin the group. I stood there in total shock as his words left me reeling. Could it be? Could Lucky really be in danger from Ed and Gloria Durant? No. No way. I'd met them personally many times, and Lucky would have told me if he was in trouble.

Wouldn't he?

Surely, Calvin was just trying to stir shit up.

But the reminder of that lone tear slipping down his face hit me right in the gut, and I knew without a shadow of a doubt that I needed to figure out what the hell was really going on.

When I emerged into the sunshine of the meadow, the bears were gone and the boys had broken into song again as they skipped through the wildflowers and joked about being in a movie. All except Lucky and Calvin. Lucky was kneeling by a tree, his hands roaming over Bear's big body, while Calvin was sending the younger guy covert glances as he pretended to tie his shoe.

Xander cocked a brow at me as I approached him, and he asked what was wrong.

"Tell you later," I said in a low voice. "I might need your advice about this one."

~

Once we arrived at Gin Lake, the boys set up camp like pros. It was satisfying to see each boy falling into his role within the smaller tent groups. Some snapped together poles, others shook out the nylon tent shells over ground cover tarps, and they all seemed to be joking around while doing it. It was a striking contrast to only a few days before when Xander had demonstrated those skills over and over to the group of city kids who'd never seen even a tarp in their lives, much less a small gas-powered camp stove.

I saw Frankie following Calvin around like a puppy while shooting hard looks at Lucky, and wondered if I needed to say something to Calvin about how his behavior toward Lucky was rubbing off on his sidekick. I decided to wait for a less-conspicuous opportunity and turned to head to the water's edge to rinse off my hands.

Aiden approached and crouched down next to me to fill a collapsible water jug we used for cooking. He hadn't said much since blowing up at Xander and me the night before.

"Hey," I said tentatively. "I had a talk with Calvin earlier, and I think there's more to his story than just being a regular bully."

Aiden turned his head toward me and smiled. "There usually is, Bennett. You should know that by now."

Heat filled my face as I realized he was right and I was an idiot. I hadn't even thought to examine Calvin's point of view and what might be causing him to target Lucky. Not that there was any excuse for his behavior, but often kids who abused others lashed out because they were victims of their own abuse.

"Yeah, well. I see that now. Forgive me if I've been a bit preoccupied." My words came out sharper than I'd intended, but I clamped my jaw together to keep from apologizing. I was still annoyed at Aiden for being such an ass to Xander.

"And how is your... ah, *preoccupation* going?" Aiden's smile turned into a smirk as he stood, preparing to close the now full jug.

"Fine."

He barked out a laugh, drawing the attention of a few kids nearby.

"No, sir. I'm going to need more details than that. Go ahead and tell me. You know you will eventually, anyway."

I sighed, knowing he was right. After looking around to make sure none of the kids were close enough to hear, I started talking.

"He fucked me," I said as quietly as humanly possible.

The jug hit the ground and water came spouting out of the narrow opening in the top.

"Shit," he said, scrambling to upright the jug and close it. He wound up drenched in water, and when he looked up at me, he looked like he'd been sprayed with a hose. "Say that again?"

I rolled my eyes at him. "You heard me. Plus, I thought you knew. You implied it when you chewed us out last night."

"Yeah, I thought you were *making out*. I didn't think you were fucking in the goddamned woods!"

My face flooded with more heat and I couldn't help but look around again, this time trying to make sure Xander was well out of hearing range. I couldn't spot him through the clusters of trees surrounding the campsite, so I could only hope he wasn't nearby.

"And?" Aiden asked so loudly and enthusiastically, I jumped in surprise.

"And, what?"

"Jesusfuckingchrist, out with it. How was it?"

"I... ah... well... it was..." How did you describe something that was so quick and dirty it belonged in a porn scene, but at the same time so perfect and meaningful, it was too sweet to put into words?

"Good."

"Good?" Aiden's eyebrows were in his hairline. "That's it? Good? After all that? Christ, do you need me to take you into the woods and teach you a few things?"

I narrowed my eyes at him. "I believe I've learned everything you have to teach already."

"Oh, you're cute, Bennett Crawford, if you think you've seen all my tricks. You haven't even scratched the surface of what I have to teach. Get naked, let's go," he said with a grin as he stood. "I've always fantasized about fucking you in the forest," he added cheekily as his eyes drifted past my shoulder.

He knew I wasn't about to follow him into the woods for sex, but I turned around anyway to walk back to my tent and ran straight into a solid mass. Xander's chest.

His arms came out to steady me so I didn't stumble back into the lake, and I gasped in surprise.

"Don't let me stop you." Xander's voice was cold enough to send shivers down my spine, and my stomach clenched at the look on his face. He'd obviously heard at least part of the conversation.

"I'm not going there. I mean the woods. Anywhere really," I stammered. "I mean, with him. With Aiden. I'm not going to the woods with Aiden. For sex."

*Holy mother of god, shut the fuck up, you idiot.*

Xander cocked a brow at me, but didn't say anything.

"Fuck," I muttered, shooting a glare at Aiden because I knew he had to have seen Xander behind me when he'd said all that shit. "You're an ass."

As I stalked off toward my tent, I heard Aiden laughing behind me. "You're welcome," he called to my back. I was too pissed to even care that I was leaving the two men alone together. Let the fuckers tear each other a new one. I was damn tired of all of it— Aiden's "help" and Xander choosing to believe everyone else but me.

I shook my head as I walked away, not realizing until I reached my tent that Bear had followed me back. "What do you say, Bear?" I asked as I knelt down to pet the dog. "It's just you and me from here on out, okay? They can both go fuck themselves," I said sourly.

Luckily, the dog agreed with me, if the wet tongue that drenched my face was anything to go by. Finally, someone who took my side.

# CHAPTER 19

## XANDER

Hearing Aiden make a suggestive comment about fucking Bennett, along with Bennett's silence, was a brutal reminder that Bennett wasn't really mine. Of course, he wasn't mine. But the idea of Aiden, or anyone else for that matter, putting hands on Bennett's naked body made me physically sick. And truth be told, after his kiss by the fire the night before, a part of me had started to wish for things to be different. I'd even toyed with the idea of putting the past in the past where it belonged and seeing where things could go with Bennett, even if it was just for a few days until he left. But even if I could have managed it, I knew I didn't want just three days of Bennett. I wanted all or nothing. And that was something I just couldn't have.

I watched Bennett long enough to see him disappear into his tent, but when I turned to go, Aiden stopped me. I was expecting him to give me a cocky smirk and then rub Bennett's preference for him in my face. So I was shocked when he gently said, "He really likes you, you know." He shook his head as he fiddled with the cap on the water jug. "This shit with you has been eating him up. Don't let my teasing make you mad at him again, Xander. I was just giving him a hard time. It's what good friends do."

I took a moment to study him, wondering what his agenda was. Guys like Aiden always had one. I'd known a million Aidens in my lifetime and every spoiled trust fund kid I'd ever known, with the exception of Bennett, was always out for himself first, and everyone and everything else came second.

"He says you're not together anymore, but everything I've seen says something different," I said, hoping I didn't sound as petulant as I felt.

"We're not... haven't been since freshman year in college." There was a subtle shift in his voice as he glanced at Bennett's tent. It was heavier somehow... and there was something there. Regret? No, that couldn't be right. I really, really didn't want it to be right.

"You touch him... constantly. You say things that normal friends don't say to each other. I don't go around telling my friends I want to fuck them in the woods."

"Normal," Aiden said with a quiet chuckle. He shook his head and then motioned to a nearby rock before sitting down on it. I reluctantly sat down next to him, but he didn't speak again until he'd taken his boots off and hung his bare feet in the lake.

"You want to know why it didn't work out between him and me, Xander? I mean, do you really want to know, or do you want to keep making assumptions?"

I ignored the subtle jab and said, "Tell me."

"He needed more than I could give him. I knew that pretty much the second we went from being guys who happened to live in the same dorm to friends, then lovers."

I flinched at the last words. Even though it wasn't news to me, the reminder still stung, and I knew it likely always would in some way.

"His heart was so damn big, and he gave as much of it as he could to me right away."

"What does that mean, 'as much as he could'?"

His eyes slid to mine. "You know what it means."

The bottom of my stomach dropped out at that. No, he couldn't possibly mean...

"No," I said. "It wasn't like that between us… ever. We were kids… we were just friends."

"Jesus, watching you two is downright painful," he said softly. "Fine, I'll let you live in your little world of denial. I'm not that guy, Xander. I'm not a relationship guy, never was, never will be. Yes, I tried for Bennett, because he meant that much to me and no one deserved rainbows and sunshine more than him."

He swirled his toes in the water, flicking up clear droplets and watching them fall back down to the surface. "But Bennett is Bennett, and I could see that pretending I was enough for him wasn't going to work. Not for him, not for me. Yes, I touch him and I joke around with him, but only because I know it doesn't mean anything to him… or me."

I looked over at the man beside me. He was tall and muscular— the kind of guy who was probably captain of the football team at his prep school and president of the fraternity in college. He was exactly the kind of guy I would have pictured Bennett with.

"You're perfect for him," I murmured. "You have everything a guy like Bennett could ever want."

He looked at me and shook his head. "You really don't get it, do you?"

"Get what?"

"Just fucking look at him, Xander. I mean really *look*. Stop seeing that kid who turned his back on you and see the man he's become. And no, he never told me the details about what happened that night, but I know whatever it was, it changed him just like it changed you."

I held my tongue, even as the instinct to lash out hit me.

"But he's still that same kid who thought you hung the fucking moon." Aiden let out a rough breath and then settled his eyes on the horizon. I knew what he was seeing— Woodland Rise. It was a view I lived for, but now I couldn't see it. I was too hung up on everything Aiden had said.

"He used to call out for you."

I jerked my head in his direction. "What?"

"In his sleep. He'd say your name and the word 'sorry.' Sometimes he'd cry. Never remembered it when he woke up, though. Ripped my fucking heart out every damn time."

I swallowed hard as my throat threatened to close up. I didn't want to believe him, but as much as I wished it was all lies, I knew it wasn't.

"You know why I touch him all the time and say that shit to him?" he asked.

I shook my head. I didn't want to look at him. I just wanted to escape. I'd been ready to call foul on all his bullshit, but he'd hit me with something I never would have expected from a guy like him.

The truth.

"Because it helps me remember what we are: friends. It makes me not want more. But I still get that little piece of him that's just so... Bennett."

I knew exactly what he was talking about, and I wondered what this man's life must be like to warrant his need for the light that being around Bennett brought into it.

Aiden pulled his feet from the water and grabbed his shoes and socks. "He's going to stop fighting at some point. He's strong, but he's not made of stone, Xander. He might not be there when you finally decide to man up and figure all this shit out."

"It doesn't matter," I said quietly, even as my insides churned. "You guys are leaving in a few days. He has a whole other life. We both do... even just being friends again would be tough."

"He doesn't need any more fucking friends," Aiden bit out as he stood and stomped his feet into the boots without putting his socks on. "He needs you!" He shook his head and angrily said, "Part of me wants you to stay the hell away from him just so you don't break his heart again. But since it never really healed, I guess it doesn't matter. Know this, Xander, you hurt him and you'll answer to me. You might think I'm just some rich prick who doesn't know his asshole from his elbow, but I assure you, when it comes to protecting Bennett, I do know the difference and I'll kick your ass if you hurt him any more than you already have."

And with that, Aiden stalked off, leaving me to deal with the shit storm of emotions he'd left behind. When I finally did move nearly an hour later, it wasn't my tent I began walking towards.

# CHAPTER 20

## BENNETT

I was startled awake by Bear's big tail thumping in my face. At some point after I'd fallen asleep, the dog must have turned around, because when I'd laid down to grab a few minutes of much-needed rest before dinner, the dog's cold nose had been pressed up against my neck.

"Bennett?"

Xander's voice had me jerking to an upright position. Holy hell, I'd completely forgotten about leaving him and Aiden alone by the lake.

"What?" I yelled as I jumped to my feet and jerked at the zipper of the tent. "Who's bleeding?" I asked as I practically fell out of the entrance to the tent.

Xander's hand shot out to catch me when I tripped on a rock.

"Where is he? I'll get the first aid kit," I said as I turned to go back in my tent.

"Relax," Xander said with a light laugh. "He's fine. Still breathing."

I eyed him suspiciously. Why wasn't he pissed? Last time I'd seen him, he'd been ready to rip me a new one.

"Come take a walk with me."

"What? Where? Why?"

"You know, Bennett, just because pot's legal in Colorado now, doesn't mean you should be trying it again. You remember what happened last time you did?"

I cringed at the memory. It had been the summer before we'd started high school. Our last summer together. A kid at the summer camp my parents had forced me to attend every summer for two weeks had given me a joint as a parting gift the day camp had ended. Xander and I had smoked the thing one night while my parents had been out of town. I'd spent the weekend at Xander's, and Mr. Reed had been asleep when we'd snuck outside. We'd gone to our special spot by the fish pond to smoke it. After two puffs, I'd been high as a kite and had ended up wading into the water so I could take a piss.

"Shut up," I groused.

"Come take a walk with me."

"Why?" I repeated.

"Because I asked you to."

"Why?"

"Jesus, Bennett, because I want to fucking apologize to you!" he said, throwing up his hands.

"You do?"

He glared at me.

"Okay," I said. "Fine, let's… walk."

I noticed most of the kids were using their free time to explore the water's shoreline. Aiden was having an in-depth conversation with a couple of the kids about something, but it wasn't until I heard him mention Batman that I realized he was having the same fight he'd had with me countless times. The man was convinced Batman would win in a fight against Superman. I personally didn't know the first thing about either character beyond what I'd seen in the movies Aiden had forced me to watch, but I usually picked the opposing character just to mess with him.

I scanned the area for Lucky, but didn't see him. I knew it was possible he was off getting firewood, since he'd been assigned the task for the evening, but I still felt my concern edge up. Especially when I also couldn't find Calvin.

"Have you seen Calvin or Lucky?" I asked Xander as we left the clearing.

"Um, yeah, I saw Lucky a minute ago. He was going to get the firewood for the night."

I nodded absently.

"Bennett," Xander said, but when he didn't say anything else, I turned my attention on him, and I realized that was what he'd been waiting for.

"Sorry," I murmured.

He shook his head and laughed. "You're kind of stealing my thunder, here."

"Oh, sorry."

At his chuckle, I shook my head and smiled. "Just gonna shut up now."

We kept walking, but this time I kept my attention on him.

"I believe you," he finally said. "About Aiden. And I'm sorry for not trusting that you were telling me the truth."

"Thank you," I said. "Aiden didn't exactly help things," I added.

Xander shrugged. "He cares about you."

I expected him to say more... to make some remark about what an ass Aiden was, but to my surprise, he said nothing. I was about to ask him exactly what had happened between him and the other man after I'd left, but movement to my right caught my eye. As soon as I realized who it was, I grabbed Xander's arm and pulled him to a stop and then quickly shoved him behind a tree.

"Bennett, what the—"

I slapped my hand over his mouth. "Look," I said softly.

He turned and looked in the direction I was pointing. "Oh," he said in surprise.

It was a feeling I shared because I couldn't believe what I was seeing. Less than a hundred feet away, Calvin had Lucky pressed back against a tree and they were softly kissing. From my conversation with Calvin yesterday, I'd figured he was struggling with his sexuality, but I hadn't been one hundred percent sure.

The boys separated after a few seconds, and Calvin stepped back, a startled expression on his face as he touched his fingers to his mouth. I tensed up as he stared at Lucky, but instead of lashing out at him like I expected him to, Calvin hurried past the shorter boy and began trotting back to camp. Lucky, for his part, stood there against the tree for several long seconds, looking as equally stunned as Calvin before he finally bent down and gathered up the pieces of wood scattered at his feet.

Xander drew me back behind the tree as Lucky walked back towards camp. I ended up standing closer to Xander than I realized, and when I looked up at him once Lucky was out of sight, I knew he was feeling the same thing as me. Had it really been less than twenty-four hours since he'd had me pressed up against a tree just like this one, his thick length buried deep inside my body?

"So, um, yeah, that's new," Xander said as he motioned to the spot Lucky and Calvin had been.

I nodded. "Yeah."

"Was that what you wanted to talk to me about?"

"What?" I asked.

"Earlier when we saw the bears. You took Calvin aside and then said you might need my advice."

"Oh, yeah," I said. "I mean, no, not that exactly." I sucked in a breath and took a few more steps back to put some space between us so I could think more clearly. "Calvin said something today, but I'm not sure if I should believe it. But after seeing that," I said as I motioned to the tree Calvin had had Lucky pressed up against, "I'm thinking maybe he was telling the truth."

"What did he say?"

"He said Lucky's foster parents were hurting him. Abusing him." Even the thought had me wanting to go find Lucky and force him to tell me the truth. "But I know Ed and Gloria… they're good people. At least, I thought they were."

"Did you talk to Lucky about it? Has he ever even hinted that something could be wrong?"

"No," I began, but then a memory popped into my head.

"What?" Xander asked gently and I felt his hand close over my arm.

"A few weeks ago, he had a bruise on his stomach. I only saw it because we were playing basketball and his shirt rode up when he was taking a shot. He said he got it during gym. I... I didn't have any reason to think he wasn't telling me the truth." I shook my head. "A few nights before we left to come out here, he asked if he could spend the night at my house. I thought he just wanted to talk about the trip because he was so excited and he liked going over the maps Gary sent us... I told him yes, but that I had to work late and I couldn't pick him up until after dinner. He told me never mind and then changed the subject."

I looked at Xander. "He wanted me to pick him up from school. What if he didn't want to go home, Xander? What if I missed something and he—"

"Don't," Xander cut in and then both of his hands curled around my upper arms. "Don't do that to yourself, Bennett. If something did happen, there was no way you could have known."

Bile rose in my throat as I began questioning more and more encounters I'd had with Lucky where he'd been acting strangely. Either quieter than usual or he'd been moving slower. What if he'd been hiding something each time? Like the bruise I'd seen on his stomach.

"Oh God."

"Bennett, look at me."

I shook my head as I tried to pull free of him. "I missed it," I whispered, in disbelief. I began struggling violently against Xander's hold. "Let me go! I have to talk to him." I could feel hot tears starting to slide down my face, but I didn't care. My only thought was to get to Lucky. "Xander, let go!" I yelled. "I have to help him!"

"Baby, *stop,*" Xander said firmly as he turned us so that my back was to the tree. "You need to calm down."

"No! He needs me!"

"He's safe, Bennett." He gave me a little shake and said, "He's safe."

The reminder helped my racing heart start to slow, but the shame quickly took over and coursed through me like a living thing. "I failed him, Xander. He trusted me to protect him and I failed him."

"No, baby, you didn't," Xander whispered and then he was tugging me forward. His arms went around me and I felt his lips skim my temple.

"I don't know what to do," I admitted. My insides felt like they'd been scraped raw.

"You're going to help him, Benny," Xander murmured against my ear. "Because that's what you do." His hand came up to hold the back of my head, and I just stood there and soaked in the comfort he was offering. When I finally felt like I could breathe again, I pulled back.

"I need to talk to him."

"I know you do, but can I suggest something?"

I nodded and looked up at him.

"Give him this trip. Let him have the next few days where he doesn't have to think about the shit back home. You guys will have a couple days at the lodge before you have to go home. On the last day, talk to him. That will give you time to figure things out. What to say, who you'll need to talk to about what happens next."

He was right.

"Okay, yeah," I said.

"He's going to be okay, Bennett."

"He has to be," I whispered.

"He will," Xander said and then he pulled me back in his arms and I happily went.

# CHAPTER 21

## XANDER

The following day was our last full day in the backcountry and the kids woke up hyper as hell. Everyone scrambled to pack their gear so they could be the first to report to me for their solo route assignments. We were departing from Gin Lake and would be camping that evening at Caldera Lake. To get from one lake to the other, we had to navigate over Mount Wodash in between.

This was the pinnacle of excitement for most kids on these wilderness adventure trips— the solo hike. I'd spent time every day going over the tools needed to make it from point A to point B in the backcountry, and I'd surreptitiously quizzed each kid's navigation skills the previous day. Everyone had passed with flying colors, and the route I'd chosen was a fairly straightforward one.

Mount Wodash sported a high pass with a large, open view of the valley below leading down to the lake. Any lost hikers would be easily spotted from that vista as I came through last to pick up any stragglers. The kids didn't know that it was almost impossible to get lost between Gin and Caldera Lakes, so hopefully they would feel a massive sense of accomplishment by nightfall.

One of my favorite parts of these trips was the final night's campfire where everyone would be chattering excitedly about their solo adventures. A storm was threatening far off in the distance, but if I had to guess, I'd say it was more likely to spoil our final short hike to the trailhead the following day rather than mess up the solos or our celebration night.

Bear lifted his head from where it had been resting on his paws as I heard someone approach.

"Xander?"

"Hey, Lucky. You ready for your solo today?" I asked with a smile. I tried to hide my concern for him by turning to dig his copy of today's topo map out of my bag.

"Well, yes. Sort of," he said hesitantly. "I mean, I'm almost ready, but I think one of the other guys is really worried about it. I heard Frankie crying in his tent this morning when I walked past on my way to take a pee."

I glanced in the direction of Frankie and Calvin's tent group and noticed Frankie sitting on his pack with his face in his hands.

"Xander, do you think maybe I should offer to go with him so he's not alone?" Lucky asked, reaching down to give Bear the petting he'd started nudging for.

"No, Lucky. I don't want your solo experience impaired. If I need to hike with him, it's not a problem, okay? Finish up packing your gear and let me handle it."

"M'kay," he replied, still focused on my pushy dog. We stood together in silence for a few moments before I caught him sneaking a peek back at Frankie and then at me. He kept quiet and continued petting the beast.

"Lucky?" I asked quietly. "What's really bothering you about Frankie?"

"No, no. It's not that," he said quickly. "It's not Frankie."

"Alright. Do you want to talk about it? Whatever *it* is?" I asked carefully as I thought about what Bennett had told me the day before. The thought of someone who'd been entrusted to care for this boy, but had abused him instead, made me physically ill, and I wanted to reassure him no one would ever dare lay a hand on him again. It was a promise I couldn't make, but I sure as hell wished I could. For his sake... and Bennett's.

More dog pets and more sneaking glances back toward the group of kids packing by the tents. It occurred to me that he likely wasn't looking to talk to me about his foster parents at all because he was just too light and relaxed.

"It's just... I mean. I guess I was wondering..."

A blush had started to rise on his cheeks, and in that instant, he reminded me so much of Bennett, it almost made me laugh— so bumbling, and awkward, and eager. So, I did what I'd always done with Bennett— offered a lighter non-subject to buy him some time to get his thoughts together.

"Hey, would you mind walking Bear down to the lake for one last drink before we set off? I need to double-check these maps to make sure I have enough."

Lucky's head snapped up and a grin widened on his face. "Yeah, sure. C'mon, Bear."

As I watched the two of them wander down to the water's edge, I caught Bennett's eye where he was burying the remnants of our fire from the night before. He shot me a soft smile and then cocked an eyebrow with a nod in Lucky's direction.

I held up an "ok" symbol with my fingers, and he responded immediately with a swift combination of hand gestures that had me desperately trying to stifle my laughter. When I failed miserably, I shook my head at him. A massive grin broke out on his pretty mouth before he turned back to what he was doing.

When we'd been in the fifth grade, I hadn't made the cut to get into Spanish class with the cool kids, so I'd been stuck in American Sign Language class instead. I'd struggled like crazy just trying to learn the basics until Bennett had finally gotten sick of me whining about it and had tried to help me study. We'd watched a video to learn how to sign "Hello, my name is Xander" and every time after that, anytime something was confusing or we just wanted to make someone think we were talking in code, we'd sign to each other, "Hello, my name is Xander."

It had nearly gotten us in trouble on more than one occasion, like the time we'd almost earned ourselves a trip to the principal's office when we'd been playing a softball game in gym class one day in middle school, and Bennett had been the pitcher. I'd signed parts of that sentence to him every time someone new had been at bat so it would look like I was making pitch suggestions like in the big leagues. He'd nodded his approval or shaken his head and asked for another until it had driven our classmates up the fucking wall. Bennett had finally started laughing so hard, it had set me off, and the coach had threatened to bring the principal, Mr. Titweiler, into the picture. And since neither of us had been able say the principal's last name without laughing our asses off, we'd begged and pleaded with the coach to give us a second chance. We'd only managed to avoid a stint in detention by using our gloves to cover our faces whenever we'd looked at each other and started laughing all over again.

When I finally managed to get myself under control and turned back to check my maps, Lucky was coming back up from the lake with a noticeably wet Bear.

"Hey, you big oaf. I told you no morning swims," I lectured the giant fuzzball. He just lolled out his tongue and grinned at me right alongside a smiling Lucky.

"Sorry, Xander. I told him not to, but he didn't listen."

"Sure, sure. That's a likely excuse. At least you didn't decide to go in too," I teased, handing him a copy of the map. "Did you think about what you wanted to ask me?"

He ran a hand through his hair as he shoved the map into his pocket with the other. "Uh, yeah. I guess. It's just… how do you know if it's okay to like someone?"

"What do you mean?" I asked, even though I was pretty sure what he meant.

"Well, you see… There's this guy, and I kind of like him. But he's been an asshole to me in the past. Like really hurt my feelings, you know?"

"Yeah. Go on," I said carefully.

"Well, how do you decide what kind of things are unforgivable? If, like, you like someone and want to be with them, but you can't forget the things they've said that hurt you."

"First of all, want to be with them how? Like as friends? Or more—like kissing?" I didn't dare mention sex because I just wasn't prepared to go there with a sixteen-year-old kid.

His face turned even redder. "The kissing one," he said.

"Well, first of all, you're still a kid so it's not like you're making a permanent decision. So, really, you're wondering if it's okay to enjoy being physical with someone, even though they may have said and done shitty things to you in the past. Right?"

"Yeah, exactly."

I tried to think about what the right advice was before saying something that might steer him wrong. "I think that you have to consider how they feel about you now. Do they still have negative feelings toward you or have they changed? Plenty of people seem incapable of changing, but with kids your age, it's different. There are people trying shit on and learning lessons from their mistakes, you know?"

"Yeah. I do."

"So I'd hate to say that someone saying something bad to you at this age is unforgivable when I really think you should allow people to change as they grow up and mature. Plus, holding a grudge against someone sometimes does more harm to the holder of the grudge than the person they're mad at."

A sliver of recognition snaked through my gut at my stupid-ass words, but I did my best to ignore it.

"So, you think it's okay?" Lucky asked.

"What's okay?" I said, realizing my eyes had strayed back to Bennett, who was obviously stalling the kids to keep them from approaching me for their assignments. I knew Lucky and I didn't have much time left before Bennett wouldn't be able to hold them back any longer.

"To kiss someone," Lucky said sheepishly.

"It's okay to kiss someone, Lucky," I said, putting a hand on his shoulder and meeting his eyes. "It's when you go to give them your whole heart that you need to be really careful. It doesn't take much to get it broken."

"Is that what happened to you?"

His question startled me and I automatically glanced at Bennett. Was that what had happened? Could you even get your heart broken if you'd never actually given it away? I saw Bennett's eyebrows furrow, and I realized he must have seen a change in my expression or something. His gentle smile faded away and I saw a flicker of worry go through his gaze.

"Xander?"

"Huh?" I asked as I forced myself to look at Lucky again. "Um, no, not really," I stammered.

He was quiet for a moment before he smiled shyly and asked, "What was it like? Your first kiss, I mean."

I tilted my head at the question. "What? Oh. Hm. First kiss? Who was that… a guy named Ronnie or Ricky maybe? Reggie?" I felt my lips tilt up as the memory returned. "Don't really remember his name. I just remember being ramped up after a pickup basketball game and yanking the guy behind the equipment shed in the park. It was nice."

"Bullshit," A familiar voice sounded from behind me. "Your first kiss was with Madison Franklin."

I turned around in time to see Bennett's mischievous wink at Lucky. His eyes returned to mine and I saw the silent question there.

*Are we okay?*

I didn't blame him for wondering if he'd done something to cause my momentary mood change after Lucky had asked me about my own experience with nursing a broken heart. After all, all I'd been doing from the moment he'd stepped off that bus was blame him for everything that had gone wrong in my life after my dad had died.

"Who? Madison Franklin? Oh, hell. That didn't count," I said lightly.

"It sure did. It counted because I saw it and you never told me about it, which pissed me the hell off." Bennett was laughing, but there was something off.

"What? That stupid kiss? It definitely didn't count. She caught me unaware at that middle school graduation party and just laid one on me before I could stop her. And I didn't tell you because it was noth—"

"Dude, it counted. There was tongue."

My jaw dropped, and I stared at him. He'd seen a girl kiss me the spring before my dad died and thought I'd *liked* it? While I'd been going crazy with dealing with my newfound attraction to *him*, he'd thought I was feeling those same things for *girls*?

"No, there wasn't," I said more sharply than I'd intended. "No tongue. I swear."

Lucky snorted and Bennett laughed. "Xander, you should see your face right now," Lucky guffawed. "You're redder than Toby's hair!"

"I heard that!" Toby called as he and a couple of the other boys caught up to us. The older boy glanced at me and shook his head. "Dude," he said with pity, and then he was brushing past me, grabbing Lucky's arm as he went.

"He's right, you know," Bennett said. "Only time I've ever seen your cheeks that red was when you stole my mom's lipstick and smeared it all over your face."

"You know why, asshole," I groused. "We were ten and I was going as Ickis from Real Monsters for Halloween, but I lost the mask so I had to paint my face to match the rest of the costume."

Bennett laughed and said, "Whatever. You kissed a girl."

I gave him a hard shove, but immediately latched onto his arm at the same time so I wouldn't actually knock him down. He quieted and his eyes fell to where my fingers were curled around his elbow. Electricity fired up through my fingers and into my arm and I was drawing him forward before I even realized what I was doing. "It should have been you," I murmured as my eyes fell briefly to his mouth.

"Wh... what?" he stammered.

"You should have been my first kiss."

"Yo, B! It's catching!" Lucky called, and we both turned to see the entire group of boys watching us with varying degrees of smirks on their faces. Bennett lifted his hand to his now very pink cheeks and then laughed. "So it would seem," he said softly.

I forced myself to release him so he could step past me and head towards the kids who immediately began singing, *Xander and Bennett sitting in a tree.*

Bennett spoke quickly. "Okay, okay, last guy to stop singing has to sleep in my tent with Bear tonight!" Since my dog had gained quite the reputation for his potent flatulence problem, all the kids fell silent instantly. "Thought so," Bennett said with amusement as he cast me a smile over his shoulder. Then I saw it.

And I couldn't fucking believe it.

That wink.

That goddamned heart-stopping, soul-sucking, perfect wink that I'd been waiting a lifetime to see again.

Bennett turned his focus back to the boys, completely unaware of what he'd just done to me. "You guys ready to get your route assignments from Xander? Who's ready to move on from here?"

His enthusiasm was contagious. I was engulfed by a pack of excited kids ready to begin the day's adventure, so I didn't get a chance to mull over everything that had just happened or what any of it meant. Once the kids were all on their way, I let my thoughts drift to the question Bennett had asked them just before we'd sent them on their way.

*Who's ready to move on from here?*

When he'd said it, I'd known he was referring to leaving the Gin Lake campsite, but I couldn't help but think about it in larger terms. After what I'd said to Lucky about allowing people to change, I thought back over all of my feelings for Bennett and wondered if I would ever take my own fucking advice and move past the bullshit with him. I hated the weird middle ground we seemed to have found with each other. We seemed to be old friends who'd been reunited as cordial acquaintances. And it didn't fucking fit.

I didn't want to be just old friends. I certainly didn't want to be a cordial acquaintance. And with only a few days left before he flew back to a world I never wanted to be a part of again, we couldn't be anything more than that. So, there we were— in this awkward no-man's land of people who had a shared past but no shared future. And it fucking burned me up inside.

As I staggered each boy's departure from Gin Lake, I thought about trying to relax and just enjoy the company of my old friend for the time we had left together. It wouldn't fix anything and it wouldn't let me have all of Bennett like I really wanted, but it would have to do.

Because I knew that if I didn't use the next three days to soak up as much of Bennett Crawford as I could before I lost him again, I'd regret it for the rest of my life.

# CHAPTER 22

## BENNETT

*It should have been you.*

Part of me was actually pissed at Xander for what he'd said, but the rest of me was reeling with the implications. And it was bringing me to my fucking knees— to think of what we could have had together if we'd just been given the chance.

If his father hadn't died.

If mine hadn't been such a selfish son of a bitch who'd cared more about appearances than he had about his own kid.

If I'd cast open that door to Xander instead of shutting it that fateful night.

I would have held on and never let go. He would have been my first everything and I, his.

Xander and I both spent the first part of the hike lost in thought, but as the day went on, I forced myself to focus on drawing us both out of our funk. With so little time left with him, the last thing I wanted to do was wallow in regret and lost chances. There'd be plenty of time for that once I got home. Not to mention the near-constant worry I had for Lucky. I'd barely managed to avoid grabbing him last night and again this morning to demand he tell me what his foster parents had been doing to him. But Xander had been right. Lucky deserved these last days to enjoy what remained of the trip. Reality would return soon enough.

It didn't take much more than a few stupid knock-knock jokes to get Xander talking, and within an hour we were dueling to see who could make the other laugh harder.

Aiden had left the campsite first thing that morning to get a head start so he could arrive at Caldera Lake before the first boy, so it was just Xander and me hiking together to bring up the rear in case of stragglers.

Once the joke-off came to an end, we spent several hours talking about lots of different things. The more he began to relax and open up, the more he started telling me about his time leading wilderness trips and some of his craziest adventures. He wound up talking a lot about his Aunt Lolly who, despite being a little bit nutty, sounded like a loving woman who'd provided him with a much-needed soft place to land after Mr. Reed's death.

When it was my turn to talk, I told him more about the foundation at work and how I'd managed to grow it through fundraising events and word of mouth. I explained some of the pilot programs we'd introduced with high-risk youth in fine arts programs after school.

I couldn't keep from laughing when I described how Daryl, one of the program teachers, had asked me out for a drink to tell me about what had happened with the kids one day. "He was so upset, I was worried he was going to quit."

"Why?" Xander asked. "What happened?"

"Apparently when he told the kids they were going to the park for a painting class, some of them assumed he meant graffiti. So, they brought spray paint and were prepared to start tagging shit. You should have seen the look on his face when he told me."

I put the back of my hand across my forehead the way Daryl had and sighed dramatically. "'But Bennett, the *police*. What if the police had seen us? I'm too pretty to survive a night in central lockup,' he said. I thought I was going to choke on my beer."

"Did he quit?" Xander asked.

"Nah. I sweet-talked him into staying on and treated him to a nice dinner. He's been teaching that class now for six months and the kids love him."

"What else do you like to do besides work and volunteering?" he asked as we approached the top of the pass. "Do you spend time with your family?"

I looked over at Xander and saw him looking at the ground in front of him while he walked. It was unusual for him. Throughout the trip, I'd noticed that Xander always looked ahead or around him, taking in the views and his surroundings like it was the very air that sustained him. But when he was unsure, he kept his eyes down.

"Yeah, I guess I do."

He looked up at me then with a quirked brow, so I explained. "Well, I mean, I work with my dad, so I see him a lot. And I have plenty of obligations to see them at company functions. But they also expect me for family things like birthdays and holidays."

"You make it sound like a bad thing," he observed.

I sighed and looked away, trying to put my thoughts into words. "You know how they are... were," I began, glancing at him to make sure he was okay with what I'd said.

"You always felt trapped," he said softly. "Is it still like that with them?"

I shrugged. "Can you be trapped if you've never actually tried to escape?" I asked absently. I shook my head and said, "I think I keep waiting for that moment, you know?"

"What moment?"

"You know... *the* moment."

Xander smiled. "Ah, *the moment*. I'd forgotten about that."

"No," I cried, clutching my heart dramatically. Xander laughed and I gave him a gentle slap on the arm. "You said you loved those movies just as much as I did."

"I never said that. I said I loved that *you* loved them."

"What's the difference?"

"The difference is that I didn't stay up night after night memorizing the lines from those *moments* and force you to act them out over and over again." He had me there. I'd had a weird obsession with movies when we'd been thirteen. I'd honed in on the moments where the big gesture happened. Whether it was the hero telling the heroine he was sorry for whatever folly had befallen the couple or the poor bullied kid turning the tables on his tormentor… it hadn't mattered. I'd waited breathlessly each time for "the moment" and the ones that had left some indelible mark on me, I'd forced Xander to reenact with me, which he'd done so without question. My favorite had always been about the kid at odds with his parents. It was pathetic, but every time the parents had wrapped their arms around their kid after some near-death experience or event that had made them appreciate their child more, I'd dreamed it was me. That it would be my mom and dad hugging me so tight I could barely breathe and I'd feel their tears against my skin as they told me over and over how much they loved me.

"So you never got it?" Xander asked, pulling me back to the present. "Your *moment*?"

I shook my head. "You think there's a use-by date on those things?" I asked jokingly, but he didn't smile. "Anyway, as you can imagine, the gay thing didn't go over well."

"Shit, Bennett," he said. "What happened?"

"Well, I kept putting off telling them. Didn't even consider coming out until I had my first real boyfriend in college, and even then, I chickened out. Finally, I knew I had to tell them because the stress of keeping it a secret was making me sick."

"How'd you do it? What did you say?"

"I was all set to tell them. We were going to be having dinner together one Friday night at their house, and I knew it would be the perfect chance to tell them in private. That way I could leave if things got tense. But right when we sat down at the table, my dad beat me to the punch. Looked right at me and asked me what the hell I thought I was doing."

I took a deep breath as memories of that night threatened to bring back long-forgotten emotions. "I didn't know what he was talking about, and my mom must have seen the confusion on my face. She told me that Dad had run into one of my Harvard classmates on the golf course that day and he'd introduced Dad to my boyfriend. I thought I was going to die."

"Oh shit, Benny," Xander murmured and the sound of my nickname helped tame some of the rampant emotions I was feeling as I recalled my father's fury. I doubted Xander was even aware that he'd slipped back into calling me that more and more these past couple of days, and I treasured every instance like it was gold.

"Yeah. It turns out it was Aiden, and he'd tried to stop it." I slid a quick look at Xander when I mentioned Aiden's name. They'd been getting along better, but I wasn't sure how he'd feel about me bringing up the fact that I'd had a romantic relationship with the other man. Hell, I didn't even know if he'd figured out that Aiden had been the guy I'd lost my virginity to. But Xander didn't look upset. At most, there was a slight tension in his jawline, but it disappeared quickly, so I continued.

"He knew I wasn't out to my parents, so he made a big joke about it. Said something like, 'Ha-ha Brett, that's hilarious. Nah, Mr. Crawford. Bennett and I are just friends. Nice to meet you, sir.' He played it off, but I guess Brett's face gave it away to my dad. And maybe that's just when everything fell into place. It's not like he didn't already know."

"What do you mean? You think he already knew you were gay?"

"He suspected it when you and I were in eighth grade. Seemed to be antsy about it. That's why he—" I stopped myself. Shit. I'd been about to mention my dad's warning about keeping things just friends with Xander, but I didn't want to go there with him. It would bring up things between us that would most likely cause tension again. And I sure as hell didn't want tension between us when we were alone together, sharing a beautiful hike on a perfect day.

"Why he, what?" Xander asked before whistling to get Bear's attention from where he'd wandered a little too far.

"Nothing. I don't want to talk about my parents anymore. Tell me about your coming out. Does Lolly know?"

Xander barked out a laugh. "Yes, Lolly knows. She thinks it's the greatest thing ever and gets mildly inappropriate asking for details of all my relationships."

I felt unease in my gut and tried to stop myself from asking the question, but it was no use. "Your relationships? How many have there been, exactly?"

Xander's face flushed, reminding me of the shy boy I'd known so many years before. Fucking cute as hell. "None. I mean— well, that's not entirely true. I've dated some guys, but nothing super-serious. I shouldn't have said relationships. I just didn't want to say my aunt was asking for details of my hookups. Sounds gross."

I chuckled. "Yeah, kinda. But why haven't you had any serious relationships? Just haven't met the right guy yet?"

Xander looked at me with a small quirk of his lip. "Who wants to know?"

Now it was my turn to blush. "Never mind. Let's change the subject."

He bumped his shoulder into mine before mentioning that we'd reached the top of the pass. "We need to stop and use the binoculars to make a note of where everyone is," he said.

Oh, right. The kids. I'd gotten so wrapped up in my hike with Xander, I'd forgotten about keeping track of the boys on their solo excursions. I reminded myself that it was a day to focus on the safety of the kids, but I began to wonder if I could find more time with Xander alone once we returned to the lodge the following day. Our group was scheduled to spend a couple of additional days there before returning home, and I could only hope Xander would be there too.

And that maybe he was feeling the same way... that it wasn't time to say goodbye yet.

# CHAPTER 23

## XANDER

I was in the process of pulling out my binoculars when Bear suddenly let out a few sharp barks and took off up a small rise to our right. "Bear!" I called, but he'd already disappeared through the heavy cluster of trees. I let out a sharp whistle.

"Think he heard or saw something?" Bennett asked.

"Maybe," I responded as I tried to listen for the sound of his barking. I could usually tell a lot by the types of barks he let out. But there was nothing, and that had me worried. "Stay here," I said. "I'll be back in a second."

"No way, I'm coming with you. If it's a bear or something, I should be there."

I shot him a glance and said, "So you can do what? Become the bear whisperer and save my ass?"

"Shut up," he groused. "I had those koi eating out of the palm of my hand. I'm a natural with animals. Besides, it's not *your* ass I'm worried about."

I began climbing up the sharp incline. When I heard Bennett struggling behind me, his boots sliding through the soft dirt, I reached my hand out. He automatically grabbed it like it was the most natural thing in the world.

"So you're coming with me so you can save my dog?"

"What can I say, I've grown fond of him. Besides, he smells better than you."

I chuckled. "My fart factory of a dog smells better than me? Thanks."

Bennett started to speak, but the sound of Bear barking had us both stopping in our tracks. Once I pinpointed where the barking was coming from, I turned in that direction and practically dragged Bennett behind me. It was several hundred feet up the incline before we reached a small clearing. It took just seconds to locate Bear by a small outcropping of boulders.

And he wasn't alone.

"Lucky?" I called when I recognized the boy's red shirt. He was walking towards us, along with Frankie. Both boys looked over at us.

"We're okay," Lucky returned as they trotted towards us, followed closely by Bear.

"What happened?" I asked. "Why'd you go off the trail?"

"Um, I caught up to Frankie and we thought we heard something—"

"That's not true. It was me," Frankie cut in. "I got scared because I thought I saw something on the trail and just panicked and ran. I couldn't figure out how to get back so I started calling for help."

I noticed the teenager's eyes were red-rimmed. After Lucky had told me he'd seen Frankie crying earlier this morning, I'd done a check-in with Frankie to make sure he was okay, but he'd brushed my concerns aside with a cocky remark about all the shit he'd seen living in the city and these woods being "a walk in the park."

"Lucky heard me and came to show me how to get back."

Lucky dropped his eyes and I saw some color seep into his cheeks. "It was nothing," he murmured. "I marked the map with the alternate route like you said so I didn't get lost."

"I'm really proud of you, Lucky. That was good thinking," I said as I patted him on the shoulder. I turned to find Bennett staring at Lucky with a wide grin on his face. His love for the boy was so apparent that it made my heart hurt to think about how tough it would be for him when he got back home and had to deal with what was happening with Lucky. Not only would he be carrying around a massive amount of guilt, he'd be struggling with having to let the boy go into a whole new situation.

I led the small group back down to the main trail and Bennett and I held back, letting Frankie and Lucky walk ahead of us. I noticed Bear was practically attached to Lucky's hip the entire time.

"He's a great kid," I said to Bennett.

"He really is. I know I'm not supposed to get overly attached to them—"

"Bullshit," I interjected and waited until Bennett was looking at me to say, "You wouldn't be you if you didn't get attached."

He nodded. "Thank you," he said softly, and then suddenly his fingers curled into my hand. When he linked our fingers, it felt like my heart was going to burst out of my chest.

Because it was so fucking perfect.

And I knew in that moment I could do it. I could let the past go and focus on the future.

A future with him. But as quickly as the thought entered my brain, reality crashed down, because Bennett said, "They're my life, you know?"

"I do," I managed to say. And that was the crux of it. Even wanting Bennett wasn't enough. He had a whole life waiting for him back in New York, and mine was here. I didn't even begin to know how to make something like that work. It wasn't like we could date while living 2000 miles apart. Not to mention that nothing about our lives would mesh. He'd told me he was being groomed to take over the investment firm his father had founded. He'd have everything at that point— wealth, status, power. And I'd still be me. Xander Reed, caretaker's-son-turned-wilderness-guide. I was the hired help. Even if Bennett could see past that, his friends and family never would.

I forced myself to release Bennett's hand when he relaxed his fingers. I listened as the boys chatted with each other, and pride swelled in my chest when Lucky offered to let Frankie walk ahead of us so it would look like he'd finished the hike on his own. For whatever reason, Frankie declined, which surprised me because I was certain he'd jump at the chance to save face. But the young man took it a step further, because as soon as we reached camp, he went straight to where everyone was setting up camp and began telling them exactly what Lucky had done. Lucky was treated to a variety of accolades, but his eyes lit up when Calvin got the group to start chanting Lucky's name and then led the boys in a raucous round of applause. As the excitement died down and the boys began sharing enthusiastic stories about their solo hikes, I wondered if this trip had sparked a desire in any of them to spend more time researching or trying to get back into the wilderness. It made me wonder if there was a way I could help other kids have similar experiences.

They hadn't been the first group of city kids I'd led on an expedition, but for some reason they'd been the ones who'd seemed to benefit the most from it. Maybe it was because I knew none of them had ever been out of the city— never slept under the canopy of aspen leaves and listened to their soft whirring sounds as an evening breeze passed through. Each of the boys in Bennett and Aiden's group had needed this. Needed open space and fresh air and the time to use their imaginations without electronics, chores, or parents.

I looked around at eight smiling faces and had a moment of such gratitude for where my life had taken me, I wished I could have called Aunt Lolly and told her about it. When she'd finally settled us down in Colorado, I'd found my true home and purpose. And as much as it had killed me to lose both my dad and Bennett, I couldn't imagine how different my life would have been had I stayed in the northeast.

Before I had a chance to get too emotional, I heard an unexpected squawk from my backpack. I rustled through the deep pockets until I found the wilderness radio I carried for emergencies. It was Gary. Probably trying to raise me on the radio to confirm our pickup at the trailhead the following day.

"Yeah," I said into the radio. "I'm here. Hey, Gary."

"Xander, good. I'm glad I got you. I think you were out of range earlier today. Everything okay out there?"

"Yeah. Just arrived at Caldera after the solo. All good. We should be to the pickup on time tomorrow."

"That's what I'm calling about, actually. We have a problem."

"What's up?" I asked as I noticed Bear following Bennett into the woods. I stifled a smile, thinking about Bennett's reaction to whipping out his dick for a piss and finding a very large dog staring at him.

"It's Jake. He's injured," Gary said through the radio. The sound was muffled through radio static, so I asked him to repeat it as nerves caused my heart rate to increase.

"Is he okay? What happened? How bad?" My words came tumbling out as I thought about my friend, as well as the group of younger children in his care.

"Just a sprained ankle, he thinks. The problem is, it happened after one of the kids went missing. He found the boy, but now he can't get back by himself."

"I'll go," I said without thinking. "I'll go get him. Where is he?"

"On the northern slope of Lower Bower. He found a rocky overhang and set up a tent. Says he has plenty of food and the river is close enough for water. It's just a matter of someone getting there and helping him get the kid back."

I saw Bennett emerge from the woods, talking to Bear and shaking a finger at him. After waving to get his attention, I gestured for him and Aiden to join me while I told Gary to hang on. I told Aiden and Bennett what was happening and then clicked the radio back on.

"Gary, I can get there. There's a shortcut between Caldera and Lower Bower. Aiden and Bennett can get this group to the trailhead tomorrow without me. It's a straight shot." I eyed the falling darkness around us. As badly as I wanted to get to Jake and the boy, I needed to be smart about it. "Gary, you said Jake is set for provisions and the kid's not hurt?"

"Yep, they're both okay. He said he and the boy decided to have an extra adventure."

I understood what he was telling me. The boy would have been within earshot when Jake radioed in. He'd probably called the whole thing an adventure so the kid wouldn't get scared.

"I'll leave at first light. I should be able to make it there by nightfall or the very next morning."

Bennett started to speak, but I held up a hand to stop him. He narrowed his eyes at me, but kept his mouth closed.

"Xander, there's a giant river between you and Lower Bower. I'm not okay with you doing that river crossing alone," Gary said.

Bennett grabbed the radio from my hand and pressed the button. "Gary, this is Bennett Crawford. He's not going alone. I'm going with him. That's one of my kids out there. Who is it?" I stiffened at Bennett's words, but I didn't interrupt the conversation since I could tell Bennett was desperate to know which kid was involved.

There was a pause while Gary seemed to regroup. "Mr. Crawford. I'm sorry about this. I promise you—"

"I understand, Gary. Just tell me. Who is it?" Bennett interrupted.

"Jimmy. And he's fine. Just took off to see some snow, apparently. Jake says they're holed up safely and playing lots of games to learn about plants and animals."

I heard Bennett let out a sigh of relief before answering. "We'll go get him. Aiden will bring this group to the trailhead."

I grabbed the radio. "Gary, Mr. Crawford misspoke. He and Mr. Vale will be bringing the kids down the trailhead," I said firmly.

"I'm going," Bennett said stubbornly and crossed his arms together in front of him. For once, Aiden was uncharacteristically silent, and I knew that probably wasn't a good thing.

"You're not," I repeated.

It wasn't until I heard Gary clear his throat that I realized I'd had my finger on the call button so Gary had heard everything.

"Uh, I'll hike in first thing in the morning to Caldera and help... whoever... bring the crew out," he said awkwardly. Gary signed off after that and Aiden mumbled some excuse about going to tell the kids what was happening.

"I'm going," Bennett repeated, and then began walking away like that was the end of it.

"No, you're not," I said as I grabbed his arm. "I can get there faster on my own." I didn't tell him the real reason I didn't want him coming along— that I was scared shitless he'd get hurt. Even though it was a relatively safe hike, there was always an inherent risk in going off trail. But I couldn't tell him I was terrified of him getting hurt, because then he'd know that things had started to change for me. And *that* was a conversation I just wasn't ready to have yet.

"Yes. I. Am."

Before I could say anything, he continued. "I am responsible for each and every one of these kids, Xander. I'm the one who promised their parents I'd bring them home safely, and I'm the one who told these boys I'd always take care of them, no matter what. Jimmy is a great kid, but he's still just a boy. What are you going to do if he gets scared or needs help on the trail while you're helping Jake?" Bennett asked.

It was something I hadn't considered. I mulled over his words and finally nodded. I wasn't happy about it, a fact he was well aware of if the hard set of his jaw was anything to go by, but I'd figure it out. I'd keep him safe if it killed me. Because I'd have to let Bennett go when this was all over, but he'd sure as hell be going in one piece. And truth be told, the idea of spending even one day alone with him wasn't a hardship in any way, shape or form.

Except maybe on my heart.

But I'd look at it as a chance to spend some time with an old friend, revisiting old memories and maybe even making a few new ones. At least that way I'd have something of Bennett to hang onto once he was gone.

"Fine," I said. "But you do as I say, you got that?"

Bennett bristled, but nodded. Then he turned on his heel and marched back to camp. I may or may not have ogled his ass as he went. Just like I may or may not have fallen asleep later that night to dreams of all the things Bennett and I could do the following night when we would be forced to share a very small and very cozy tent together.

# CHAPTER 24

## BENNETT

As we got ready to go the following morning, I was still pissed at Xander for trying to talk me out of coming with him. As if I was too weak to make the trip, or what I wanted didn't matter. It made me feel unimportant and stupid, and I wasn't used to feeling either of those things. Especially with him. Not to mention his parting shot the night before about me having to do what he said. Okay, yeah, so his words had both infuriated me and excited me at the same time. No way I'd ever tell him that.

I hadn't slept well, and not just because I'd been worried about Jimmy. Although the boy had a tendency to get easily distracted, he was a good kid who wasn't prone to questioning authority, so I knew he'd do whatever Jake told him. And while I didn't know this Jake guy at all, I had to trust that he was good at his job and would be able to take care of Jimmy until Xander and I could reach them.

After saying goodbye to the kids and Aiden, I gave a last hug to Lucky.

"Take care of Bear, okay?" I asked, seeing the boy's chest puff up with pride.

"I will, B. I promise. I told Xander I'd walk him when we got back and make sure he had plenty of food and water."

Xander had decided the dog would be better off returning to the lodge with the group, since we had a river crossing that he'd said wouldn't be easy for the animal to navigate, and the current was too strong to risk letting the dog swim across.

"I know you will. He's lucky to be staying with you. I know Xander must think a lot of you to trust you with him," I said, scratching the dog's head. I glanced up at Lucky and waited until I caught his eye.

"You going to be okay?" I asked quietly. "You need anything?" I wanted so badly to ask him about his foster family, but I knew Xander was right— I didn't want to spoil his fun on the last day of the hike, and there would be time enough for us to deal with it when I got back from helping Jimmy.

"Nah, I'm good," he said with a small smile. "Aiden asked me the same thing. I think he's trying to take over as my Bennett while you're gone."

My heart expanded in my chest— both for the kid who recognized that he was cared for and my friend who knew without asking that I'd be worried about Lucky while I was gone.

"Alright. Well, keep an eye out for Aiden too. He probably needs looking after more than you do," I said with a wink.

"Hey, B?" Lucky asked.

"Yeah?"

He looked down at his feet before grinning back up at me mischievously. "Are *you* going to be okay?"

"What do you mean? Of course I am. Why wouldn't I be?"

"Well, it'll just be you and Xander out there until you get to Jimmy. I'm worried you're either going to kill each other or… you know..."

"Know what?" I asked dumbly.

Lucky looked around us and then dropped his voice and sang, "Xander and Bennett sitting in a tree…" He waggled his eyebrows at me.

I stared at him, feeling my face turn crimson. "Wh-what? Jesus, Lucky. No. I mean, that's none of your… it's… we're just friends. It's fine. I've known Xander for a long time. We're past the kill each other phase. I promise."

He snorted. "Sure, B. If you say so. If not the killing, then I guess it'll be the other thing." He lifted an eyebrow at me, and I rolled my eyes.

"Go," I said, flapping my hand at him. "Get out of here with that mangy beast, and stop trying to ruffle my feathers."

He wandered off laughing and quickly joined the other boys who were finishing up breakfast. Before he got too far away, he turned back.

"Yo, B! Don't do anything I wouldn't do," he shouted for everyone in the campsite to hear.

I stood there frozen, feeling my face incinerate as Aiden barked out a laugh and slapped Lucky on the back as he approached the remaining campers.

"I hope you aren't going to listen to him."

The low, warm voice snuck into my ear from somewhere behind me and I closed my eyes to suppress a moan. Wait, I was pissed at him. Which meant I couldn't go all gooey on the inside when he said that crap to me. My flirt was officially on the fritz.

"You wish," I muttered to Xander. "I'm not doing shit. You can forget it."

His smile drooped a bit and his eyebrows furrowed in confusion. "What's wrong? You mad at me for some reason?"

*Fuck*. Why did he look so goddamned cute all the fucking time? I needed him to look ugly and mean. Was that too much to ask? I wondered idly if Lucky had been right. Was I going to pick option number two when it came to Xander? I couldn't say I hadn't considered the idea.

I glanced down at his legs— curvy and muscled between the worn edge of his hiking shorts and the scrunched top of his wool socks and leather hiking boots. I wanted to lick his legs.

Was that weird?

As I fantasized about running my tongue up the inside of one of his thighs while my hand ran up the inside of the other, into his shorts, I felt my cock stir in my own shorts.

"So do you?" Xander said. My head snapped up to meet his eyes.

"Do I what?"

"Want a taste?"

"What?" I barked, my voice going ultrasonic. How the fuck was he reading my mind? And more importantly, why was he bringing it up here and now when I couldn't do a goddamned thing about it? "No! No, I don't," I blurted before noticing he was holding out some kind of pressed fruit bar to me. "Shit," I muttered.

There was a noticeable twinkle in his eye as he lifted the bar to his lips and made a big fucking production out of wrapping his tongue around it before gently pulling off a piece with his teeth.

He never took his eyes off mine the entire time, and by the time he was finished, my dick was leaking into my fucking underwear.

It was going to be a long day.

~

"What do you mean, we have to wait?" I asked impatiently. I scanned the sky above the mountain pass ahead of us and it looked fine to me. Sure, there was some lightning, but it was barely noticeable. It made no sense why Xander would say we couldn't cross the pass because of it.

"It's not safe, Bennett. Lightning strikes the tallest thing and we'd be the tallest things on the pass. A high mountain pass is one of the worst places to be when lightning strikes," Xander said as he began removing his pack. He leaned back against a tree and pulled the hair tie from his hair, releasing the gorgeous locks. I desperately wanted to run my hands through the soft tangle of wavy hair.

"I thought it wasn't safe to stand near trees during lightning," I groused, looking around at the thick cluster of pines around us. I worked my own pack off and let it fall to the ground. We'd been hiking for hours and unlike with the kids, the pace had been much quicker and the terrain more difficult. I'd known that the several breaks Xander had made us take throughout the morning hadn't been for *his* benefit, and that had just pissed me off. For some reason I didn't want to think too much about, I wanted him to see me as his equal... especially out here.

In his world.

"Bennett, just take a few minutes to catch your breath," he said gently.

If he'd said it with a pissy attitude, I would have been fine. But knowing it was exactly as I'd thought— that he was doing all this for my benefit— set me off. I jerked my pack off the ground and said, "Stop fucking around, Xander."

Then I was striding towards the clearing. I ignored him when he shouted my name, but I couldn't ignore it when he grabbed my arm.

"What the fuck are you doing?" he yelled as he dragged me backwards.

"Let go!" I snapped as I turned to swipe at him. But he was stronger than me, and he easily pulled me back into the woods and then slammed me up against the tree he'd been leaning against moments earlier.

"I told you it wasn't safe!" he bit out.

"And I'm calling bullshit," I retorted. "Stop fucking babying me, Xander. You made your point, okay!"

"What point?" His fingers were biting into my arms and the pack was digging into my back, but I didn't give a shit. All the emotions I'd been holding in for the past few days came rushing forward all at once and full force.

"That I don't fit! That I don't belong here!"

"What the hell are you talking about?"

"I know you think what I did to you when we were kids was about that, but it wasn't!"

I needed to stop, because I was saying things I'd vowed to leave behind us. But it was like my mouth was on autopilot. "You want to get back at me, fine! But don't do it while one of my kids is out there!"

Xander released me and stepped back. He shook his head. "What are you saying, Bennett? You think I'm getting some kind of revenge on you by what? Slowing us down? Purposely keeping us from reaching Jake and Jimmy?"

"Yes… no… I don't fucking know. I think you're pissed I insisted on coming, and I think you want me to know that I don't belong out here. That I don't belong with…"

"With what?"

But my brain finally caught up with my mouth and I snapped it shut. "Never mind." Since he'd released me, I lowered the pack to the ground just to give my hands something to do.

"Answer me, damn it," Xander bit out.

"No. It's not important."

He was on me just like that. His big body forced mine flush with the tree and he pinned me in with his arms. "Do you actually think I see you as less? Like the way people saw me when we were kids?"

His voice was so soft and gentle; it was my undoing.

"I think you see me as one of *them*." I swallowed hard and whispered, "I hate it."

"I don't," he said with a shake of his head. "I could never see you that way, Benny."

I wanted to believe him. I really did. "Then why didn't you want me to come with you? Why did you make that crack about me needing to do everything you told me to?"

"Jesus, Bennett," he said with a heavy sigh as he straightened and ran his fingers through his hair, pushing it back off his face. "I said that because I need to be able to keep you safe. I told you I didn't want you to come because I was worried about you getting hurt."

"What?" I asked.

"Worried isn't even the right word," he muttered. "I'm so freaking terrified of what could happen to you…" He shook his head. "Yes, it's a relatively safe hike, but you're never truly safe out here," he said as he motioned to the woods around us. "And I took lots of breaks today to make sure you were okay and not pushing yourself too hard, because I know what a stubborn ass you can be and that you wouldn't tell me when you needed to rest."

I would have laughed if I wasn't reeling from everything he'd said.

And the way he'd said it.

I sagged back against the tree. "I'm sorry, Xander. I thought..." I paused because I didn't even know how to make him understand.

Suddenly his hands were on my face and he was tilting my head up. "I don't care, Benny," he said urgently. "I don't care," he repeated, and then his mouth was closing over mine. His tongue surged between my lips and I let out a cry of relief. It had only been days since he'd kissed me like this, but it may as well have been a thousand lifetimes.

Only, unlike last time, I was going to take everything I wanted from him. I hungrily kissed him back, even as I straightened my body to its full height. I used my hands on Xander's shoulders to spin us so it was his back against the tree, and then I went all in. I nipped at his jaw, licked the corded muscles of his neck, and kissed my way down to where the collar of his shirt hid his delicious skin from view. I fisted my hand in the hem of his shirt and lifted it as I sank to my knees and settled my mouth on his tight abs.

"Fuck," Xander groaned as I licked my way down each ridge of muscle and then nuzzled his happy trail, breathing in his unique scent. I sensed Xander taking off his shirt completely, but as much as I wanted to explore the rest of his gorgeous chest with my mouth, my hands would have to do, because I had another target in mind for my unslaked lust.

But first, I had to get to said target. I quickly worked Xander's shorts open and pulled his turgid flesh free of his underwear. His cock was thick and leaking like a faucet. I lifted my eyes to his for the briefest of moments before I went in for the kill.

His reaction to my mouth on his dick was instantaneous and almost painful because his fingers fisted in my hair. If I hadn't been holding his base, he'd have jammed all eight inches of perfection down my throat before I was ready to take him that deep.

I teased the ridge of his crown with tiny licks, then tickled his slit a few times before closing my lips around the head and sucking up the pre-cum that kept bubbling up. I used my free hand to play with his heavy balls.

"Benny," I heard him whisper. I kept his dick in my mouth as I looked up at him. His eyes were wide, the pupils blown. I knew what he wanted… needed. It was an amazing feeling to know how badly he needed me in this moment. To know that I finally had the chance to give him something that should have been his all along.

I held his gaze for a moment longer, then closed my eyes and sucked him deep to the back of my throat before swallowing. He shouted and began fucking my mouth, and I let him. My lips ached because they were stretched so wide, but I still wanted more of him. I managed to relax my jaw even more and focused on my gag reflex until Xander was hitting the back of my throat with every pump and my nose was pressed against his groin. I lifted one hand so I could stroke it across his chest while I grabbed his ass with the other hand and massaged the perfectly rounded flesh.

Tears began to sting my eyes as Xander used my mouth, but the last thing I wanted was for him to stop, so I increased the suction and hummed around his shaft. Xander let out a ragged moan as he pulled out of me. Before I could protest, his mouth was on mine, and then he pushed me to my back on the ground.

"So fucking hot," he practically snarled against my lips. "Need inside you."

"Yes," I moaned. I would have been happy to have him shoot his load down my throat, but this was so much fucking better. All that hot flesh buried inside of me again… no way I was going to pass that up.

Fingers plucked at the button and zipper of my shorts and then they were yanked down. Xander released my mouth, but only to put it someplace I wasn't expecting. And it wasn't my dick.

Nope.

He flipped me over, split my ass open with his big hands, and went in for the kill.

# CHAPTER 25

## XANDER

If I stopped to think too much about having Bennett Crawford, my Benny, bare-assed and on his hands and knees in front of me, I'd come before I even got inside him. He moaned and whimpered with every pass of my tongue across his gorgeous hole.

The man's ass was perfection. Two tight, rounded cheeks at the base of a beautifully arched spine. My hands didn't know where to be — squeezing those ass cheeks or wandering up and down the long, lean muscles of his back.

My mouth, however, knew exactly where it wanted to be. I used the tip of my tongue to toy with the puckered skin around his entrance and felt him contract around me. Fuck, he was tight and hot. I wanted inside him so badly, but I wanted to make sure he was plenty ready for me when the time came.

I used my tongue to stretch him out as I heard him mumble and babble incoherently. He sounded so lost in pleasure, I wanted to laugh.

"You okay up there?" I asked, pulling my mouth away long enough to slide a finger inside him in place of my tongue.

"Mngh," he groaned. "Don't stop. *Fuck.*"

I pulled my finger out and rubbed it gently around the outside of his hole. The touch was soft and reverent as I enjoyed the sight of him and anticipated pushing into all that tight heat.

"Dammit, Xander, stop fucking around," he griped. "Get my wallet. In my shorts. Condom. Lube."

His words came out in a staccato rhythm punctuated with gasping breaths. My own breathing was just as rapid and heavy, but I was doing a better job of hiding it from him. For some reason, I didn't want him to know the effect he had on me— that the idea of fucking him again in these mountains was enough to make my head spin and my heart nearly explode out of my chest.

I fumbled through the shorts still tangled around his lower legs and came out with his wallet. My hands shook as the wallet opened to reveal a New York driver's license. I flipped past it as quickly as I could, hell-bent on blocking out all reminders that Bennett didn't live here— that he had his own life to go back to, so very far away from mine.

I found the condom and lube and grabbed them, shoving the wallet back in the shorts pocket as quickly as I could while sneaking another nibble of one of Bennett's ass cheeks at the same time.

"Xander," he warned.

"Patience, Benny," I teased. "Good things come to those who wait."

"No, the early bird gets the worm, jackass. Now get that anaconda in here."

I finally couldn't help it and barked out a laugh, ripping open the condom and rolling it on as quickly as I could. I wasn't sure I'd ever felt this light and happy during sex before. In fact, I couldn't remember the last time I felt this light and happy at all. Being back around my best friend was like finding a part of myself I hadn't realized was missing— the ability to fully relax and just have fun. To stop taking everything so goddamned seriously.

My hands were kneading Bennett's ass as I stared at his hole and the back side of his balls hanging down. I felt my mouth water as I tried to figure out how to have him in my mouth at the same time I was fucking him. I didn't even realize I was just kneeling there, drooling, when he straightened up on his knees and turned to face me.

"What the hell are you doing?" His frustration was fucking adorable, and I was pretty sure I just grinned at him stupidly. "Do you need a map?"

I grinned some more. God, he was even cuter when he was miffed.

"Xander?" he asked. "Babe, are you even in there? Did you have a stroke?"

"Just enjoying the view," I said, raising my eyebrows and looking him up and down slowly.

His skin flushed pinker and his lips dropped open in response to my words. I took the opportunity to lean in for a kiss, brushing my lips softly over his before pressing harder and invading his mouth with my tongue. My hand went to his cock to stroke it in time with the thrusts of my tongue into his mouth. By the time I was done with the kiss, his pupils were blown, and he was mumbling unintelligible shit again.

"What, baby?" I teased again. "Are you trying to say something?"

"Huh?" he asked, blinking.

"Turn over and get on your hands and knees," I commanded in a low voice. "I'm going to fuck you until you can't remember anything except the feeling of my body inside of yours."

Bennett whimpered and turned to resume the position. I opened the lube and quickly slathered it on myself before rubbing it onto the outside of his hole and pressing lubed fingers inside of him.

Once finished with the lube, I leaned over his back until my lips brushed his ear. "You're so beautiful, Benny," I whispered. I felt his entire body shudder before I moved my cock to his entrance and began to push inside of him. "I want you so badly. The way you make me feel, the way you trust me with your body..."

His muscles tightened around me for a moment before relaxing enough to let me in.

"That's it, baby," I murmured. "Let me in. Want to feel you." I pushed carefully until my entire length was encased in his warmth, and I let out a groan of my own. He felt amazing— like his body had been molded specially to fit me and I was the only person meant to be inside him like this.

One of Bennett's hands reached over his head to slide fingers into my hair, pulling my head tighter against his face.

"Xander," he breathed. "*Xander.*"

"I know, baby," I cooed in his ear. "I'm here."

I began to move slowly in and out until I couldn't keep myself from picking up the pace and slamming into him. He dropped his hand from my head back to the ground to hold himself up— to keep from collapsing onto the rough forest floor from the impact of my thrusts.

The need to own him came over me like a fog of aggressive lust. Suddenly, I found myself fucking him with everything I had. Sharp pine needles bit into the skin of my knees with every shift of my weight, but I didn't care. Cold pinpricks of rain stung our heated skin, but we barely noticed.

It was just me inside of the one person on earth who had the power to both fill me up and leave me empty and alone. And in that moment, he was filling me up. Every sound, every clench of his responsiveness made me feel alive and on fire. I felt wanted and needed, like I was the only person who could bring Bennett to his knees with pleasure and make him feel whole again.

Was that actually the case? Surely not. But in that moment, I felt like we were both giving each other everything we'd ever needed— trust, pleasure, comfort, warmth, and the absolute knowledge of being safe and cared for above all else.

"Xander, I can't... I want... Have to—"

"S'okay," I grunted. "Come."

I reached around and grabbed his cock over his own grip and helped him stroke himself until hot shots of fluid coated our joined hands. His shouts echoed in the trees around us and seemed to be joined by thunderous growls from the skies above us. The sky had grown dark and the rain was pelting down in the pass nearby as my own release struck, and I cried out— slamming into him one last time and feeling his channel tighten around me again in response.

After the pulses of my orgasm died down, I realized I'd pushed Bennett face-first into the forest floor. I was collapsed on top of him, and I quickly pulled out before helping him sit up so that he was on his knees. I shucked off the condom, tying it off before gathering the trash bits and shoving them into a little trash bag in a pocket of my backpack.

As I began to straighten my clothes, I realized Bennett was still kneeling, bare-assed on the ground. I dropped to the ground next to him. Fuck, had I hurt him somehow?

"Benny?" I asked softly, stroking his damp hair back from his forehead. "You okay?"

"Hmm," was all he said as he turned and gave me a goofy grin. His eyes were at half-mast and he looked completely blissed out.

"It's raining. It'll start filtering through the trees here in a minute and drench us. C'mon, let's get our rain gear on before we get soaked."

He looked around in a daze. "Is it storming? God, were we going at it that long?"

I let out a laugh. "Not really. Thunderstorms come in fast and leave just as quickly out here. We just need to hunker down until it passes."

Once we got our rain gear on and our packs covered in Bennett's tarp, we used my tarp to huddle under together while the storm blew across our area. We sat so we could look out over the pass in front of us and watch the dark clouds pass overhead.

As the air cooled around us from the rainstorm, I could feel the heat of Bennett's body against my side. We'd been sitting for a few minutes in easy silence, but I was curious about how he was feeling after we'd had sex. I wasn't sure if I wanted to ask him about it. Hell, I wasn't sure if I was actually brave enough to ask him about it.

A hand reached out for mine, and I felt Bennett's long fingers thread through mine.

"You okay?" he asked me softly. "You're being awfully quiet over there."

I squeezed his hand and leaned over to brush a kiss across his jaw. "Yeah. I'm okay. More than okay, really."

He quirked a brow at me, but didn't ask me to elaborate. I felt I owed it to him to tell him exactly how I was feeling after the hell I'd put him through this past week and even this morning.

"I'm really happy we're here together," I admitted. "It's… it's something I never even let myself dream about, you know? Sharing this with you." I nodded to all that was around us— the trees above us, the expanse of loose rock leading to the pass in front of us, and the peaks beyond.

He leaned his head on my shoulder and let out a breath. "Yeah. I know. It's kind of surreal."

There wasn't anything else that needed to be said in that moment. We just let the sounds of the storm surround us and the feel of each other's bodies sustain us.

It was everything I'd ever wanted.

And yet I knew it could never last.

# CHAPTER 26

## BENNETT

I must have dozed off on Xander's shoulder to the sounds of the low grumble of thunder and the steady patter of the rain on the plastic tarp above us, because I awoke to the feel of Xander's rough palm stroking my cheek.

"Bennett, wake up. We need to get going," he said in a soft voice. "The rain stopped."

I opened my eyes and saw rays of sunlight breaking through the clouds over the mountains. Rain drops still fell intermittently on the tarp Xander held around us, and I noticed the ground around us hadn't gotten too wet.

"How long was I out?" I asked, lifting my head from his shoulder and stretching. "What time is it?"

"You were only asleep for about twenty minutes. It's three o'clock. We only have about four hours of hiking ahead of us before we get to where Jake and Jimmy are."

We stood up and shook off the tarps before folding them up and strapping them to the outside of our packs. We'd sent as many of our non-essential supplies back with Aiden and the group as we could, since we'd need to divvy up Jake's stuff for the hike out. We were left with essentials like food, a first aid kit, sleeping bags, bad weather gear, and one tent. We'd left behind extra clothes, my tent, and most of the climbing gear Xander had been carrying.

Packing lighter meant we were able to move faster. As we escaped the drippy canopy of the trees, we worked to ascend the pass as quickly as we could, but it was slow going. The rain had softened the earth enough that it was difficult to get traction, so, it took even longer when we began our descent down the other side. Before we made it back down into the tree line on the far side of what Xander had called Doser Pass, he stopped me to point out a few landmarks.

"See that kind of rounded lump in front of the jagged peak behind it?" Xander asked, pointing with an outstretched arm.

"Yeah?"

"Jake and Jimmy are in a protected area on the close side of that lump. That's Lower Bower."

I glanced at my watch. Darkness would be falling within a couple of hours. "Can we still make it to them today?"

"No, probably not. Hiking after nightfall is dangerous."

"We can't leave them for another night, Xander." Fear curled in my belly for Jimmy.

Xander's face softened and he brought a hand up to grip the back of my neck. "They're safe, Benny. Jake will know the weather probably slowed us down and once we make camp, we can radio him and Gary to let them know what's going on. Jake had enough provisions for at least a few days and he's great with kids— Jimmy is probably having the time of his life. When we radio Jake, I'll make sure you get a chance to talk to Jimmy, okay?"

I nodded. "I trust you," I said softly. "If you say they're safe, then I know they are."

My answer seemed to satisfy him.

"Let's go for another hour and then we'll make camp and radio Jake and Gary. Then we can make my specialty pasta dish and snuggle together in our tent for the rest of the night. Okay?"

The thought of enjoying a hot meal after confirming that Jimmy was safe was enough to get my legs moving again. And I spent the next hour of our trek daydreaming about getting my hands on Xander again once we were alone in the tent.

"Usually you're the chatty one," Xander said from behind me at one point. We were passing across the far side of a plateau area full of scattered boulders, and I was struck by how different it looked from anyplace I'd ever been. I caught myself wishing Lucky and the other boys had been there to see it.

"Sorry. I was just thinking about what you said about sharing a tent tonight," I admitted, smiling to myself.

"Oh yeah? Did you have some thoughts about that, or were you trying to figure out how to get out of it? I promise I don't fart as much as Bear."

I snorted. "Are you trying to sell me on what a good tent-mate you are? As if we haven't shared a tent a thousand times before? Hell, for that matter, we've even shared a sleeping bag a million times before," I reminded him, making my way through the sparse damp grass of the plateau. "I'd be happy to share one again. Of course I would. Only this time, can we be naked? I'd like to try it that way for once. Naked sleeping bag sharing. I think we should make it a thing. Don't you? I could get used to that."

I kept walking for a few beats before I realized he hadn't responded.

I stopped and turned around to see why he'd gone quiet. Xander stood still and stared at me with his head cocked. My nerves kicked into gear and I wondered if I'd said something wrong.

"Xander? I'm sorry. I didn't mean—"

"Shh," he said quickly. "Do you hear that?"

I stopped to listen and realized there was a loud sound of water rushing nearby. "Is it a waterfall or something?" I asked.

"That's the river we're supposed to cross. But it sounds really high and fast. C'mon. There's a spot we can scout it from up here before we go down the plateau and lose sight of the best place to cross."

I followed him for a few more minutes until we got to the edge of the plateau. Down below, in a canyon of sorts, was the river. Water gushed over rocks and across downed tree trunks, and I looked upriver to see if I could find out where the sheer volume of water was coming from. There was a waterfall feeding it, but it was way off in the distance. I wondered if the storm could have created enough water to make the river that full.

Without realizing it, I'd snuck my hand into Xander's and linked my fingers with his.

"How're we going to get across?" I asked, nerves snaking in my gut.

He shook his head. "We might have to wait until the water dies down a little. It's too dangerous to try right now."

"There has to be a way to get across. What about that rope system you told me about? The Tyrolean something."

"Tyrolean Traverse. One of us has to be able to get across to set up the anchor on the far side," he explained.

"Well, shit. If you can do that, we might as well both get across without all the bother," I muttered, trying to look up and down the river to see any slower spots or wider areas where the water would be much shallower. "Wait… right there," I said, pointing to an area where several large boulders crossed the width of the river.

Xander followed my gaze until he spotted the area. He pursed his lips and furrowed his brow. "Maybe…"

"Let's go check it out, at least. We won't know how it really looks till we get there."

I began to walk toward the edge of the plateau in the direction of that spot on the river, but Xander reached out and grabbed my pack to stop me.

"Hold on there, hotshot. Let me call Gary first and check in, okay? While we're still high up, it'll be easier for the radio to reach him. We'll call Jake afterwards."

I blew out a breath and nodded. Once I heard Jimmy's voice, maybe I could stop worrying so much. Yeah, right— as if I would stop worrying about one of the boys in my care.

While Xander tried to raise Gary on the radio, I dropped my pack and wandered off to take a leak. When I returned, Xander was finishing up the call.

"What'd he say?" I asked.

"He talked to Jake, and he and Jimmy are fine, but apparently there's a giant storm coming this way. This afternoon's shower was just the front of it. Gary said we should try and get to them before it hits so we can all be together in that lower altitude. The storm won't be as dangerous down there where they are, and we might still be able to hike out even if it's raining. But if we don't get down in altitude, we could get stuck."

I knew he didn't like the idea of hiking through the darkness, but it was clear we no longer had a choice. "Okay, well, I guess we should get moving." Without waiting for a response, I began walking down the side of the plateau and into the trees in the direction of the portion of the river we'd pinpointed. By the time we arrived at the side of the river, the sky had darkened again with more storm clouds.

"I don't like this," Xander said as we stood and assessed the boulder crossing. "The rocks are wet and slippery. All it would take is one slip."

I knew he was right, but I also knew we needed to get to Lower Bower before the storm hit.

"Xander, it's only going to get worse according to Gary, so unless you have a different plan, we need to do this."

"Okay. But you have to listen to me, Bennett," he said. Worry lines creased his forehead, and I wanted to reach out and smooth them. But I kept my hands to myself and gave him what I knew he needed— my full attention.

"I'll go first," Xander began. "The most dangerous part of a river crossing is drowning, obviously, and your backpack can make it ten times worse. So, make sure your waist belt is unclipped. If anything goes wrong, Bennett, let the pack go. Do you hear me? Nothing in that bag is worth dying for."

His gaze was intense and I could tell he was worried about me. "Ok. I promise," I said, unclipping the belt and feeling the weight of the pack rest down on my shoulders. "What else?"

"Remember what I taught the kids about rock climbing. Your hands and your feet are like four table legs— use them wisely to keep your table upright. The most stable way to travel is by having three of the four legs anchored while you move the fourth. Go slowly and take your time."

The sun came out between a break in the clouds and shone down on the river in front of us, making the water sparkle and everything around us look less scary. I looked up at Xander with a smile.

"I think that's a sign. Let's do this. First one across gets to give the other one a blow—"

"Benny—" he growled.

"I'm kidding. But I think we should get this show on the road, don't you?"

I could tell he still wasn't happy about it, but it wasn't like we had much of a choice. Xander unhooked his waist belt and began to step onto the first boulder. He bent his knees and stayed low, keeping his center of gravity down and taking time to scope out the next boulder. Once he made the step onto the next one, I stepped carefully onto the spot he'd vacated.

We continued that way, carefully picking the most stable path across the wet rocks we could and trying to avoid extra slick spots where the rocks had built up a level of slippery moss. It was slow-going. Xander had been right when he'd said that our backpacks would cause the most problems. Without the waist belt fastened, the pack shifted more than I expected, throwing off my balance when I moved suddenly or wasn't careful. I knew that what he'd tried to warn me about was true— river crossings were way dicier than they looked.

As the sun hid behind another cloud, the bright light disappeared, leaving everything looking flat and the same. Picking out slippery spots on the rocks wasn't as easy in the dim light, and I reminded myself to take it slowly.

Xander was almost to the other side when he stopped and turned around. He called something out across the sound of the rushing water, but I couldn't hear him over the roar. I shook my head and pointed to my ear. He flashed me the okay symbol with a questioning glance on his face.

Just as I began to throw him back some sign language shade, I saw a massive cluster of huge branches and downed tree trunks break off from where they'd been lodged between a large boulder and the riverbank upstream from us. The debris rushed toward Xander, and I turned my head to warn him.

My mouth opened to scream, but all I heard was the raging river. Before Xander could turn all the way around to see the debris coming at him, I knew it would be too late— the logs and branches would be on him, knocking him into the river and pushing him under. I couldn't even fathom it. I had to get him across to the other side before it could happen.

So, I dropped my pack and lunged.

# CHAPTER 27

## XANDER

It was true what people said about traumatic events happening in slow motion. One minute Bennett was moving his fingers through some sign language, and the next his face had gone deathly pale and he was screaming for me to jump across the final rock to the riverbank.

I turned to see what he was trying to warn me about and saw an enormous log heading right for me. Just as I crouched down to get momentum in a jump, something landed against me, launching me forward onto the wet ground of the bank. I landed hard on one shoulder and would have rolled if my pack hadn't run into something and stopped me short. I was left lying on my side just in time to see a flash of familiar blue go into the water. Bennett's shirt.

My Bennett. In the raging river.

I scrambled out of my pack, screaming, as time sped up. Luckily, I remembered to grab the coil of rope I'd clipped to the outside of my pack for this very reason before I started running downstream.

"BENNY!" I screamed. "Let go of your pack!" I didn't know if he still had his pack on or not. I just knew if he did, he was a dead man. I ran down the river bank as fast as I could, catching glimpses of Bennett as he fought to stay above water. His arm was caught in a tangle of small branches and I knew if he didn't get free of them, they could catch on a rock and pull him under.

"BENNY!" I screamed again, only this time it was more of a sob as I saw him go under. No, *no no no*. I had to get to him. To pull him out before he hit his head on a rock and got knocked out or was pinned against a boulder and forced under the water forever.

"Benny, I'm coming," I cried through tears and nausea as I stumbled to unlace my boots and throw them behind me. I saw him reach up again and try to grab hold of the branches he was tangled in as if they were a flotation device instead of one of the worst hazards in the river with him.

"Let go of the branches!" I yelled. I got ahead of him down the river a few yards and threw the rope across the expanse of the water.

"Grab the rope!" I shouted. He must have heard me because he scrambled to get to the brightly-colored rope, but it slipped through his grasp. I quickly coiled it as I ran down farther to try again.

"Benny," I sobbed again, losing hope. I considered just throwing myself into the river after him, in hopes we'd end up near each other somehow and I could pull him to safety, but every water rescue course I'd ever done was screaming at me to do the right thing— to give him the best chance possible by following the rules.

I threw the rope across again, trying my hardest to place it perfectly so he couldn't help but grab it. This time it was in the right spot and he grabbed onto it, using it to help him get his legs under him so he could push toward the side of the river. I quickly ran the rope around a nearby tree to help me get leverage and shouted encouragement as he got closer.

"That's it, baby," I called out. "You're doing it. Come on, come to me. You got this. Just a little bit more."

I could tell it was taking every ounce of his energy to make it to the river bank. The water was snowmelt from the alpine peaks, and I knew we had precious little time before hypothermia would drain what little energy he had left. He was already white as a sheet and completely waterlogged, and I sent up a prayer for him to just hang in there a little longer.

He stopped pulling and looked at me, and I knew in that moment he didn't have enough energy left to keep going.

"I can't," he mumbled. I couldn't hear the words as much as read his lips.

"I know you're tired, baby, but just a little more. *Please.*"

The current knocked him sideways and his head went under. He was struggling so hard to keep a hold of the rope, but when he popped back up, I could see his hands slipping. He looked at me with the most heartbreaking expression of apology.

"No!" I screamed through my own tears. "Don't you fucking dare! Hold that rope. Hold it Bennett Crawford, goddammit, *do you hear me?*"

I knotted the rope where it was and ran after him, knowing I had seconds before the current would rip the rope out of his hands, and I'd lose him forever. It was my only shot. If I couldn't get to him in time, I might as well throw myself in the river and go with him.

Because a life without him in it was a life I was no longer interested in living.

I scrambled out into the water and grabbed for him, managing to snag his shirt with my hand until I got a better grip on one of his arms. As I pulled him toward me, I saw some gashes on his skin—watery blood pooling for a second before being washed away by the river every time he was splashed. The current tried to pull him out of my grasp, but I held onto him for dear life.

If the river wanted him, it was damn well going to have to take me too.

My stockinged feet slipped in the shallow water as I pulled him closer to the bank. I could already feel the numbing of my own feet and was terrified of what that meant for Bennett, who'd been in the water longer. I needed to get him dry and warm as fast as possible.

Even when I was finally able to pull him to safety, that wasn't the end of the danger. He was unconscious by then, so I quickly tilted him on the ground to try and get the water out of his mouth and lungs before assessing him. His skin was white and freezing cold. He had a nasty-looking gash on his temple and some scratches on his arm, but those were the only injuries I could see.

I whacked him on the back and he began sputtering, water coming out of his mouth and nose in choking gasps.

Once I felt like he was breathing well enough, I grabbed him up in a fireman's carry, thanking god he wasn't quite as big or built as I was. I quickly made my way up the riverbank to where I'd left my pack, looking around for a safe place to set up the tent to get Bennett dry and warm.

Only about fifteen yards away from the bank was a canyon wall with a kind of overhang; it wasn't really a cave, but it would provide shelter from the wind and the worst of the coming rain.

Despite my burning muscles, I worked as fast as I could— talking out loud to Bennett, even though I knew he was out of it.

"Just gonna get the tent put up real quick and then we'll get you warm," I murmured, snapping poles and secretly thanking my years of loyalty to the same tent I'd bought as a newbie backpacker. I could put the thing together in my sleep, and this shock was about as close as I'd probably come to doing just that.

Once the tent was up, I unfurled the sleeping bag and threw it inside, turning to where I'd rested Bennett against the rock wall and my pack. He was in and out of lucidity and mumbled periodically, asking if I was okay.

"You hurt?" he asked with his eyes closed.

"No, baby. Just scared for you. Come on, let's get you undressed as fast as we can."

He snorted. "F'you say so."

I couldn't help but smile as I yanked his shirt off him and used my own semi-dry shirt to dry the river water from his skin and hair and mop up the blood on his face and arm. Luckily, both wounds had stopped bleeding. By the time I got him completely naked and inside the sleeping bag, I was half-naked myself. I'd used my drier clothes to dry him off, and then I searched for the small camp stove in my bag to get some water boiling for hot chocolate. I had to get a warm drink in him as soon as possible.

While the stove took its time heating the water, I stripped the rest of the way and slid inside of the bag next to him. His skin was like ice, and I gathered him up with my arms and legs to try and get as much of my warmer skin against his freezing skin as I could.

He was shivering terribly and I stared out through the tent flap, willing the water to start producing steam. It seemed to take forever, but I finally saw a tiny white puff of steam unfurl from the pot. I crawled out of the bag to the sound of Bennett's whimper of complaint.

"Getting you something warm to drink. Be right back," I said over my shoulder. When I returned with the giant mug of hot cocoa, I had to prop him up, his back against my front, so I could help him drink it.

"Just want to sleep, Xander."

"I know, baby. But you'll sleep better once you're warm, okay? Did you hit your head on a rock? Do you know?"

I felt his head shake against my chest. "Not sure. Scratched my head," he said as he lifted his hand to his head but stopped short of touching the bandage I'd covered the wound with. "And bumped my shoulder. My hip…"

"What's my middle name?" I asked, trying to remember concussion assessment.

"Something dorky," he muttered. "Like Kevin."

Unfortunately, he was right.

"Who's the president?"

"Are you trying to upset me?"

I dropped a kiss on his head and helped him take another few sips. "Okay, I think you're fine to take a nap, but I'm going to wake you up every once in a while, just to be on the safe side."

I emptied the mug of hot chocolate quickly and reached to set it outside the tent before I noticed Bennett try to get up. I held him tight to my chest. "What're you doing?"

"Gotta go get Jimmy," he said. "I'll be fine."

"Oh, no you're not. You just need a little rest first. They'll be okay," I said as calmly as I could. I wasn't about to tell him that even if he was feeling strong and healthy, we stood zero chance of making it to Jake's camp before the big storm hit. We were going to shelter in place until the worst of the storm was over. That could be just the night or two days, for all we knew.

"But—" he said sleepily. "I'm fine, I promise."

"I know, baby. But I'm really tired. Would it be okay with you if we just rested a little bit? I don't think I can walk all that way just yet. I'm sorry," I said softly, feeling his breathing regulate before I even got the words out.

By the time I got us laid back down in the sleeping bag, he was snoring gently in my arms, and I tried my hardest not to hold him to me in a death grip to make up for nearly costing him everything.

Instead of falling asleep with him, all I could think about was how many stupid ways I'd let him down or hurt him. Everything from ripping into him the moment he'd stepped off that bus, to fucking him in the woods against a tree and then accusing him of cheating, to letting him attempt a river crossing that was way too fucking dangerous. I'd known better. I'd known better and yet I'd let us try it anyway against my better judgement. And then I'd almost lost him.

Again.

# CHAPTER 28

## BENNETT

I was finally warm. Warmer than I'd been in a long time. It kind of made me wonder if I was dead. But were you supposed to still feel pain when you were dead? Because both my head and arm hurt, though not badly.

When enough awareness returned that I could feel the hot, rough fingers skimming up and down my spine, I knew that, despite the pain, I had to be dead.

Because there was only one person's fingers they could be. And the fact that I could feel them on my skin meant one thing.

I was finally where I'd wanted to be for so very long.

Naked in bed with Xander.

Okay, so bed was a stretch, but the sleeping bag was almost better. Even if the ground was hard beneath us, sharing one bag meant there was no choice but to be pressed up against one another. I wanted to believe I was draped across his chest with my palm laying directly over his heart because he wanted me there, but I wasn't going to hope for something that would only cause me pain when reality intruded once again.

"Where are we?" I asked.

"We're still by the river. We need to wait for the storm to pass."

His voice was strange. It was off somehow, but I couldn't put my finger on what the problem was.

"Are you okay, Xander?" I asked. I didn't shift my position because I almost didn't want to look at him. I was afraid I'd see something in his eyes that I didn't want to see.

"No, Bennett," he responded quietly. "I'm not okay."

His fingers kept stroking over my spine, so I remained where I was. He sounded so… broken. It made me afraid to ask him what was wrong. Maybe he was mad at me for what I'd done, but I wouldn't apologize for it. I'd never apologize for keeping him safe.

"Tell me about that night."

I stiffened at that because it was the last thing I'd been expecting. Of course, I knew what night he was talking about. But he'd made it clear he didn't want me to bring it up ever again. "You said—"

"I'm ready to hear it now." He paused and said, "All of it."

I knew what he was asking, and while the knowledge that he was ready to listen to my side of the story should have been a relief, I was oddly reluctant to talk about it. Despite my hesitation, I knew it was something we needed to lay to rest, and that could never happen if we didn't face it head on.

"I had crew practice that afternoon, so I didn't hear about what had happened until I got home and my mom told me. I begged her to take me to the hospital, but she said no— that it wouldn't be appropriate."

It had been and still was one of my mother's favorite words. Things were never wrong or right or good or bad. They were just appropriate… or not.

"I went to my room and tried calling the hospital, but they said they couldn't give me information about your dad. When I asked to talk to you, they said they couldn't tie up the phone for personal conversations. I felt so… helpless. I knew you were waiting for me." I felt tears sting the backs of my eyes and I barely managed to keep them in check when Xander stiffened beneath me just the slightest bit. The move was a confirmation of sorts.

He *had* been waiting for me.

"I'm sorry, Xander, I wanted to be there..."

He didn't say anything, but I felt his lips press against the top of my head. The tender gesture was nearly my undoing. But I held myself together so I could continue.

I owed him that.

"When my dad got home, I was crazy with worry. And then he told me your dad... that he was gone, and I just couldn't believe it. I begged him to take me to see you. When he said no, I lost it and began screaming at him. I told him you needed me. He was so pissed," I murmured as I recalled the fury in my father's eyes as I'd stood up to him for the first time in my life.

"Did he hurt you?" Xander asked. I felt the fingers of his other hand come up to play with my hair.

I shook my head. "No, he just grabbed me and told me never to speak to him like that again. Then he reminded me of our deal."

Xander's body locked up and suddenly he was rolling me onto my back and leaning over me. "What deal?"

I didn't realize I'd started chewing on my lower lip until his thumb came up to force my teeth to let go of the tender flesh, and then he was stroking over the sore spot with the pad of his finger. The need to be doing something with my own hands had me reaching up to clasp his arm. I let my fingers trace over the muscles there and immediately felt more relaxed.

"Right before school started, my dad confronted me and said some stuff. He thought we were getting too close... closer than friends should be. He wanted it to stop. I knew what he was talking about, because I'd started feeling things for you that went beyond friendship," I admitted.

"Me too," he whispered, and then he leaned down to brush his mouth over mine. Pain ratcheted through my entire body at the reminder of everything I'd given up because I hadn't been brave enough to admit who I was back then.

"Keep going," Xander murmured as he let his fingers stroke over my cheek. Having some of his weight pressing down on me was oddly grounding and gave me the strength I needed to continue.

"He said if I didn't put some distance between us, he'd have the school revoke your scholarship, and he'd fire your dad. He said you guys would have to move out of Greenwich."

Xander's eyes flared with anger. But his touch remained gentle.

"I couldn't lose you, Xander. I just couldn't. So, I did it. That day in school… our first day…" I began, but my voice cracked so badly I couldn't continue.

Xander pressed his forehead to mine. "I get it, baby," he said softly. "It's okay."

I shook my head. "No, it's not. I saw your face. I know what you thought." Before he could deny it to try and spare my feelings, I hurried on. "The night your dad died, my dad said that I was going to have the pool party for the guys from my crew team as planned, and that if I talked to you at all, he'd follow through on having your scholarship taken away. But if I did what he said, he'd let you and your aunt live in the caretaker's cottage for free until you finished school." I shook my head. "I thought losing you for one night would be better than losing you forever, Xander," I croaked.

"Benny—"

"No, let me finish, please," I managed to get out. I wiped at the tears that had started to fall against my will.

"I was like a zombie when the guys started showing up. I didn't swim at all… just sat in one of the patio chairs the whole time while I watched those guys swimming in my pool, eating my food… it was all so fucking normal. But inside I was screaming. I wanted to tell them all to get the fuck out so I could find you. I wanted to crawl into your bed and hang onto you and tell you that everything would be okay, even though I knew it wouldn't be."

"Fuck, Benny," Xander whispered, and then he was lying on his side and pulling me against his chest so his lips were pressed against my forehead. I welcomed the ability to press my face against his throat. His arms were like steel bands around my upper body.

"My dad came to tell me that you were at the door. He said if I didn't turn you away…"

I didn't finish the statement because I didn't need to. I couldn't bring myself to rehash those few moments when Xander had reached for me, tears slipping down his cheeks, arms stretched out, my name a broken whisper on his lips. But just because I couldn't say it, didn't mean I wasn't reliving it.

"Oh God, Xander, I'm so fucking sorry." I curled myself into his chest, grateful that he wasn't pushing me away, because I'd never needed anything more in that moment than to feel him holding me so tight that I'd never have to worry about him letting me go. It was so much more than I'd given him fifteen years ago. I didn't deserve it, but I took it anyway.

"Shhh, it's okay Benny, I understand."

I shook my head violently as my tears soaked his chest. "I chose wrong," I whispered harshly. "You needed me! But I was only thinking about me. About what I'd lose."

"Stop it," he said, his voice thick with anger. "Don't you dare blame yourself, Bennett Crawford." He used his fingers to gently tilt my head back enough so I could look into his eyes. "You were a kid. You were faced with an impossible choice... you couldn't have known how it would turn out."

I shook my head because I couldn't accept him just letting me off the hook like that. Not knowing how he'd suffered so much more than just the loss of his father that night.

"You said you came to see me that night," Xander finally said softly after I'd quieted.

I nodded against his chest. "After I sent you away, I went to my room and cried. I didn't care what my father thought at that point, and I didn't care what those assholes at the party thought. I waited long enough for everyone to go home and my parents to go to sleep, and then I snuck out of the house."

"But I was already gone."

"When I saw all your clothes were gone, I was so fucking scared what it meant. But I told myself it wasn't true. So, I got in your bed and I waited for you. My dad found me there the next morning. Said you were gone and you weren't coming back." I pulled back enough so

I could look at him. "What happened to you? Why did you leave Greenwich so fast? What about your father's funeral?"

"We didn't, Bennett," he said quietly. "Yes, we left the house because I told Aunt Lolly I couldn't spend another second there. But we just went to a hotel."

"What?" I asked, scrambling back enough so I could really see him.

"We stayed in Greenwich for another week. Long enough for the funeral and for my aunt to get the rest of our stuff from the house... she gave all the furniture and stuff to charity."

I suddenly felt too stifled, so I quickly unzipped the sleeping bag and sat up. My heart felt like it was going to pound out of my chest.

"He said you were gone!" I yelled. "That's why I didn't ask him to let me go to the funeral. I couldn't go without you."

Disbelief tore through me. The betrayal cut so deep that I couldn't breathe. I'd known my father had been obsessed with keeping me and Xander apart, but to go to such lengths? To blatantly lie to my face, even after knowing how much I'd been suffering. How much Xander had been suffering.

I felt Xander's hand come up to rest on my back. "Take deep breaths, Bennett," he urged as he rubbed circles into my skin. I tried to do as he said, but nothing I did made the breaths come any easier. Xander pressed his forehead against the side of my head and clasped his hand around my throat. "I'm here, baby. He didn't win."

Except he had won. He'd driven us apart.

"Benny, please, just breathe."

The fear in his voice had me focusing on him instead of the agony slicing through my insides. The constriction in my lungs finally seemed to ease and then I was pushing myself into his arms. "I'm sorry, Xander."

"Please don't say those words to me ever again, Bennett," he said hoarsely. "I should have had more faith in you... in us." I began to shake my head, but he kissed me hard before I could say anything. "I thought I lost you, Benny. I saw you go into that river and I couldn't find you at first and then I was watching you struggle to hang on to the rope... seeing you fucking saying goodbye to me..."

He was shaking violently, so I quickly put my arms around him and pressed a kiss against his neck. "I'm safe, baby," I whispered in his ear. "You saved me."

I felt hot tears sliding down my skin, but this time they weren't mine. I kept murmuring in Xander's ear that I was safe and that we were together until he calmed. When we separated just enough to try and catch our breaths I said, "Let's not let him or anyone or anything else take these last couple of days from us, okay?"

He nodded. "Yeah," he agreed as he wiped at his eyes. "God, I've missed you so much, Benny."

"Show me, Xander. Show me how much."

He let out a choked little sob, and then he was drawing me forward and settling his mouth on mine. Unlike all our previous kisses, this one was unhurried and gentle. That should have made it less intense, but it was the opposite. Because I felt everything he couldn't put into words in that one kiss.

And it broke my fucking heart.

Because I knew whatever happened these last couple of days together, it wouldn't change anything. We would still have to walk away from each other when it was over.

I refused to let myself dwell on that, though. I kissed him back and then pushed forward until I was straddling his lap. His hands closed around my ass to hold me in place as we kissed. I could feel his erection pressing against mine, but there was no frenzy to do anything about it. The wind whipping the tent around ceased to exist and the rain splattering the sides of the nylon shell became our soundtrack as we took our time exploring each other's bodies. Hands on heated skin, seeking mouths, dancing tongues… it was speaking without speaking. Loving each other in the only way we could.

Xander carefully lowered me down into the folds of the sleeping bag. I welcomed the weight of his body as he covered me from head to toe, and I gladly made room for him by spreading my legs wide. I'd never had sex with a guy face to face, just because it was a level of intimacy I'd never wanted. Even with Aiden, I'd only ever let him take me from behind.

Looking into Xander's eyes, I knew why.

Because I'd been too afraid that I'd look into my partner's eyes and find them lacking. And then I'd have to face a truth I hadn't wanted to acknowledge.

That nothing they did or said would ever be enough. Not because there was anything wrong with them… but because they just weren't Xander. They'd never hold that place in my heart that he'd had from the day I'd met him.

I'd loved Xander from the moment I'd spied him through the car window, sitting on that swing, his sad eyes on his faded Transformers sneakers. It had been a child's love then, but it had never waned, only grown. I didn't even know when it had changed to loving him in a different way. But it had. And it had happened long before I'd stepped off that bus seven days ago.

But I couldn't tell him that. It would just hurt him… and me.

And the last thing I wanted tonight to be about was pain... and regret. We'd both had enough of that to last a lifetime.

So no, I couldn't tell him how much I really did love him. But I sure as hell could show him.

And that was exactly what I did.

# CHAPTER 29

## XANDER

It had been too close.

Way too fucking close.

Even now with Bennett lying beneath me, his mouth eagerly sipping at mine, I still had this irrational fear that it was a dream. That I was lying out on the banks of that river looking at the spot I'd seen Bennett go under for the last time. Even the thought had tears threatening to start all over again.

It shouldn't have taken almost losing him to know that I was in love with him. That I'd always been in love with him, even when I thought I'd hated him.

The hate he hadn't deserved.

Because he'd been forced to make an impossible decision that no teenager ever should have to make. And because I hadn't had the faith in him I should have had. Even after I'd left Greenwich, I'd had a million chances to call him... to give him a chance to explain himself.

But I'd been so certain that he'd become just another rich asshole who thought he was better than me, that I'd refused to even give him the benefit of the doubt.

My stubbornness had cost us fifteen years we couldn't get back. And worse, I'd set us on a course that meant we'd never be together. If

I'd sucked it up and called him, I could have kept that connection with him and maybe once he'd been old enough to tell his parents to go to hell, we could have been together. I wanted to rage at that… to find something that I could take my fury out on until I didn't have to feel the regret seeping through my every nerve ending, through every cell in my body.

"Xander, baby, please don't." I hadn't even realized I'd stopped kissing Bennett at some point and I was braced above him, my elbows locked to keep my weight off his upper body. He pulled me down for a kiss and whispered, "Stay with me."

Yes. I would do that. Because he was still here. I'd lost what we could have had, but I hadn't lost *him*.

"Always," I murmured against his lips, and then I sealed my mouth over his and settled my weight back down on him. I let the past and the future go and focused solely on him. My body ached to be inside of him, but my soul ached for something more. I needed more time so I could slow down and drink my fill of everything about him. I needed to be able to hang on to all the things he'd changed for me in the past seven days. I'd become *his* Xander again, and even if I couldn't be with him once he got on that bus that would take him back to his life, I'd still always be his.

We kissed for a long time… soft, slow, hard, desperate— didn't matter. Every touch sent us higher and higher and our need for one another grew. Pre-cum was making our cocks slide deliciously against one another and I had no doubt it was a mix of both of our desire.

"Fuck, need you so bad," Bennett breathed against my mouth. His hips were bucking up against mine and his feet were locked around the backs of my thighs as if to hold me in place. I rocked into him a few times and drank down his moans of pleasure. But it wasn't until his hands gripped my ass so he could grind our bodies together, that the rush of need became too much to ignore.

"Benny," I said harshly. "Are you negative?"

"Wha… what?" he asked. His fingers were digging into the globes of my ass and I wondered if I'd have bruises tomorrow. God, I hoped so. I wanted Benny's mark all over me. Just like I wanted to leave my mark on him… in him.

"I don't have any more condoms. Do you?"

He stilled, but luckily, he didn't remove his hands. Who would have guessed I'd have such a thing for his hands on my ass?

"No," he said dejectedly.

I shouldn't have been glad, but I was.

Hell, glad wasn't even the right word.

"Are you negative, Benny?" I murmured against his mouth as I pressed gentle kisses against his lips. He kissed me back, but I kept the pecks light so he could focus.

His eyes widened as he finally seemed to understand what I was asking. He began nodding. "Yes… yes."

"Me too," I said. I kissed him deeply and asked, "Do you want it, Benny? Me inside of you? All of me?"

"Are you really asking me that?" he asked, his lips drawing into an exaggerated frown. His hand came down on my ass with a crack, causing me to jump in surprise.

"Was that supposed to be some kind of punishment?" I drawled as I enjoyed the warmth that flooded through my skin the second the slight sting faded away.

"Not working?" he asked as he smoothed his palm over my globe. "Guess I'll have to think of something else." He arched his eyebrows as if deep in thought and then pulled his hands from my backside.

"No fucking way," I snarled, and then I searched his hands out and put them right back where they'd been. I kissed him hard and deep until he was squirming against me again and his fingertips were clutching my flesh. But he wasn't satisfied with the simple act of gripping me. Because as I fucked his mouth with my tongue, one of his long fingers traced the crack of my ass and then he was breaching it and searching out my hole. I'd been with a few guys who'd tried to play with my ass before, but it wasn't something I'd ever been into. But Bennett wasn't just some guy and even if the sensations were new ones, I welcomed them. Hell, if he'd told me to turn over in that moment so he could shove inside of me, I would have gladly done it, despite the fact that I'd never let a guy fuck me before.

"Yes!" I cried out when he began massaging my hole.

"God, Xander, you feel so good," he murmured against my mouth. I wanted to tell him what he was doing to me felt amazing, but figured I'd show him instead. I reached behind me and grabbed his hand. I held his gaze as I pulled his fingers to my mouth and slowly bent every finger down until only the one that had been pressed against me remained. I slowly sucked it into my mouth and licked all around it as if it was his cock in my mouth. His eyes went wide and he inhaled sharply. When I released his finger, it was covered in spit and I carefully returned it to my ass.

Bennett hesitated for several long seconds before he pushed against me.

"Go slow, I've never..."

I let my words drop off and Bennett completely froze. "What?"

I dropped down to kiss him. "You're going to be my first, baby." I nipped at his lower lip. "I need you too bad to let you fuck me tonight, but I'm going to have every part of you before you leave, Bennett. I promise you that."

"I've never either... done that to a guy, I mean," he stuttered.

I smiled against his mouth. "So we still get to be each other's firsts after all," I whispered.

He let out a little cry and then his mouth crashed against mine. His kiss was hungry and passionate, even as his finger gently began to probe me. It wasn't until he began adding pressure that he gentled the kisses, making them slow and deep. It stung when his finger popped through my outer muscles, but the burn that followed didn't feel at all bad. And the sensation when he pulled his finger back just a little bit before pushing it in again was heaven.

"Fuck, yes," I said on a breathy sigh.

"So tight, baby. You're going to feel so good wrapped around my dick."

I'd already known Bennett was demanding, even when he was the one getting fucked, but the heavy timbre of his voice as he plied me with dirty talk had me wondering if I shouldn't be reconsidering having him take me tonight. It was my last coherent thought, because just as Bennett's tongue slipped between my lips, he hit something inside me that sent shockwaves throughout my entire body.

"*Jesusfuckingchrist*!"

I dropped my head against Bennett's shoulder and heard him chuckle in my ear. "Now you know what you do to *me*," he said softly.

I couldn't even muster a response because he was massaging my prostate with finesse. He might not have ever fucked a guy before, but his touch had me guessing he'd probably at least done this part. It felt so good, I didn't even have the energy to feel jealous about that fact.

He plunged his finger into me several more times before I had to reach behind me to stop him. "I'm too close," I said. Even now, the orgasm was right there, waiting for that last touch that would send me over. And I definitely didn't want to go over without him.

Bennett gently withdrew his finger and then we were kissing again. Our dicks were spikes between us. As much as I wanted to tease him with pleasure like he had me, I was too far gone for it. I reared up and began searching through my pack. I nearly jumped out of my skin when Bennett's hand wrapped around both his dick and mine and began jerking us off. But he knew exactly where to draw the line to keep us riding the edge of pleasure, but not toppling over it.

"What are you looking for?" he asked lazily, though I could tell from his bright eyes that he was as ready to blow as me.

"Something to use as lube," I said.

"You don't have any more?"

I looked at him. "Seriously?" I asked. "Why would I be carrying lube around out here? Who exactly do you think I'm going to fuck out in the middle of nowhere?"

He shrugged. "You did have an unnatural obsession with your teddy bear when we were little, and you did name your dog Bear."

"This coming from someone whose room looked like a *Barney the Dinosaur* store."

"Hey, he was popular when we were kids."

"Yeah, for like five-year-olds. You were almost twelve when your mom made you redecorate. You cried your ass off!"

My chuckle was cut off when he gripped my dick hard.

I leaned down to kiss him and said, "Remember, turnabout's fair play."

He gasped at my words and I eagerly drank the sound down as I kissed him. I remembered what I'd been doing before we'd gotten sidetracked and resumed the search of my pack. When I finally found what I was looking for, Bennett stopped playing with our cocks.

"What is that?" he asked as he eyed the small white lump in the plastic jar I was holding in my hand.

"You know what it is," I said.

"No, I don't," he shot back. "It looks like the coconut oil we use for cooking, but I know that can't be what it is because there's no way you're sticking that up my ass."

"Don't worry, Aunt Lolly swears by this stuff."

"What?" he asked, his mouth agape.

I chuckled and leaned down to kiss him. "It's this or nothing," I said. "And by nothing, I mean that tight little ass of yours stays empty."

"Just use some spit."

"No," I responded. "Not risking hurting you… except for in a good way," I added suggestively. "And trust me, the pounding I'm going to give you, you're going to want something more than spit between my dick and that tight little hole of yours."

I kissed him again and once he was completely pliant, I said, "It's perfectly safe, Bennett. It's all natural."

He nodded, his eyes glassy. "Yeah, okay. God, just fuck me already, Xander." He was practically writhing beneath me. I wasn't faring much better. I knocked his hand away from our dicks and slathered some of the oil, which had a texture like butter, on my cock. I put a generous amount on my fingers and searched out Bennett's hole, but as soon as I slipped a finger inside of him he said, "Don't play with me, okay? I'm too close."

Joking Bennett was gone and in his place was gorgeous, needy, dangerous-to-my-heart Bennett. When I shifted slightly, Bennett grabbed my arm and said, "Xander."

When he didn't continue and color stained his cheeks, I dropped my mouth to his. "What is it, baby?"

"I need… I need…"

"What, Benny? What do you need? Anything… it's yours."

The words held more meaning than he could ever know.

"I need it to be face to face this time."

I nodded. "Me too. I need to see you…"

Bennett nodded and I knew we were on the same page. "It's another first for me, Xander. I've never let anyone else take me like that."

My heart lurched in my chest. "Me neither," I admitted. I was too overwhelmed to say anything, so instead, I settled down on him and shifted enough so I could get my hand between our bodies. I guided my cock to his entrance and began to slowly push inside of him. Bennett bore down on me and we both shuddered when my crown breached his outer muscles. I pulled out a little before sliding back in, allowing more of myself to sink into him. By the time I'd bottomed out inside of him, I was a quivering mess. I couldn't even hold myself off him because my arms felt like jelly.

"God, Benny, so good."

He grunted in my ear and then his mouth was pressing against my neck. I forced myself to lift enough so I could watch him as I began sliding in and out of his hot, tight body. The oil smoothed out my glides after a couple of strokes, so I picked up the pace. Fire coiled in my belly as I watched Bennett's eyes go wide with wonder. His hands wrapped around my forearms and I felt his ankles lock behind my ass. His inner muscles milked my cock on every pass, pulling my orgasm to the surface in record time.

I'd wanted to make it last longer, but I knew I wasn't going to be able to.

"Too close," I muttered.

"Me too," he huffed. Sweat clung to our bodies as the tide of pleasure began to consume us. I shifted my left hand so that I could clasp his and hold it against the ground near his head. I began moving my right hand between our bodies so I could jerk him off, but he grabbed it and linked our fingers instead.

He shook his head and I understood his unspoken message. He didn't need the extra stimulation. From the slickness coating my abdomen as my lower half rubbed his dick with every pass of my body, I'd guessed as much. The feeling of being bare inside of Bennett was just too much. I wasn't allowed to tell him I loved him, but I couldn't stop the words that did tumble out of my mouth as my orgasm began to wash over me.

"So many firsts we should have had together, Benny."

# CHAPTER 30

## BENNETT

*So many firsts we should have had together, Benny.*

The words were painful to hear, but I knew he was only saying the same thing I was thinking. As beautiful as this moment was, I couldn't help but recognize the regret that came along with it. We'd lost so many years of moments like this… of firsts that had been meant for each other, but that a cruel twist of fate had stolen away.

I clung to Xander as he drove into me over and over again. I didn't want it to end, but I couldn't stop the agonizing bliss that had become a living thing within me. My only purpose in life in that moment was to take the pleasure Xander was giving me and give it right back to him. I let out a scream as the violent orgasm hit me with such force, I had no choice but to close my eyes.

"No, Benny, open them," Xander ordered… demanded… begged.

I did as he said and held his gaze even as the pure beauty of what was happening to my body threatened my very consciousness. It frightened me how good it felt… pleasure that bordered on the edge of pain. Explosion after explosion detonated within my body, and I gripped Xander's fingers hard so that I'd have something to hang onto in case the climax tried to tear me from him. Seconds later, Xander dropped his lower half onto me and yanked his hands free of mine. He curled his arms around me and held me flush against his chest as he began shooting deep inside of me. I fisted my hands on his back as his release triggered another round of gut-wrenching spasms. I couldn't believe it, but more cum shot from my cock and pooled between our sweat-drenched bodies.

Xander kept fucking me through his orgasm. My well-used channel stung, but I wouldn't have changed a second of it for the world. Even when Xander's body unlocked as the climax released him from its deathly grip, he continued to push into me, his essence leaking out of my body with every thrust. He was panting heavily against my neck. My own pleasure had finally started to turn into a blissful haze of semi-awareness, but when Xander made a move as if to pull out of me, I reached down to grab his ass to keep him inside of me. His lips searched out mine and then he was kissing me.

For minutes.

For hours.

I wasn't sure.

I just knew I never wanted it to stop.

"You okay?" he asked. His hands came up to push my sweaty hair off my forehead.

"Better than," I said.

"That was..." He shook his head.

"Yeah," was all I said. There were a million things we probably needed to say to each other, but somehow it just didn't matter at the moment. Maybe because we'd said so many things without speaking. Maybe because there just weren't words for some of the other things.

Xander sighed and settled on my shoulder, his lips pressed against the pulse point of my neck. His cock was still pulsing inside of me and every once in a while, one or both of us would be hit with an aftershock, but otherwise we didn't move or speak. We just held onto each other.

Until I finally found the strength to ask something that was both a safe topic and driving me crazy with curiosity.

"Um, Xander, can I ask you something?"

"Mmmm."

I took that as a yes. "Please tell me your aunt didn't know about using the oil as lube from personal experience."

Xander laughed and it was the sweetest thing I'd heard in a long time.

Maybe ever.

~

"B!" Even though I'd known Jimmy was safe, seeing him bouncing up and down as he waved at me nearly sent me to my knees in relief. As it was, I was struggling to make it up the last little bit of the incline that led to the overhang where Jimmy and Jake were waiting.

"Give me your hand, baby," I heard Xander say. I looked up to see his worried eyes on me and his hand extended. As much as I wanted to tell him I could do it on my own, I knew I couldn't. My body was just too drained. I grabbed his hand and let him pull me up the rest of the way. As soon as I reached the overhang, Jimmy was throwing himself into my arms.

"You okay, buddy?" I asked as I wrapped my arms around him. I glanced at the man standing a couple of feet to his right. He was leaning against a large section of rock and I could see that he was favoring his left foot.

"Jake and I had an adventure!" Jimmy exclaimed.

"I heard," I said. I knew I probably needed to talk to him at some point about him wandering off on his own, but I was just too relieved to care at the moment.

Xander and I'd had a rough morning. We'd caught a break when the weather had cleared up unexpectedly, but the hike had been tough because of the wet conditions, and my injuries. The scratch on my arm wasn't really bothering me, but I'd woken with a little bit of a headache, which hadn't improved with the rough hike. My body also hurt like hell, and unfortunately, it wasn't the good kind of hurt from a night of passionate lovemaking.

Which was what we'd had.

After making love the first time, we'd both fallen asleep. Xander had woken me a couple of hours later to make sure I was doing okay, since I likely had a concussion from when my head had hit something in the water. He'd urged me to go back to sleep after he'd asked me a few questions, but I'd needed him again, so I'd crawled on top of him and easily silenced his protests about me needing to rest.

I'd spent the next twenty minutes alternating between riding his gorgeous cock and sucking it to the back of my throat. Of course, Xander hadn't been a passive participant. While I'd ridden him, he'd teased me by playing with my cock. When I'd been blowing him, he'd pulled my body around so he could suck me at the same time. Once we'd both been about to blow, I'd climbed back on top of him and ridden him as he'd thrust up into my body in such a way that he'd struck my prostate over and over again.

In the end, we'd had nearly simultaneous orgasms. I'd collapsed against his chest and fallen asleep right then and there, with him still buried deep inside my body. He'd woken me up one more time to ask me questions, then he'd let me sleep until morning. I'd wanted to stay there in our little cocoon of happiness, but the need to get to Jimmy had won out and I'd forced my tired, sore body to get moving.

"Jimmy's turned into quite the expedition guide."

I lifted my gaze to meet Jake's as he shook Xander's hand, and then Xander pulled him in for a hug and slap on the back. I hated the curl of jealousy that went through me as they exchanged words that were too softly spoken for me to hear.

"Glad to see you're okay," Xander said. He helped Jake sit down on the rock and then began looking through their small campsite. "We should get a move on while we've got a break in the weather," he murmured as he began packing things.

"Jimmy, let's get your stuff together, okay?" I said. The boy had his own pack, though it wasn't as big as the packs the kids in Xander's group had carried.

"'Kay," Jimmy said. He gave me another quick hug before rushing over to Xander and began chatting excitedly with him about the adventure he and Jake had had.

"Thank you," I said as I approached Jake and held out my hand.

"No need to thank me," he said as he shook it. "He's a great kid, but he sure moves quick."

I chuckled at that. "I lost him once on a field trip to the museum, so I know what you mean."

Jake was a good-looking guy about our age, maybe a little older. He was close to my height, but not quite as lean as I was. His hair was dark brown and a little longer on top than on the sides. He had a little bit of scruff going on, but I wasn't sure how much of that was normal or just extra growth from being out in the woods. His eyes were a striking shade of gray that reminded me of the storm clouds that had been threatening to open on us all morning long. But it wasn't just the color that caught my attention.

There was something else there— an almost haunted look.

Which didn't match the forced smile he was sending me.

"What happened?" Jake asked as he motioned to the bandage on my head.

"Accident while we were crossing a river yesterday," I said, dismissing the injury away with a wave of my hand.

Jake's solemn eyes studied me for a moment before he said, "You mind if I take a look?"

The request surprised me. Xander had already patched me up, but since I didn't want to be rude, I merely nodded. Since I didn't want Jake to have to stand, I bent over him so he could peel back the bandage. His fingers were gentle as he pressed against the tender skin around the actual cut.

"Do you know what did this?" he asked.

"Not sure… a log maybe."

"Did you lose consciousness?"

"He did," Xander cut in. I glanced at him to see him watching me with concern. "But not right away. It happened right after I got him out of the water."

I could see that Xander was reliving the moment, so I quickly said, "I'm fine, really. Just a little bit of a headache."

"Could be a concussion," Jake said as he carefully removed the bandage altogether.

"Xander kept waking me up throughout the night to ask me questions."

Jake nodded. "That's good." To Xander he said, "Can you get me my first aid kit?"

As Jake watched Xander, I watched Jake. I couldn't put my finger on it, but there was something off about the whole thing. I knew I was probably overreacting, but I couldn't get past the feeling that there was more happening here between the two men.

"Here," Xander said as he handed Jake a small bag that was similar to the one Xander carried in his bag. But it looked like Jake's was a little bigger.

"Thanks," Jake said softly as he took it.

And that was when I saw it.

It lasted only seconds, but I knew it for what it was as Jake's eyes stayed on Xander. He inhaled just the tiniest wisp of air when their fingers touched as they exchanged the bag, but whereas Xander turned away to finish packing, Jake's eyes lingered and followed him as he moved around the small campsite. When his gaze finally shifted back to me, he quickly dropped his eyes.

My stomach dropped out as it dawned on me what I'd seen.

*He has feelings for Xander.*

"Butterfly bandages might keep the scar from being as noticeable," Jake said. I was reeling from my discovery so I barely heard him.

Were he and Xander in a relationship? Or had they been? Xander had said he hadn't been in any relationships, but he'd had hookups. Was Jake one of them?

I felt sick to my stomach at the thought of this good-looking man and Xander together.

"So you swallowed some water when you fell in the river?" Jake asked.

I was numb, but I managed a nod.

"Any coughing since then?"

"What?" I asked.

"Have you been coughing since the accident? Any chest pain or trouble breathing?"

"No," I said with a shake of my head. "Why?"

"One of the risks when you breathe in water is secondary drowning."

"What is that?" Xander asked, his voice laced with concern.

"Water builds up in your lungs after the incident and causes pulmonary edema. It can happen anywhere from an hour later up to even a day later. It's rare, though."

I was surprised when Jake pulled a stethoscope from a zippered pocket on the side of the bag. It seemed like an unlikely thing for a wilderness guide to be carrying.

"Would you lift your shirt?" he asked as he climbed to his feet. Xander instantly moved to his side to support him so he wouldn't have to put too much weight on his injured foot. I did as Jake asked and followed his instructions as he had me take several deep breaths and then listened to my heart. When he was finished, he said, "You should be fine, but it might not hurt to get checked out when we get back."

I nodded and was about to ask him why he was carrying a stethoscope on a backpacking trip when Jake turned to Xander and said, "We should probably get moving."

My eyes shifted to Xander, but he wasn't looking at me. The insecurity that hit me was an ugly thing and I wanted to cast it away, but as we began the journey down the small incline, I couldn't help but watch Xander support Jake so he could walk. I wanted to believe I was simply reading something into the way Jake leaned into Xander, but I kept remembering the way he'd looked at Xander when he'd handed him the first aid kit.

"So how did you guys meet?" I found myself asking, though it wasn't the real question I wanted to ask.

I heard Jake's soft laugh before Xander spoke up. "We met several years ago on an expedition to Patagonia."

“What were you doing in Patagonia?” I asked.

Jake answered. “It was an organized trek across Nef Glacier and Soler Valley. Simply beautiful terrain. A once in a lifetime trip.”

“Bennett, you would have loved it,” Xander added. “Remember when we did that science project about glaciers and we had to learn all the terminology?”

I thought back to fifth grade. “Weird words,” I said. “I can't remember them, though.”

“Kettles and drumlin,” he reminded me.

I turned to look at him, sure the smile on my mouth matched his. “I remember now. We said it sounded more like the name of a half-decent band than parts of a glacier.”

As we came upon a large, open meadow, Jimmy took off running through the flowers to climb on a big flat boulder in the middle of the field.

“Exactly. Well, Jake and I got to see glacial kettles and drumlin in person.”

Jake cut in. “And when we got back to the hostel, I got to see what Xander here acts like when he drinks enough to get giggly.”

That swirl of jealousy went through me again, only this time because I realized Jake had known Xander as an adult. I hadn't known Xander since he'd been old enough to drink. Or smoke or do any number of other adult things. Maybe I didn't know him as well as I thought. What if he did drugs? What if he was into group sex? What if there was something about me that he found strange?

“A giggly Xander, huh?” I said, for lack of anything else clever. “I've never been around Xander when he's had anything to drink.”

“He's adorable. So funny that after I moved here, I introduced him to my homemade ale so I could get him drunk as often as possible.”

Xander laughed. “I knew you had an ulterior motive for that. I should have never introduced you to Gary. Having a brewery next door has not been good for my health.”

“You live next door to a brewery?” I asked, beginning to feel the full force of my aches and pains.

"No," Jake corrected. "I bought the cabin next door to Xander's, and I brew my own beer at home. Xander is my taste-tester."

"Wait," I said. "You two met in South America on an expedition but you live next door to each other?" Why did I feel like I was missing something?

When we caught up to Jimmy, Xander helped Jake sit on the boulder to take a breather. I'd been carrying Jake's pack and let it drop to the ground before collapsing next to it for my own breather. Part of me was concerned that once on the ground, I wouldn't be able to get back up.

"No. We met on the trek, but then I didn't hear from him again until he moved to Haven last summer. I hooked him up with Gary for a job as a beginning wilderness guide, and Gary sold him the cabin," Xander explained.

"So you two are next door neighbors. And you work together," I said, taking a sip from my water bottle. Part of me wished it was straight vodka instead. Just so I could have been put out of my misery. Had I passed out in that field of wildflowers for the next twelve hours, maybe then I could have woken up feeling stronger and better able to handle both my injuries and my petty jealousy.

I looked over at Xander as he carefully pulled Jake off the rock and put his arm back around the man's waist.

The water tasted like iodine purification tablets, and I realized I'd be glad to get back to civilization again— filtered water and a comfortable bed.

Maybe Jake was a better match for Xander after all. The guy clearly loved many of the same things Xander did. And I could never compete with someone who was that adventurous and worldly. Compared to Jake, I was just some suit from Manhattan who worked with computers and numbers.

The thought exhausted me, and it took every ounce of energy I had just to drag my sorry ass the rest of the way to the trailhead.

# CHAPTER 31

## XANDER

Despite the fun I'd had reminiscing about how Jake and I had met, I couldn't shake my concern for Bennett. I'd heard of secondary drowning as part of my first aid training, but I hadn't even considered it after pulling Bennett from the river. I'd been so focused on getting him warm and making sure he hadn't had a serious injury that I hadn't been able to think about much else. I looked ahead at Bennett who was leading our little group with Jimmy at his side. He'd been unnaturally quiet, but I also knew he was physically exhausted. His injuries had been bad enough, but to then tack on two hikes in less than ideal conditions— I knew he had to be feeling it.

Still, I didn't like the silence.

But he wasn't exhibiting any of the signs Jake had mentioned.

I glanced at Jake to see how he was doing. He was handling the day's hike like a champ, but I knew, like Bennett, he had to feel wiped out from both his injury and the stress he'd been experiencing the past couple days.

"You going to tell me about how you knew all that stuff back there?" I asked. Jake was leaning on me more heavily now, presumably because his ankle was starting to hurt more and more.

"What stuff?"

"That secondary drowning shit. Carrying a stethoscope around," I said.

"Just like to be prepared."

"Bullshit."

He shot me a look, but he quickly shuttered whatever emotion had been in his eyes for the briefest of moments.

Although I'd gotten to know Jake somewhat better once he'd made the move to Colorado, he was still a complete enigma. I could count on one hand the things I knew about him. And even then, I'd have fingers left over. I'd always let it go because I figured, like me, he was running from something in his past. But I was beginning to wonder if maybe what he was running from was much more than the broken heart I'd been trying to deal with for the past fifteen years.

"Just let it go, Xander," he said. "That's not our thing, remember?"

I knew what he was talking about. Somehow we'd reached a silent agreement that whatever was in the past was better off left there. It was a rule I'd gladly adhered to after I'd gotten drunk one night and told Jake about Bennett's defection when we were kids. I hadn't told him any of the details, but he'd learned enough to know I'd carried the scars for a long time. Luckily, he'd never pressed me for more, and I'd respected the same boundary with him.

Which meant I'd have to respect it now.

"Thank you," I said.

"For what?"

"For checking him out," I said as I motioned ahead of us. I knew Bennett was too far ahead to hear our conversation. We were on the last leg of the trail which was a straight shot to the trailhead, so I didn't have to worry about him and Jimmy getting a little farther ahead of us.

Jake nodded. "He seems like a good guy."

His comment surprised me since last time he'd seen Bennett, I'd been in the process of trying to get away from my former friend. I would have expected him to be lashing out at Bennett in some attempt to protect me. Before I could say anything, he continued.

"You guys talked it out, didn't you? Fixed whatever was wrong between you?"

"We did," I said. "How did you know?"

He shrugged. "It's written all over your faces. Even the one time you told me about him, there was something in your eyes..." His voice fell off briefly before his gaze connected with mine. "It's still there."

I sighed. "It always will be. But we only fixed some things. Some things just can't be changed."

"Like what?"

"Like the fact that he lives 2000 miles away. That he's a part of a world I never want to go back to."

"What, because he's got money?"

"Not just that... he's *someone* out there. His name means something. He's got a successful career ahead of him running the family business. Even if I wanted to, I wouldn't fit."

"Hmmm, never pegged you for a pussy."

I was so startled by his comment that I actually stopped walking. Jake wasn't big on confrontation and had a habit of keeping his thoughts to himself. If I wanted his opinion on something, I usually had to drag it out of him.

"What is it? Is everything okay?" Bennett asked as he glanced over his shoulder at us.

"Yeah, sorry, all good," I said quickly and got us moving again. I waited until Bennett and Jimmy had put several yards between us before I said, "I guess when you've got something to say, you don't pull any punches, huh?"

"I learned a long time ago that life's too short not to say what you mean. While you're fiddling around trying to find the right words or the courage to say what's in your heart, you might just lose your chance altogether."

"Thank you, Professor Nietzsche," I said.

Jake chuckled and a small smile drifted across his lips. But for once, it was a real smile. It *almost* reached his eyes.

Almost.

But not quite.

"What if he doesn't need you to fit into his world? What if he just needs you?"

"So what? I'm supposed to ask him to give up everything to be with me?" I asked. Even as I spoke, Jake's words had planted a little sliver of hope deep inside of me that began to unfurl and curl throughout my body. Maybe there was a way I could make it work. Maybe I didn't need to ask Bennett to give anything up. As much as I hated the idea of living in New York, maybe I could stomach it if it meant I got to be with him. I could pretend that his friends and family didn't think I was trash. I'd still have to travel for work, but it would be a hell of a lot better than not being a part of his life. I could make it through just about anything if it meant I could go home to Bennett each day.

I knew I was getting ahead of myself, but I couldn't help it. This past week had shown me that as much as I loved my life, there was a gaping hole in it that only one man could fill.

I finally realized Jake hadn't answered me, and I glanced at him to see his eyes were on the ground in front of us. "You okay?" I asked. He'd always been the quiet, solemn type, but there was just something off about him today.

"Yeah, I'm good. Just tired." His eyes met mine, but it seemed like he had to force the connection. "Thanks for coming to get us."

"That's what friends do, right?"

But he didn't answer me, and in a strange way, I felt like I'd just lost a part of him. Which made no sense since he was right there next to me. Before I could question him, though, he said, "Look."

I looked up to see Gary striding towards us, a look of utter relief on his face. We were less than a mile from the trailhead. Which meant that even at Jake's slow pace, it was less than an hour before we reached the lodge and all of its offerings.

Warm beds.

Hot showers.

Amazing food.

And I got to share them all with Bennett. Before talking to Jake, I'd figured I'd get a day or two at most to make love to Bennett on a soft mattress or talk to him over a hot meal, but now I was wondering if it couldn't be more than that. If those things could become my new normal.

Once Gary reached us, I let him take over helping Jake so I could run ahead and make sure Bennett was okay.

"Hey," I said. "It's not much farther. You doing okay?" I asked. I closed my hand around his elbow, both to support him if he needed it and also just to feel his warm skin, but I was shocked when he moved away from me.

"Yeah, we're good," he said as he put his arm around Jimmy's shoulders.

His defection hurt, but I knew it was likely the exhaustion talking. Not to mention he might not be comfortable showing affection around Jimmy.

Except he'd been fine with the boys in our group assuming we were together.

Uncertainty shimmied through me as we walked in silence.

"I thought I'd stay at the lodge for a couple days," I said, more to get him talking than anything else. I let my words drop off because Bennett didn't even look at me as I spoke. "You okay?" I asked again.

"Fine," he said. "Just tired. Ready to go home."

*Home.*

Did he mean the lodge or did he mean New York? Doubt began to creep in. What if I'd read last night wrong? What if everything he'd said and done hadn't really meant anything? I'd been so certain after we'd made love the second time that he was feeling the same things I was, but what if I was wrong? What if he was content with how things had ended up, after all? He could certainly regret what had happened fifteen years ago, but that didn't mean he wanted things to change now.

"So I thought I'd stay at the lodge," I said again, hoping, praying for some kind of reaction from him.

"Probably a good idea," he said. "I'm sure you're tired and could use some rest before you head home."

"Yeah, right," I said. A familiar churning in my belly had me slowing my step. The sensation continued all the way back to the lodge. I barely managed to interact with Lucky who, along with Bear, Aiden and one of the chaperones I recognized from Jake's group, was waiting for us by the entrance to the lodge. Gary helped Jake into the lodge while the other chaperone took charge of Jimmy, leaving just me, Bennett, Aiden and Lucky standing there. Thunder rumbled in the distance, a reminder that although we'd beaten the storm back to the lodge, we were still in for a good soaker.

As Lucky told me all about how he'd taken care of Bear for me, I watched Bennett approach Aiden. The other man looked from Bennett to me. I saw him say something to Bennett, but Bennett just shook his head. I watched in disbelief as the man I loved more than anything else in this world sought comfort in another man's arms.

This couldn't be fucking happening. Not twice in one lifetime. It just couldn't.

"He's an awesome dog, Xander. I'm gonna miss him."

I forced my attention to Lucky and said, "I appreciate you taking such good care of him for me, Lucky. I know he's going to miss you too. I will too, for that matter."

"This was the best trip ever," Lucky said with a huge smile, and then he was wrapping his arms around me. I hugged him back as I fought the emotion that was threatening to close up my throat.

I watched Lucky head back to the lodge. Aiden put his arm around the boy's thin shoulders as they disappeared through the front entrance. It took everything in me to stand there and face Bennett, because I knew what was coming.

He was going to tear my fucking heart out. I just knew it.

Just like when he'd pushed me to safety on that river crossing the day before, everything slowed down. Only this time, I knew the outcome wouldn't be in my favor.

He finally turned to face me. He looked pale and sickly, and despite the agony that was threatening to send me to my knees, I was worried about him.

"Xander, I—"

"You should go inside, Bennett. You need to get warm and rest. If you can, try to go see a doctor before you head home."

"Um, yeah," he murmured. "I should do that... I just wanted to say—"

"You don't have to say it," I said. I'd thought I could do it— listen to him give me the brush-off— but I wasn't strong enough. I was way too close to doing what I'd done that night so many years ago... something I'd done when my mother had walked out of my life for the last time.

Begging.

I might still be that unlovable kid, but I'd be damned if I was going to give him the satisfaction of ripping my heart to shreds again.

"A walk down memory lane and a few hot fucks was a good way to pass the time, but we both know it's not something you can build a future on," I said.

He looked stricken, but he nodded. "Yeah... yeah, you're right."

"Have a safe flight home, Bennett," I managed to get out before I felt my throat completely close up.

I was dimly aware of him saying something equally polite to me, but I didn't even wait for him to finish before I turned on my heel and began walking.

Because I'd be damned if I let Bennett be the one to turn his back on me first.

Not again.

# CHAPTER 32

## BENNETT

"B, please, you need to eat."

I shook my head. I knew if I ate a thing, it would just come back up. After all, that's what had happened as soon as Xander had turned his back on me. I'd barely managed to wait until he was out of sight before I'd rushed around the side of the lodge and thrown up in some bushes. Aiden had been the one to find me on my knees, my arms wrapped around my waist as I'd sobbed so hard that I'd made myself sick again and I'd retched a second time, though there'd been nothing left in my stomach at that point to expel.

I heard Aiden sigh. I was dimly aware of him setting the tray of food on the small table in the room, but I didn't bother telling him he should just take the damn thing away because the food would likely be spoiled by the time the pain in my belly eased enough to let me even try filling it with something.

*He left me.*

I still couldn't believe it. I didn't even know how it happened. One second I'd been prepared to throw myself to my knees to beg him to pick me over Jake, the next he'd been telling me fucking me had been a great distraction.

The mattress shifted as Aiden climbed into the bed with me and lay down so that he was facing me. His fingers came out to skim the wound on my head. He'd been oddly quiet himself after I'd told him about the cause of my injuries.

Quiet and almost clingy.

Normal Aiden would have been telling me that Xander could go fuck himself, but this Aiden hadn't said much after I'd told him everything that had happened between me and Xander after we'd split off from the rest of the group.

I almost wanted asshole Aiden back.

"Something must have happened, B," he said softly as he toyed with my hair. "From everything you told me after the river—"

"Jake happened," I cut in. "You should have seen them together, Aid. The way they talked about all the trips they'd been on. Even if they aren't together, they should be. He's everything I'm not."

"What does that even mean?"

I wiped at the tears that wouldn't stop randomly leaking from my eyes. "He likes the same things as Xander. The outdoorsy shit. And he's beautiful." I shook my head. "He isn't a smart-ass, he isn't klutzy, he doesn't get pissy…"

"You met the guy for like five minutes, Bennett. You sure you're just not projecting stuff on him?"

"Are you seriously going all shrinky on me?" I asked. "I saw the way Jake was looking at him. I didn't need more than thirty seconds to know there was something there. And the whole way back they were talking like I wasn't even there."

"Did you try talking to Xander about it?"

"Talk about what? What was I supposed to say? *Hey Xander, I'm head over heels in love with you and have been my whole life, so dump the hot wilderness guy who also happens to live within spitting distance of you and pick me, a guy whose family put you through hell and who lives 2000 miles away in a world that you yourself said you could never live in again.*"

"Sounds perfect to me." Aiden grinned at me and I couldn't stop the smile that stole across my mouth. But it didn't last.

"He couldn't get away from me fast enough, Aid. Last night… last night happened because he was feeling guilty about what happened at the river."

"Jesus, B, for someone who graduated with honors, you're so damn stupid sometimes."

"Thanks?" I said.

Aiden sighed and said, "Bennett, tell me something, okay. And think about it before you answer."

I nodded.

"What's your first reaction when you start doubting yourself?"

"What do you mean?"

Another sigh. "Okay, let's look at it this way. When we broke up, what did you say?"

"Really?" I asked in disbelief. "I just got my heart stomped on and you're bringing *that* up?"

"Shut up," he said impatiently. "You and I both know that what you were feeling then isn't anything even in the same universe as what you're feeling now."

He was right, but that didn't make me feel any better. Aiden had been my first real boyfriend, not to mention the one who'd introduced me to sex. I hadn't loved him, but I thought I had at the time. When he'd ended things, I'd been heartbroken, but not for the right reasons.

"I made a joke about having to cancel our wedding registry," I said.

"Right. You made a couple more equally stupid cracks, and then what happened?"

I narrowed my eyes at him because they'd been perfectly good jokes. "You said we should be friends."

"Right, and how did that go over at first?"

It finally dawned on me what he was getting at. "I told you that sounded like a good idea."

"And then?"

"And then I avoided you like the plague."

"You pulled away from me. And it started the second I told you it wasn't going to work out between us."

"We'd broken up, Aiden. You gave me the 'it's not you, it's me' line. What was I supposed to do?"

"What about your parents, then?"

"What about them?"

"All the times they told you how things were going to be... when you admitted you were gay and your dad told you he never wanted to hear those words come out of your mouth again, what did you do?"

"Why are you doing this?" I whispered as I closed my eyes.

I felt his hand cup my cheek. "Because I'm tired of you not standing up for what you want, Bennett... for what you deserve. And because I know what happened out there on that trail when you decided Jake was a better man for Xander. The same thing that happened tonight when you guys got back here. You withdrew... you tried to convince yourself that you were okay, that you weren't hurting. You use words to mask what you're feeling, B. Whether it be jokes or just out and out lies, you pretend you're okay when you aren't."

I wanted to deny it, but I couldn't. I'd never been allowed to say what I was really feeling as a kid, because that wasn't the Crawford way. My life had been mapped out from birth, and wanting something different hadn't been an option. It was like I'd been given a part to play and I'd spent my entire life perfecting that part.

Bennett Crawford, son of a prominent businessman, heir to a vast fortune, successful Harvard graduate, member of Greenwich's elite upper crust. Even my work with my father's company's foundation had been an acceptable prop, since what I did was considered philanthropy. If I'd done the same kind of work under the title of teacher or social worker, it would have been nixed from the get-go.

I wasn't just masking my feelings like Aiden said, I was *wearing* a mask. It had become a part of who I was. Aiden could see past the mask, but I hadn't actually ever felt comfortable enough to take it off around him. I was still Bennett Crawford to him.

"He's the only one, Aiden," I whispered. "He's the only one who ever just let me be me. His Benny."

"So why won't you fight for that?" he asked softly.

I forced my eyes open. "Who will I be if he says no? When I lost him the first time, it was different. I still had…"

"Hope," Aiden finished for me. "You had hope you'd find him again."

I nodded.

"Bennett, I can't pretend to know what you're feeling, but I do know this. If you get on that plane without having tried, it's not hope you'll be taking home with you. It'll be regret. I don't know about you, but I sure as shit know which one I'd rather wake up with every day."

He leaned forward and kissed me on the forehead before climbing off the bed. "Aiden," I called just as I heard him open the door. I sat up and kicked the covers off. "Can you ask Gary if he has a car I can borrow, and get me directions to Xander's cabin? I need to change."

"Well, I did have plans to check in on Larry," he mused. "But I suppose it can wait a few minutes."

"Let it go, Aid. The man's straight. He's not going to cave."

Larry was one of the chaperones who'd accompanied us on the trip and had been helping out with the group of younger boys that Jake had been leading. Aiden had been shamelessly flirting with him, but the single dad was completely clueless.

"We'll see," Aiden said. I reached him before he could leave the room.

"Thank you," I said softly, and then I was brushing a kiss over his cheek.

"Go get 'em, B," was all he said. His eyes twinkled as he shot me a soft smile and closed the door behind him.

# CHAPTER 33

## XANDER

The rain was so loud on the roof of the cabin, I didn't even hear the knocking at first. It was only Bear's incessant barking that had me climbing out of bed. I didn't need to look at the clock on my nightstand to know what time it was, because I'd been staring at the damn thing for the past three hours. I'd managed to pretend things were normal after I'd left the lodge, but it hadn't lasted longer than me making it home and climbing in the shower. That was when the gig had been up and I hadn't been able to pretend that I was in any way, shape or form okay with losing Bennett all over again. I'd ended up sitting on the shower floor crying my ass off until the water had turned so cold, I'd had no choice but to get out. But I hadn't gone very far.

My bedroom, to be exact.

I hadn't even bothered to dry off after I'd forced myself up off that floor. I'd gone straight for my bed and crawled between the sheets, not caring that they'd get wet. I hadn't cried anymore because I hadn't had any tears left, but I'd felt too numb to do anything but lie there. Jake had called me a few times, probably because he'd expected me to spend the night at the lodge. I hadn't answered. After the first few calls, I'd silenced the phone and turned it over so I wouldn't be tempted to check the screen.

So I wouldn't have to be disappointed when Bennett's name didn't show up on the Caller ID.

I knew I was being ridiculous, because we hadn't even exchanged numbers.

The floor was cold beneath my feet as I padded over to my dresser and grabbed a pair of jeans and pulled them on. Concern went through me as I realized my visitor was probably Jake coming to check on me. With his left foot being the injured one, he could have driven up the mountain road without too much trouble.

I flipped lights on as I went through the cabin. It wasn't a big place, but it suited me perfectly.

I was all prepared to apologize for worrying Jake by not answering his calls, but my words died off when I yanked the door open and saw who was standing there.

"Bennett," I said in disbelief. "What are you—"

"You need to pick me, Xander," he said, raising his voice so I could hear him over the rain. It was coming down in sheets. He was completely soaked, but he didn't even seem to notice. Before I could even respond, he said, "You need to pick me because I'm the one who knows how to make you laugh and I'm the one who knows where you're ticklish and I'm the one who knows you're afraid of spiders and I… I… I'm your Benny. You can't just give me that nickname and let me be all weird and crazy and stupid and then pick him!"

"Bennett—"

"I know what I did on the trail. I know it. I pulled away from you. When you talked about staying at the lodge, I pushed you away. I was a coward because I knew you'd be better off with him. I knew he was perfect for you and I'm not and we have so many things between us that don't seem to make sense, but they do, Xander. They do. "

I heard his voice catch and tried to reach for him so I could at least get him out of the rain, but he stepped out of my reach. "No! I have to finish!" he practically yelled. "I can love you better than he can, Xander. I've been doing it my whole life! He doesn't know you!"

Bennett jabbed his finger in the direction of Jake's cabin, and I finally realized what he was saying. And right after that realization, the rest of what he'd said hit me.

He loved me?

"I love you so much, Xander," he said, his voice dropping so low that I had to step out onto the small covered porch to hear him. Cold rain began to pelt my body from the side, but I didn't care. In fact, I was glad for it.

Because it meant maybe I wasn't dreaming.

Maybe he was really here, telling me what I'd been waiting a lifetime to hear.

"And not just because you see *me* when we're together. But because you let me see *you*." A sob tore from his throat. "Please, Xander, I can't lose you again. I won't survive it." He shook his head. Shock reverberated through me as I realized everything I'd ever wanted was literally within reach.

He loved me.

Which meant I was enough for him.

I heard a choked cry spill from his mouth, and then he was turning away from me and I realized I'd been too slow to respond. He'd taken my shocked silence for cold rejection instead.

I was on him in two strides, ignoring the rain as it soaked through my hair and jeans the second I stepped off the porch. I grabbed his elbow and yanked him back hard enough to have him spinning and slamming against my chest. I didn't let him get another word in before I crashed my mouth down on his.

Because he didn't need to say another word.

He'd said enough.

More than enough.

Bennett let out another soft cry and then he was kissing me back. His arms wound around my neck, and as soon as I lifted him by the backs of the thighs, he wrapped his legs around my waist. I barely felt his weight as I carried him up the steps and into the cabin, kicking the door shut behind me. He never stopped kissing me as I carried him to my bedroom. Bear wisely sought out his own bed in the corner of the room.

I lowered Bennett across the foot of the bed, not caring about our wet clothes. I released his mouth and used my hands to push the mop of hair off his face. His beautiful eyes held mine. They were filled with a mix of relief and uncertainty.

And I knew why.

"My Benny," I whispered as I let my fingers trail down his face. "Don't you know?" I asked as I let my finger glide over his perfect lips. Lips that were all mine now. "It's always been you," I told him. "Only you."

He sucked in a breath, but before he could say anything, I kissed him. I held my mouth against his for the briefest of moments before lifting my head.

Because I wanted him to see my eyes when I spoke.

So he'd know I was telling the truth.

"I love you, Benny. I've loved you from the moment you sat down on that swing next to me. I can't pick you because it's always *been* you."

"Really?" he asked, his lips pulling into a soft smile.

"Really."

"I love you so much, Xander."

I kissed him slow and deep, but it didn't take long before my wanting him turned feral— like a living, breathing thing. My hands couldn't get enough of him, and I found myself practically tearing off his clothes to get to him. I wanted him and I wanted him now. As if even my body had a need to cement what we'd just admitted to each other.

"Need you," I mumbled, trying to find his fly with shaking hands. Bennett gasped as my fingers brushed the bare skin behind his waistband, and I felt the tip of his cock. "Fuck, get these pants off."

I heard him chuckle as his hands released my face and joined mine to try and get his damned zipper down. He sucked in a breath when I started to yank. "Shit, babe. Careful. No underwear."

"Oh my god," I groaned. "Are you trying to make me come right now?"

"Kinda, yeah," he said with a soft laugh before latching his lips onto the base of my throat and sucking.

I felt him abuse the skin hard enough to leave a mark, and I was secretly grateful. I wanted to have proof of this coming together so that even if he did have to go home until we figured shit out, I'd know he was mine and I was his.

"Clothes off," I commanded, standing up and shucking my own pants faster than I ever had before. By the time he shook off his lust-filled haze and got the remaining articles of damp clothing off, I had a bottle of lube in one hand and a condom in the other. I held the condom up with a raised brow, but before I even had a chance to ask him the question, he was shaking his head violently.

"No, never again," he said with wide eyes. "Nothing between us."

Even though the words referred to the condom, I felt like he was making me a promise that ran deeper. I took a moment to lean back over him and place a gentle kiss on his soft lips. "Love you," I murmured against his lips.

His mouth turned up in a familiar grin. "Thank you. Now stop talking and get to work," he teased. His eyes twinkled and his hands came around to squeeze my ass encouragingly. "Get in there before I flip you over and show you what it looks like when a bossy bottom becomes a bossy top."

I felt my own grin widen and couldn't believe how fucking happy I felt. Light and happy and free. My lubed fingers found their way to his tight entrance and I massaged my way in, triggering curses and moans from the gorgeous man in my bed.

Maybe my man needed a reminder of who was in charge tonight. "Baby, you can fuck me all you want in the morning. But right now, your ass is mine. I'm going to do this fast and dirty, because I can't wait another minute to get inside that sweet ass. "

I nipped at his lips as I spoke while I fingered him. First with one, then two. By the time I added a third just to see what he'd do, he began writhing on the bed, his fingers clutching the bedding.

"Fuck, god, need you so bad!" he cried, his bright eyes catching mine. "Please, Xander."

I carefully pulled my fingers free before pushing inside him hard and fast, bottoming out in one swift surge. Bennett yelled something unintelligible, and then he was trying to drive his hips up to meet my urgent thrusts as I began pounding into him. I slipped my hand between our bodies and began jerking him off to make sure he was as close as me.

"Yes, just like that— love you so much," he babbled.

I leaned down to kiss him. "Love you, baby," I murmured just before I sent him over. His hot release coated my stomach and then dripped down my hand. My own orgasm ripped through me, and all I could do was hang onto Bennett until it eased enough that I could lift some of my weight off his sweaty chest. As he opened his eyes, I couldn't hold back the sense of pride I felt at knowing I'd put that look of satisfaction there.

I carefully pulled out of him and then slid down his body and began cleaning him up with my tongue. Bennett's fingers sifted through my hair when I got to his semi-hard cock and gently began sucking him, lapping up the remnants of his cum. I moved back up his body and sealed my mouth over his. He let out a gasp of surprise when I let some of his release slide over his tongue. But it lasted mere seconds, and then he was hungrily kissing me back.

By the time I got him settled under the covers, he was half-asleep. I curled my body against his back and pressed kisses against the back of his neck and down his shoulder.

"Bennett," I said softly.

"Mmmmm?"

I chuckled at his inability to form an actual sentence. "Thank you."

He was quiet for a moment and then he turned in my arms. "For what, baby?"

"For coming to find me. Tonight… that night fifteen years ago."

His hand came up to caress my face. "Always, Xander." He kissed me and then nestled his face in the crook of my neck. "Don't let me go, okay? Want to wake up just like this."

"I won't, Benny. Never letting you go again."

# CHAPTER 34

## BENNETT

Xander had been telling the truth when he'd promised to hold me all night. I slept deeply and peacefully, only waking when I heard Bear's nails click on the hardwood floor. From the soft light sneaking through the window blinds, I guessed it was very early morning. I untangled myself from Xander's warm body and found my way out of the bedroom to let the big dog out the front door.

As I waited for him to return, I looked around the main room of the cabin. I hadn't had much time to notice Xander's home before he'd carried me into his bedroom, and I was pleasantly surprised at what a nice, comfortable place he had. There was a tidy area in one corner of the main room that housed snow skis, a snowboard, and plastic milk crates full of what appeared to be rock climbing equipment. The rest of the room held a large, comfortable sofa along with two overstuffed chairs. The seating faced a well-used stone fireplace, and I realized I hadn't seen a television anywhere.

Off the side of the main room was an open kitchen with a large round table and chairs. I padded over to the kitchen and found what I needed to start a pot of coffee and feed Bear before letting him back in the front door.

By the time I got back to the bedroom, my head was spinning with ideas about how I wanted to wake Xander up. I caught myself grinning like a fool as I took in the long form of his body outlined under the bedcovers. His long hair lay tangled on the pillow around his head and my fingers twitched with the need to touch it— to touch him. Anywhere and everywhere I could get my hands on.

I slipped the covers back and feasted my eyes on his naked body. There wasn't a shred left of the little boy body I'd known so well, yet every single part of him was familiar to me in a way. I wanted to lick every fucking millimeter of his skin and run my hands over every part of him. The idea that I'd have an infinite number of opportunities to explore this body in the coming days, weeks, months and years made my stomach turn somersaults.

I laid a knee on the edge of the bed and stretched forward to drop soft kisses on the inside of his thigh. The curve of his quads leading up to his hip was firm under my hand, and that was all it took for my dick to harden and my balls to wake up.

Xander murmured something I couldn't quite make out as he shifted in bed, his legs opening wider to expose himself further.

I quickly dragged my mouth up to brush against his sac before running my tongue against the smooth skin of his morning wood. I heard a quick intake of breath, followed by a groan, but I ignored it—instead, I focused on getting my lips around his thick cock.

He gasped again and brought his hands to my head, fingers forking into my hair and gripping it before he was even fully awake.

"Benny," he croaked. "Fuck, don't stop."

I shook my head and hummed around him instead of answering with words, and his cock pulsed in my mouth in response.

"Oh god. Jesus," he murmured. "Fuck that feels good, baby. So good."

My tongue danced around the head of his cock before I took him all the way to the back of my throat. I tried to ignore the tightening fingers in my hair and focused on suppressing my gag reflex so I could take him down as deep as I could. The sounds coming out of him bore witness to my success and before I knew it, he was trying to pull me off him.

"No, dammit. You're gonna make me come," he grumbled. "I want inside you."

I pulled off and locked eyes with him before speaking. "Un-uh. I'm in charge this time, babe."

Xander's eyes widened in surprise for a brief moment before he rolled them and fell back onto the pillow. "You're always the one in charge," he complained. "Now you're going to tease me and make me cry and beg."

I barked out a laugh.

"You love it when I tease you," I said. I ran the tip of my tongue around his nipple before pulling it into my mouth and sucking. My teeth grazed against the hard nub and he thrust his hard cock up into my belly.

"I do not," he gasped, even though his leaking cock betrayed his words.

I leaned up and bit the lobe of one ear. "Do too," I whispered into his ear. He let out a whimper as my fingers teased the hair just below his happy trail. I felt the cool touch of precum brush against the back of my knuckles, but I ignored that part of him for now.

"Fuck you. Touch it. Do it," he growled.

"Nah. Not yet. You're being awfully growly right now. I think maybe you need a reminder of who's in charge here. I recall you seeming to have a certain fascination with my hand spanking this perfect ass of yours." As I spoke, I let my hand slip between the bedding so I could grip his ass.

Precum dripped all over my other hand after my words sunk in and I finally couldn't resist grabbing him and stroking. I used his fluid to coat the skin of his cock before sliding my fist up and down his length. Xander let out a groan of relief and punched his hips up into me.

I let him have a few strokes before I moved my fingers lower to tickle his balls.

"Benny," he breathed. "Benny, please, baby. You're killing me."

His breathing was labored and his hands reached for the sides of my face to force me to look at him. His eyes were wild and his skin was flushed. Fuck, he was stunning like this.

"You've reached the begging stage already? Hm, I like it." While I spoke, I moved my fingers even lower to massage the skin below his sac and sneak a fingertip farther back to tap lightly on the crinkled skin of his hole. Xander sucked in a breath as his eyes searched mine.

"Do it," he whispered. "Want you to feel good. Just go easy, okay?"

The fact that he was going to let me fuck him because he knew it would make me feel good was enough to make my heart swell. I just wished I wasn't so goddamned scared of fucking it up somehow and disappointing him.

"You sure?" I asked around the lump that was forming in my throat. "We don't have to. You know I love bottoming too."

His face softened into a smile as he gazed at me. "I'm very sure. I love you. I want to feel you and be with you every different way possible, Benny."

I reached over to grab the bottle of lube on the bedside table and dropped it on the bed by his hip. Then I kissed my way across his stomach to his cock again and gave it several more good sucks and pulls.

"Turn over, babe," I said, raising up on my knees and patting his thigh. He flipped over without question and tucked his knees underneath him.

I felt my breathing speed up as I looked at the long expanse of his beautiful back and the rounded cheeks of his muscular ass. I leaned down to kiss and nip at those glorious cheeks before moving my hands to pull them apart.

"Benny…?" Xander looked over his shoulder, realizing what I was getting ready to do. My mouth landed on his hole. "Oh my fucking god!" His voice cracked as I laid into him with my tongue. "Mmpfh… mm-hmm… more," he begged.

I knew the more time I spent rimming him, the better off he'd be when I entered him. But the more I feasted on him, the harder I got, until I just couldn't wait any longer. I grabbed the lube and opened the cap before squeezing some out. It was cool and slick on my fingers as I finished stretching him out.

I forced my eyes away from his opening to see how he was doing. From the sounds of his sweet gasps and moans, he was feeling just fine. His face was mashed into the bed covers and his ass was propped in the air. I wrapped one arm around his waist and leaned across his back to kiss the side of his face.

"Please," he whimpered. "I need you."

I flipped him over onto his back and settled my cock against his. Xander's legs immediately wrapped around me, ankles locking behind me. "Want to look into your beautiful face as I take you," I murmured. "Want to know I'm finally inside you in every way."

"Bennett," he breathed. His eyes were wide and reverent, and I knew he was completely with me in that moment.

*"Xander."* I moved my hips until the head of my cock pressed into him. The hot squeeze of his body around mine was unlike anything I'd ever felt before.

Absolute heaven.

# CHAPTER 35

## XANDER

I was pleasantly surprised at the lack of pain when Bennett's dick slid into me. He'd relaxed me to the point of a horny nirvana before entering me, and my body stretched to accommodate him with little trouble. He kept mumbling comforting words, reminding me to breathe and push out, but he went so slowly it drove me crazy. His body hovered above me and his eyes locked onto mine. Little divots of worry marred his forehead, and I reached up without thinking to grasp the sides of his face so I could pull him down to kiss away the worry lines.

"S'okay," I said with my lips against his skin. "Feels good, baby, but please move, okay? Wanna feel you."

Bennett began to pulse his hips, dragging his cock out before pushing it back in again. With every move he made, his length went deeper and deeper until I finally felt his balls brush against my ass. His taut abdominal muscles pressed into my erection, dragging the skin up and down with each stroke into me. My nerves were firing in every direction and I couldn't focus on what felt better— the delicious slide of Bennett's stomach against my cock or the complete fullness of his dick inside of me. I felt him everywhere at once and it still wasn't enough.

He shifted his hips. "*Benny*," I cried out as the new angle caused him to brush against a sensitive spot that had me seeing stars. "Oh god, oh god. Please, Benny. Please do that again."

His thrusts sped up until he was nailing my prostate with every stroke and I thought I would come completely undone. Bennett's face was intense, and I could tell he was close to finishing.

"Xander, come with me," he gasped.

"Go. Want to see you, feel you," I reassured him. Before the words were out, he was screaming my name and pushing even deeper into me. I felt the warmth of his release and the pulse of his cock as it emptied inside of me. It felt amazing.

But I still wanted more. It was like he'd ignited something inside of me, and I couldn't get enough of him. I felt like a caveman who wanted to do nothing more than capture the man and drag him back to my lair. To own him and fuck him and make him mine in every way. Over and over and over again.

When he pulled out of me, I immediately scrambled out from under him and pushed him down, face-first on the bed. He was half-drunk with the aftershocks of his release, but I was still hard as fuck and lucid as hell. I wanted inside his body with a single-minded focus that drove me to act.

"Gonna take you, baby. Right now, okay?" I ground out as I shoved his knees underneath him, exposing the tight pink hole in his crease. I groaned and looked away, afraid that one more look at him already well-fucked and laid out for me would push me over the edge.

He mumbled his agreement, so I grabbed the lube bottle and squeezed out what I needed. I leaned over and ran my tongue from his balls up his crease and back again, stopping only briefly to lick into him with a firm tongue.

Bennett babbled and groaned into the pillow under his face, and I took a moment to run appreciative hands up and down his spine.

"Fuck, you're beautiful, Bennett Crawford," I murmured. Was I being a selfish jackass by interrupting his post-orgasmic high to get myself off? I began to have second thoughts, even as I stroked lube onto my stiff cock. "Benny, I can't… I want… I need to—"

"Less thinking, more doing," he quipped, and I could tell from the teasing tone of his voice he was not only willing, but happy too. That was all it took.

I shoved into him with a roar before I began thrusting deep and sure. He cried out and slammed his ass back against me in response, which only served to ratchet up my pace to a fevered pitch.

Only a handful of strokes later and I was ready to spill into him—jagged shards of shimmering pleasure kicked up from my balls to my cock, and a rough cry fell from my lips against his back. Tears pricked the corners of my eyes, and I knew that I'd never be the same after that claiming. His of me and mine of him.

It was done. We were together. And it was only the beginning.

~

Several moments later, I realized I'd basically collapsed onto his back with my full body weight. I felt him struggle beneath me, and I grunted in response.

"Can't… breathe…" he croaked.

"Shit, sorry," I said, feeling a little sheepish as I rolled off him. "Guess I got carried away." I landed on my back beside him and stretched my arms above my head like a cat.

Bennett climbed on top of me and grinned down at me. The look on his face was fucking adorable as hell.

"I look forward to you getting carried away again in the future," he said.

"That can probably be arranged." I reached up to brush my fingers through his messy hair until it was sticking up even more than before. "Good morning, gorgeous. Do I smell coffee?"

"You do. Let me get cleaned off, and I'll join you for a cup."

It was only then that I noticed there were streaks of cum smeared all over his belly and chest. My eyes snapped to the sheets where he'd been lying face down, and I saw they were covered in wet spots too. I quirked a brow at him.

"You came twice?"

Bennett nodded and continued his shit-eating grin. "Didn't I tell you the early bird gets the worm? You must have been too caught up in your Neanderthal act to notice little old me getting off again."

I felt my face heat. "Baby, I'm sor—"

"Are you kidding? It was hot as hell, Xander. And if you don't believe me, believe the gallon of cum on your bed. C'mon. Let's get some coffee. While I'd love to lie here and rehash what had to have been sex for the ages, I think we have some things we need to figure out."

He leaned back over me to kiss me sweetly, and I brought my hand up to cup the back of his head. After a few moments of enjoying each other's lips and tongues, Bennett pulled back and smiled down at me.

"How's your poor little virgin hole?" he asked.

I took stock of how I was feeling back there and winced. "Not so virgin anymore. I think you might need to kiss it and make it better later."

Bennett let out a laugh. "Gladly. Now c'mon," he said, climbing off the bed and reaching out for me. "Quick shower, then coffee."

When we were finally settled with coffee and half-empty plates of scrambled eggs at the kitchen table, I took a sip of my coffee before asking, "Are the kids with Gary today for the ropes course?"

"Yeah. Aiden and Jake went to watch. Along with Kimberly and Larry, the other chaperones from the foundation. Why?"

"Just making sure they're in good hands. I was hoping to take you with me to meet Aunt Lolly." I set the mug down and reached for his hand. "But first, let's talk about Lucky. I know you're worried about him."

Bennett's eyes found mine, and I felt my heart squeeze. "C'mere, baby," I said softly, pulling him off his chair and over to the sofa in the main room. I sat down and pulled him into my lap. I wrapped my arms around him and held tight. "I want you to know without a shadow of a doubt that I'm with you. We'll figure this out together. You're not alone."

His body trembled as I held him. "What if they've hurt him? What if I have to take him home to them, Xander? I can't do it. I won't." He looked up at me with defiance.

I brushed a kiss onto his forehead. "We'll talk to him tonight to find out exactly what's going on, and you won't have to take him home to them if there's even a hint of abuse."

Bennett snuggled back into my chest, and I knew his mind was going a million different directions.

"Benny, did you ever think about taking in Lucky yourself?" I asked as an idea began to take shape in my mind.

His eyebrows furrowed in confusion. "Well, yeah. I mean, I daydreamed about it, but I'm a single guy who works sixty hours a week. That's hardly a good situation for a kid to come home to. Not to mention the fact I'm gay, and my parents would never accept it. I just assumed it wasn't even something I could seriously consider."

"What if you weren't single?" My question caused him to turn his head to look at me.

"What do you mean?"

"Well, I don't plan on losing you again, which means I'm going back to New York with you, whether you like it or not," I said with a smile. "You won't be alone anymore. The two of us can take care of Lucky together."

Bennett sat up quickly, nearly toppling off my lap with the momentum. I reached out to keep him from going too far from me.

"You… wait, what? You want us to foster Lucky together? Like a real family?" His eyes had gone wide, as if he was too afraid to hope for what I was suggesting.

"No, baby," I said. Bennett's smile began to fade, so I continued quickly. "I didn't mean foster him. I meant we can try to adopt him. If he wants us, that is. We'd have to ask him—"

Bennett launched himself at me with a yelp before squeezing his arms tightly around my neck. I automatically brought my arms around his back to hold him tight. My heart was racing from seeing him so excited, and I wondered how many other times in our lives I'd be lucky enough to see that raw joy on his face.

"Xander, are you serious right now?" He breathed against my ear. "It's okay if you aren't, but I don't want to get my hopes up if you—"

"Yes, Benny. Of course I'm serious. Lucky is a great kid, and he deserves a great dad like you."

Bennett pulled back to look at me, eyes shining with unshed tears. "Like both of us."

My chest tightened. "Think so? I wouldn't be a terrible parent?"

"Of course not. You and I learned from the best, after all. Didn't we?" His eyes were locked on mine, and I knew he meant my dad—the man who'd taken us to see our favorite bands in concert, who'd taken us to Yankees games, who'd taught us how to fish and how to light a campfire. The man who'd loved both of us unconditionally and had taught us the value of hard work and dedication to family. The man who'd let us be together without a shred of judgement. If Bennett and I were able to become good fathers, it would be because my dad had shown us by example. I felt my throat close up.

"Benny," I whispered. "I miss him so much."

"I know you do, baby. Me too."

Bennett leaned in and kissed me softly, letting our lips stay pressed together until I gathered my composure and could speak again. "Lucky needs us. This is the right thing to do. I'll move to New York. I write freelance content for several outdoor sports websites. I can probably turn that into a full-time job, so I can be there when Lucky gets home from school."

"No, Xander. I don't want you in New York. You don't belong there." Before I had a chance to lie and deny his statement, he smiled. "Lucky and I will come here. This is your home and I'm not about to let you give it up."

"No. You're the one with a big important job. There's no way you can leave the foundation," I corrected. "I'll move east."

Bennett let out a big breath and turned to face me on the sofa, crossing his legs and taking both of my hands in his.

"Xander, from here on out, *you* are my big important job. You, and hopefully Lucky too. I think Haven, Colorado is a much better place for Lucky to finish growing up than New York. You saw how he was in the mountains. He loved it. Can't you imagine the three of us hiking and camping? Rafting and fishing? Staying in the city isn't what either of us needs. We need fresh air and space for a new start."

God, that sounded amazing. Like a dream come true. I used our joined hands to pull him forward for a kiss. "That sounds perfect. But just know that my new start is with you no matter where you are, okay?"

"Even if I decide to move to a nudist colony?" Bennett's eyes twinkled and he couldn't help but start laughing.

I narrowed my eyes at him. Maybe my love was conditional after all.

After a few moments, Bennett settled, and I gently pushed him back so I could look into his eyes. "Last night… you mentioned Jake. Why?"

His fingers reached out to tuck my hair behind my ear. "It doesn't matter. It's not important."

I ran my hands up and down the warm skin of his sides as I said, "Everything you think and feel is important to me, Bennett. There's nothing between me and Jake. Never has been."

"He has feelings for you."

"What makes you say that?" I asked, surprised by his statement and the certainty with which he'd said it.

Bennett shrugged. "Just the way he looked at you… some other things. I can't really blame him," he said with a wan smile.

The idea that my friend had been harboring feelings for me and I hadn't known it bothered me, but it didn't really change anything. "It's only you, Benny. It's always only been you and it always will be. Tell me you know that."

His eyes held mine for a moment and then his finger stroked over my cheek as he cupped my jaw. "I do know it," he finally said, and then he curled against my chest. "Why do you suppose he never told you how he felt?"

"No idea," I said. "I didn't even know he was gay." I began toying with Bennett's hair. "He said something yesterday about life being too short not to say what you mean, but I guess he didn't take his own advice."

"You think he's hiding something?" Bennett suddenly asked.

"What do you mean?"

He shifted again so he could look at me. "Dunno. Just seems like he doesn't quite fit here, you know? The stethoscope, the stuff he said about my injuries... just makes me wonder if there's something more there."

I pulled him back against my chest and ran my hand up and down his back. "Wouldn't surprise me," I admitted. "A lot of people who come out here are running away from one thing or another."

"Like you?"

"Yeah, like me."

"But not anymore," Bennett said softly as his fingers fiddled with the fabric of my shirt.

"No, not anymore." I dropped my lips to his temple. "Never again."

# CHAPTER 36

## BENNETT

On the way to meet Xander's aunt, I began getting a little nervous.

"Are you sure this place is called Bare Bottomed Acres?" I asked for the third time.

"Baby, are you seriously asking me that again?"

"I just don't think that sounds right."

He turned his head from watching the road and lifted an eyebrow at me.

"Fine," I mumbled. "But promise me again they're not going to make me get naked."

Xander took a long moment to run his gaze up and down my body, and by the time he was done, I may or may not have been breathing heavily.

"Do you *want* to get naked?" he drawled.

*I do now,* I thought. "Shut up," I said.

"Because that's always an option at Hiney's Hideaway."

I glared at him. "See? That. That right there is why I don't think you're telling me the real name of the place. So far you've referred to it as Moon Manor, Rump's Rest, and Woody's Hole. And I swear to god I heard you call it The Jiggle Jungle a little while ago. Which is it?"

His lips curved into a grin as he turned onto a narrow road. "There's the sign. See for yourself."

I turned quickly to read the sign, but by the time I saw the small wooden billboard, I was staring at the back of it.

"Motherfucker," I muttered.

We pulled up to a one-story stone building that looked like it had seen better days. As we stepped out of Xander's SUV, I noticed a small hand-painted sign next to the front door.

*Bear Trodden Acres.*

I looked over at the gorgeous jackass beside me, and he burst out laughing. Just seeing him let go and enjoy himself like that was worth every stupid name he'd called this place. I couldn't help but laugh right alongside him.

"There you are," a woman said, pushing her way out of the building via a screen door. Thankfully, she was wearing a loose-fitting sundress that flowed around her legs as she made her way toward us. "Xander, sweetie, who's this?" she asked as she pulled Xander into a big hug.

The woman was slim and tanned. I couldn't put my finger on it, but there was definitely something about her that reminded me of Xander's dad.

"Aunt Lolly, this is Bennett Crawford."

At the sound of the name, Lolly's eyes widened, and she stepped back to take stock of me for a moment before looking back and forth between Xander and me.

"*Your* Bennett?" she asked.

Xander's face softened as he looked over at me. "Yes, *my* Bennett."

Would that ever not give me stupid butterflies in my stomach?

Lolly studied me for a moment before her lips curved into a sweet smile and she walked right into my arms. As we hugged, she whispered into my ear, "I hope to god you're gay because I've had three different spiritual healers imply the two of you are soulmates, and I worried that might make things awkward for you if you weren't."

"You can stop worrying," I whispered back. "And they were right."

When she pulled away from the embrace there were tears in her eyes. "Really? You're not just pulling my leg?"

I reached out for Xander's hand. As our fingers threaded together, he lifted an eyebrow at me in question, obviously wondering what his aunt was asking about. I pulled him close enough for a quick kiss on the lips.

"Lolly wants to know if I'm gay," I explained.

"Lolly, Jesus," Xander said, frowning at her.

Before she had a chance to respond, I interjected. "I told her I wasn't originally, but you'd made a compelling argument."

Lolly stood there watching us with moony eyes, and I could tell how happy she was for Xander. "Come inside, you two. I made some lemonade and cookies."

"Oooh, what kind of cookies?" Xander asked like a little kid.

"Snicker*noodles*," she said over her shoulder as we entered the building. "I also have some store-bought ones."

"Do you have any Moon Pies?" Xander asked. I snorted and tried to stifle some nervous giggling.

"Xander," Lolly warned, but I could hear the smile in her voice.

"What about Tits Ahoy?" he asked.

"Stop that, or I'm going to whip up a quick batch of Lemon Puckers and make you eat them one at a time. Slowly," she said with a laugh. "Bennett, how about you? What kind do you like?"

"Oh, well, my favorite snack is raw nuts, but I'd be happy to nibble on a pucker if—"

Xander's hand clamped over my mouth before I could finish the sentence. By the time we settled down on the comfortable seating in the main room of what I learned was the community gathering house, the three of us were laughing so hard I could barely breathe.

A handful of older men and women came in, completely nude, and wandered over to grab a cookie off the tray on the coffee table. I tried not to look at their bare breasts and limp dicks swinging and bobbing as they walked.

"Oh Lolls, these look amazing," one woman said with a smile for

Lolly. "Any chance you made your famous chocolate starfish cookies? Those are my favorite."

"Not this time, Margaret. Sorry."

Lolly introduced us to her friends and they all welcomed us with friendly smiles. I tried so hard to be cool with the random nudity, but it was still difficult to get used to. Xander reached over to grab my hand, and I realized I'd folded a paper napkin until it was nothing but a tiny square between my fingers. I looked up at Xander. "Sorry," I mumbled.

"S'okay," he said softly with a smile. "I'd rather you be nervous than turned on." He winked at me and squeezed my hand while I rolled my eyes.

Once the group had grabbed the croquet set they were looking for, they exited the front door with waves and good wishes for a safe trip home.

Lolly turned back to look at us, but before she had a chance to speak, I opened my stupid fucking mouth.

"You can get naked if you want."

Time seemed to stop and I wondered where the lever was for the secret door in the floor.

*Dear god, tell me they have a secret door in the floor.*

"I, ah, mean…" I swallowed, unsure how to say what I'd actually meant. "Oh god."

"Benny?" Xander asked. I didn't dare look at him. I could tell from the sound of his voice that he was beyond amused.

"Shut the fuck up," I muttered. I got up the nerve to look up at Lolly and saw her eyes twinkling. Unfortunately, that's not all I saw.

"Thank god. That dress itches like a bitch. I feel better now. Thanks, Bennett. Now, spill. I want to hear everything. Does this mean you're taking my baby away from me?"

Even though there was a smile on her face, I could see worry lines around her eyes.

I tried to ignore the elephant's boobs in the room and focus on her question.

"No. We've decided to settle here, in Haven. Hope that's okay with you," I said.

She let out a sound of relief as she stood up from her chair to grab for us, pulling us both into a hug.

If you could let go of the fact she was naked when she did it, the woman was a damned good hugger, and I had the errant thought that I could get used to feeling loved by Xander's Aunt Lolly.

*Was that perverted?*

I looked at Xander as if he had the ability to read my mind and reassure me.

He winked, and I let out a sigh of relief. I tried to focus on what Lolly was saying.

"Oh my gosh, you're really moving here? You and Xander are going to stay here?" she asked after sitting back in her spot.

Xander settled his arm around my shoulders and pulled me in close to his side. "I told Bennett about Gary offering to sell me the business on our drive up here. He's hoping to retire before next year's summer season."

"Xander, that's amazing. You'll do a wonderful job with the lodge and expeditions. But, Bennett, what will you do? What do you do for a living?"

I looked at Xander before replying, "We're going to buy the business together. I can run the business side while Xander does the expeditions. Hopefully, once we get everything running smoothly, I can start a youth adventure program for underprivileged kids. That's the kind of work I've been doing in New York. I have some contacts there who might be able to help fund the first few trips to get us started. Then, if we market the concept well to other corporate foundations, we can help bring youth groups from all over the country here for backpacking, fishing and rafting trips."

Lolly clapped her hands together. "That sounds absolutely wonderful. If there's anything I can do to help, you just let me know. I just know it will be a success, though. Xander is very good with kids."

She looked at him with pride and love, and I was struck by the realization that he had indeed landed in a good place with Lolly like

I'd hoped. She clearly doted on him and seemed like a generous, loving soul. I was glad to know he'd wound up with someone as devoted to him as his father had been. But, then again, it made perfect sense. Lolly and Mr. Reed had been brother and sister. They both had the same gentle spirit and loving manner. I hoped like hell any kids we had in the future would inherit that same personality.

"Bennett, I wish Xander and I could have stayed in Greenwich. I didn't want to take him away from everything that he knew— especially you. I know you two were close. After your dad told me we couldn't stay in the cottage anymore—"

"What?" I blurted. "He kicked you out?"

Lolly glanced at Xander, who shook his head.

Her hand reached out to pat mine. "Sorry, honey. It doesn't matter now."

"I don't understand. What did my father say to you?"

"He said we couldn't stay in the cottage, and since Xander's scholarship would be revoked—"

I felt my heart rate kick up and tried not to lose it. "He said Xander's scholarship would be revoked?"

Xander put a hand on my cheek and swiveled my face so I was looking at him. "Baby, it doesn't matter now, okay? It's in the past. It's all over now, and we're together."

I knew now wasn't the time for me to rage about my father, so I forced myself to bite my tongue. As Xander told Lolly about Lucky and our trip, I only half-listened.

When Xander told Lolly about the night he caught some of the boys skinny-dipping in the lake, Lolly started giggling.

"When they grow up, send them our way," she suggested. "Bear Trodden Acres could use some fresh meat around here."

I couldn't help but laugh. Her lightness was contagious, and I found myself enjoying her company even more.

"Well, I hate to break up our conversation, but I'm joining some friends for a game of tennis in a few minutes. Would you two like to come watch?"

"Sure," I said, standing up.

Xander stood up and put his arm around my waist, squeezing my hip as if to send me a message. "No, actually. We have to get back to the lodge to check on the kids. Sorry we can't stay, Lolly."

After saying our goodbyes, we got back in the car and began driving down the lane toward the main road.

"Why didn't you want to stay? The kids are busy with the ropes course for a little bit longer," I asked.

"Babe, if you'd ever seen a naked tennis match, you'd understand."

~

"I'm nervous," I admitted as I waited for Xander to come around the car. I couldn't contain my goofy smile as he automatically reached for my hand. Damn, I could so get used to this.

I *would* get used to it.

Because Xander was mine.

I still couldn't believe everything he was willing to do for me… to be with me. The fact that everything was changing so fast should have scared me, but it felt like my life was finally starting. I didn't even care that my father would shit bricks when he found out that his plans for me had gone up in smoke the second Xander had told me he'd make the move to New York to be with me.

Because like I'd told Xander, I had no intention of remaining in New York.

Xander belonged in Colorado.

Which meant I did, too.

I'd fallen in love with this place as much as Xander had. It was scary as fuck to uproot my life, but I couldn't wait to do it.

The idea of being a full-time father to a sixteen-year-old kid, however, was a little more daunting.

Okay, that was the understatement of the decade.

I was absolutely terrified by the prospect.

But I also wanted it. I wanted to give Lucky what Xander's aunt had given him. The only question was, did Lucky want that?

First, I had to get Lucky to admit there was even a problem with his foster family. Between what Calvin had said and the bruise I'd seen for myself, along with some of the behavior Lucky had exhibited these past few months, I was pretty sure it was true.

"You're going to do great," Xander assured me. He pulled my hand to his mouth and kissed my knuckles. The move gave me the strength I needed. It took only a few minutes to find Lucky, because I'd called Aiden from the road and asked him to have Lucky waiting for us in the lodge's lobby. Sure enough, when we walked through the doors, Lucky was sitting in one of the leather armchairs in front of the fireplace. He was flipping through some kind of outdoor adventure magazine.

"Hey," I said as I led Xander to where Lucky was sitting. The kid jumped up and wrapped his arms around my waist. His eyes shifted to Xander's and my joined hands.

"So does this mean I can sing the song?" he asked. He opened his mouth as if to start singing right there in the lobby, so I quickly clapped my hand over it.

"Maybe later," I said. "And somewhere no one can hear you."

He nodded, his eyes bright with humor, as I released him. "I'm happy for you, B," he said as he gave me another quick hug. "Aiden said you wanted to talk to me," he added.

"Yeah, let's go for a walk, okay?"

Lucky nodded. I released Xander's hand so I could put my arm around Lucky's shoulders as we left the lodge and began walking along a path that surrounded the property. There was enough room for all three of us to walk side by side, but Xander held back just a little, presumably so Lucky wouldn't feel boxed in.

"Lucky, I wanted to talk to you about something before we go home."

"'Kay."

I spied a picnic bench a few feet ahead of us and said, "Why don't we sit?"

Once we were settled, with me sitting across from Lucky and Xander sitting next to me, I tried to figure out where to start.

"Lucky, I wanted to see how things were going with Gloria and Ed."

The second Lucky dropped his eyes and began scratching his fingernail along the edge of the wooden table, I knew.

*Fuck.*

I managed not to say a word, but Xander must have sensed something, because his fingers curled over the hand I had fisted on my thigh beneath the table. He linked his fingers with mine.

"Good," Lucky murmured.

"Are you having issues with them or any of the other kids staying there?" I knew Gloria and Ed were fostering four other kids, all younger than Lucky.

Lucky's only response was to shake his head. He still refused to look at me.

"Lucky, would you look at me?" I asked gently. When he looked up, I saw that his eyes had gone blank.

It wasn't the first time I'd seen that kind of reaction, but now I finally understood the reason for it. "You can tell me anything, Lucky."

His eyes shifted to look at the scenery around us. "It's not so bad," he finally said.

I squeezed Xander's hand hard and his thumb began tracing patterns into my skin. The move helped, since I had nothing else to occupy my hands like I normally did when I got anxious. I took a deep breath and focused on his touch for a few more seconds before saying, "Are they hurting you?"

Lucky refused to look at me as he spoke. "Sometimes they forget, you know?"

"Who?" I asked. "Forget what?"

He returned his eyes to the table. "The younger kids. They don't always remember the rules. Ed gets mad 'cause he likes it quiet when he gets home from work."

"When Ed gets mad at the younger kids, do you do something to make him madder?" Xander asked.

Lucky hesitated and then nodded. I squeezed Xander's hand so hard, I was shocked he didn't make a sound.

I wanted to cry. To know the kid I'd helped get off the streets had ended up in a situation that was nearly as bad as the one he'd been in broke my heart. And it didn't surprise me in the least that he'd put himself in harm's way to protect the younger kids in the house.

"I'm sorry, Lucky," I said softly. "I wanted to protect you—"

"It ain't bad, B," Lucky quickly interjected as he straightened. "It ain't all the time like it was with Mom and Jerry."

My throat felt too tight to speak and I looked helplessly at Xander. He squeezed my hand and then looked at Lucky. "Lucky, it's not about settling for the lesser of two evils. You and all those other kids deserve to feel safe and wanted and loved."

I reached across the table to cover Lucky's hand with mine. "I'll fix it when we get home, Lucky. I promise."

His eyes held mine for a moment. "I know you will, B. You always take care of us... like we're your real kids or something."

I felt tears stinging the backs of my eyes, but I managed to keep them at bay. "That's something else I wanted to talk to you about." I had to muster up the courage to continue because I was suddenly afraid Lucky would turn me down. When the hell had I already started to think of him as my kid?

I glanced at Xander and he nodded.

*Our* kid.

"Lucky, I was wondering if you might want to come live with me and Xander for a while. Well... not for a while," I babbled.

His eyes widened and he leaned back. "For real?"

Xander and I both nodded at the same time.

"So, you'd like, be my foster parents?"

"Um, no, not exactly. We... we want something more permanent. We were hoping... if you were okay with it, that is... that you might let us adopt you."

Lucky's eyes shifted back and forth between me and Xander. "You — you'd be my dads? Both of you?"

"Yeah, we would," Xander said. "Bennett would adopt you initially, but once he and I are married, I'd adopt you too."

I jerked my head to look at Xander. We hadn't talked about

marriage, but even hearing it on his lips, and said with such certainty, had my insides doing a happy dance.

*He wants to marry me.*

"You don't have to make a decision now," I quickly said as I forced my eyes back to Lucky. "There are a lot of details to work out with Children's Services to make sure I qualify and stuff, but I started making some calls and it looks really good."

"So, I'd live with you and still go to the same school and stuff?"

"Um, in the beginning, yes. But we'd probably end up leaving New York to come live out here," I said.

I felt Xander squeeze my fingers again, and I knew why. He kept seeing us living in Colorado as some kind of sacrifice on my part. So I turned to him to remind him of the same thing I'd said over and over this morning when we'd talked about what the future held for us.

"Remember what I said, babe. This is your home. New York will never be to me what this place is to you," I explained. "Hell, Greenwich hasn't even been that for me… not after you left."

He nodded and then leaned over to kiss me. "I love you," he said softly against my mouth.

"Love you too."

"Geez, are you guys gonna be playing kissy-face all the time when I come live with you? 'Cause I'm telling you now, watching your dads make out is not cool."

It took Lucky's words a moment to register. "Does… does that mean you're saying yes?"

He was barely done nodding when I reached him and pulled him into my arms. "Love you," I said as I kissed the top of his head. Xander was there a moment later, his big arms surrounding us both.

And fuck if it didn't feel like I was finally exactly where I was meant to be for the first time in my life.

# CHAPTER 37

## XANDER

Three weeks back in New York, and I was already going stir-crazy. I missed the fresh air and clean expanse of the mountains, and the feeling of pavement underneath my boots instead of dirt, rocks and grass felt wrong to me. But I'd been handsomely rewarded for giving up that part of my life, even for a little while.

Because I got to wake up in Bennett's arms every morning, and the last thing I felt every night before I fell asleep was his warm body pressed up against my side.

Upon returning to New York, Bennett had started the ball rolling on getting temporary custody of Lucky. His previous work with Children's Services through his company's foundation had proven to be an asset in fast-tracking the process of removing Lucky and the other kids from their foster home. We'd been worried that Lucky would have to spend some time in a group home or another foster home and had prepared him for that. But we'd caught a break when Bennett had gotten temporary custody of him. We'd both taken the required foster parenting courses in case that was the route we'd end up needing to go if the adoption couldn't be pushed through quickly, but Bennett was doing all the legal stuff on his own.

It wasn't ideal, since I'd already started to think of Lucky as mine, but I knew we couldn't rush into making our own relationship legal, because that could likely cause issues down the line. Additionally, we figured with me still legally living in Colorado, it would just slow things down if we both applied to adopt Lucky at the same time. Lucky himself had more say in his future since he was sixteen. He'd already met with representatives from Children's Services twice—once to talk about what Ed Durant had done to him and the other kids, and once to assure them he was completely on board with the adoption.

While the adoption might only take a couple more months, Bennett and I had talked the night before about staying in New York through the following spring so Lucky could finish out his sophomore year. I couldn't say I was thrilled about staying in the city for so long, but I'd decided to make use of my time by taking some courses in business management. Bennett and I had decided to purchase the lodge as well as the wilderness expedition business together. I'd balked at the idea of Bennett putting part of his savings towards buying Gary out, but he'd reminded me that it would be *our* business. We hadn't ironed out all the details yet, but the bottom line was that Bennett and I would be working together to make the business everything it could be.

And I couldn't wait.

For his part, Bennett was struggling with how to tell his parents both about our relationship and the fact that he wouldn't be taking over his father's company. His anger at his father for the role he'd played in splitting us up as kids had made him want to drive right out to Greenwich the moment we'd stepped off the plane, but I'd reminded him that he needed to deal with the foundation first. Knowing his father, the man would punish Bennett for his defection by taking it out on the kids Bennett loved so much.

The way Bennett had explained it, the foundation was currently more of a pet project for the investment firm. Bennett's goal was to actually have the foundation become its own entity sponsored by several companies in addition to The Crawford Group. He wanted the foundation to stand on its own so it could get donations and support from multiple sources in the community and help even more at-risk kids. But to do that, he needed his father to throw in his support long enough to ink the deal with the other potential sponsors.

That deal was happening today.

At this very moment, my man was preparing to go before a group of thirty representatives from some of the most successful companies in the city to pitch them his idea. If he was successful, he'd get enough support to finally break free of the leverage his father continued to wield over him. In as little as a few days, my Benny could finally be loose of the chains he'd worn around his neck for so long.

"Xander, you home?"

"In here, Lucky," I called as I turned the stove down to keep from burning dinner. Bear, who'd been lying by my feet, jumped up and took off towards the front door. I'd been lucky enough to have a friend drive Bear out east with him on his way to meet up with family in Boston, which meant I'd been able to fly out with Bennett, Lucky and the rest of the group.

The dog returned moments later, happily trailing Lucky who dropped his backpack onto the kitchen table and flopped down into one of the chairs. He dropped his cheek on his hand and stared into space.

"Uh oh," I said as I went to the fridge and pulled out two cans of soda. "What happened?" I asked as I slid into the chair next to him and placed the can in front of him.

"Can we just move already?" he asked.

I sighed. "What did he do this time?"

"Nothing," Lucky muttered. "Literally nothing."

Despite the kiss Bennett and I had seen Lucky and Calvin share, whatever had been blooming between the boys seemed to have run its course, at least on Calvin's side. During the remainder of the trip in Colorado, things between Lucky and Calvin had gone well and there'd been no more fights or Calvin talking shit about Lucky. Lucky had even felt confident enough to confide in us that Calvin had kissed him. But if the older boy had felt anything, it hadn't lasted. As soon as we'd stepped off the plane in New York, Calvin had iced Lucky out.

To Lucky's heartbreaking disappointment.

The only good thing was that Calvin hadn't resumed his cruel taunting of the younger boy either.

So, there was that at least.

"Did you try talking to him?" I asked.

Since I was the one home when Lucky finished school, I was often the first to hear about his problems. When Bennett got home, we usually discussed things over dinner as a family. After learning Calvin had been ignoring Lucky completely in the three weeks since we'd arrived, Bennett and I had suggested Lucky try to pull Calvin aside to try to talk to him.

Lucky nodded miserably. "Said he was too busy. I thought maybe if I told him we could talk someplace where no one would see us, he'd go for it."

While I wasn't exactly worried that Calvin might hurt Lucky if they were alone together, I couldn't discount the fact that something else could happen between the two of them. And while it freaked me out that someone as young as Lucky could be engaging in any kind of sexual activity, I wasn't completely naive either.

"Um, Lucky, we should probably talk about that…"

"About what?" he asked.

"Yeah… um… being alone with a guy you like."

"What, you mean like how we're alone right now?" he asked, curiously.

"What? No!" I nearly shouted, but then I caught the smile that flitted across his mouth. "Little shit," I said as I gently punched his shoulder.

"Don't worry. B already had 'the talk' with me."

"He did?"

Lucky nodded. "Last year. He used a cucumber to demonstrate… you know."

I laughed. "A cucumber?"

"Yeah. You should've seen him. It was a really big cucumber."

I smiled at that. I could envision Bennett getting all flustered as he tried to explain the facts of life to a teenage boy while working a too-small condom over a too-big cucumber.

"Ok, carry on then," I said with a wave of my hand.

Lucky's face fell. "He hates me," he said.

"He doesn't hate you, Lucky. My guess is he's not ready to face some things about himself."

"Yeah," Lucky said with a sigh. "I just thought..."

"What?"

"I thought he might be the one, you know?"

"Yeah, I know," I said as I put my hand over his arm. "But maybe the one is still out there for you. Could be you'll meet him tomorrow or next week or next month or next year. Could be you don't meet him for a lot of years. But believe me, it'll be worth the wait."

"Like you and B had to wait?"

"Exactly," I said. "Doesn't matter how many years you lose, the ones you share are the ones that'll stay with you."

The boy nodded and then he stood. "I should go get started on homework."

"Okay, dinner will be ready in a bit."

"B's doing his thing tonight, huh?"

"Yeah, he'll be home late. We'll go ahead and eat without him."

Lucky nodded, and then suddenly he leaned over and hugged me. "Glad you're here, X."

I smiled at the nickname. "Me too, buddy."

Once he and Bear were gone, I climbed to my feet and began pulling ingredients for salad from the fridge. Just as I began searching for the serving bowl, my phone rang. I assumed it was Bennett calling for another pep talk, or to yell at me for the suggestive text I'd sent to remind him what was waiting for him when he got home tonight besides his favorite meal.

But I didn't recognize the number.

"Hello?"

"Hello, is this Xander?"

"Yes, who's this?"

I didn't recognize the voice. The man's voice sounded shaky. "Um, it's Steve… Steve Patterson. I run Bear Trodden Acres."

I stiffened. There was only one reason he could be calling me.

"What happened? Is my aunt okay?"

"Xander, I'm sorry, there was an accident."

I felt my throat close up. Heat washed over me as I leaned hard against the counter to keep myself upright.

"Is she…"

I couldn't even say it.

"She's still alive, son, but they had to use Flight for Life to get her out of here."

I barely registered him telling me that a car had sideswiped the van she and some of the other residents had been riding in. "Where… where is she?"

"They took her to St. Elizabeth's in Denver. I tried calling there before I called you, but they wouldn't tell me anything over the phone. I'm so sorry, Xander."

I didn't even remember responding to him before I hung up. With shaky fingers, I pulled up the browser on my phone. It seemed to take forever to find the number. My knees felt weak, so I stumbled to one of the kitchen chairs as I hit the dial button.

*Please god, don't let me lose her too.*

It took forever for someone to answer on the other end, and I was immediately put on hold. When a young woman came on the line, I didn't even let her finish her greeting. "Yes, I need some information on a patient. Lois Reed. She was brought there by Flight for Life… she was in a car accident. I'm her nephew."

"One moment, please."

As the seconds dragged on, I could feel the tears coursing down my cheeks.

She was alive. She had to be.

"Sir, what's your name?" came a man's voice over the line.

"Xander Reed," I croaked. "Lolly is my aunt."

"Mr. Reed, your aunt arrived twenty minutes ago and was rushed directly to surgery. I'm sorry, but I don't have an update for you at this time."

"But… she's alive?"

"She's alive."

"I'm in New York… I'll catch the next flight out. Can you call me if you hear something? I'll use the Wi-Fi on the plane to check my email."

"Of course. Give me your number and your email address."

My tongue felt thick as I gave him the information and hung up.

Bennett. I needed Bennett. I began dialing, but stopped before hitting the send button. I knew that he'd drop everything to be by my side, but the cost was just too high. From everything he'd said, his presentation was a one-shot deal. It had taken months to get all these people together in one room. The kids who benefited from all the hard work Bennett had done were counting on him to make this happen. As badly as I needed him, they needed him more.

"Lucky!" I called as I wiped at my eyes and stood. I turned off the stove and hurried to Bennett's and my room, making plans in my head as I went.

Mostly so I wouldn't have to think what it would mean if I lost the only woman who'd ever been a real mother to me.

# CHAPTER 38

## BENNETT

*Kiss their asses, then come home and take mine.*

I could feel the heat rising in my cheeks as I reread Xander's text. I was going to have fun punishing him for sending me such a provocative message. It had been on the forefront of my mind for the last two hours as I'd prepared my speech. And the image of Xander lying face down on our bed, his gorgeous backside waiting for me, was all I could think about even as my father introduced me to various men and women in the room.

I still had a few minutes before I had to get up on the raised platform in front of the room and tell these people why they should help me build an organization to do good on a greater scale. The fact that it was also the key to getting me away from the man next to me for good was an added benefit. But regardless of how my pitch went, I'd find another way to make sure the kids weren't left in the lurch. Even if it meant finding other organizations to carry the load.

Because I had no doubt my father would pull the foundation from my control as soon as he found out Xander and I were building a future together.

"Bennett, pay attention," my father snapped. In the past, his irritation would have left me scrambling to get back on his good side, but tonight, it just pissed me the fuck off. How the hell had I spent so many years falling all over myself to be who this man wanted me to be?

"Gerald, this is my son, Bennett. Bennett, this is Gerald Mulvaney, head of—"

"Mulvaney Communications," I interjected. "Thank you so much for coming."

The older man nodded as he shook my hand. "Looking forward to hearing what you have in mind, Bennett," he said. "Mulvaney Communications is always looking for ways to have a greater impact on the community."

"Glad to hear it, Sir," I said.

I watched as the man wandered off to talk to some of the other patrons.

"I have to commend you, Bennett."

The remark was unexpected and I hated that, despite the fact that I was so pissed at him, a little part of me puffed up at my father's comment. He'd only ever seen the work I'd done with the foundation in terms of how good it would make the company look. Like the foundation also doing some good in the world would somehow deflect from the fact that my father's firm was about making already rich people richer.

"Getting all these potential clients in one room… a lot of new business to be had here, Son."

Disbelief went through me. "Dad," I said as I shook my head. "I didn't bring them here to—"

"Arnold!" my father called robustly as he took off to greet the next man who walked through the door. I felt sick to my stomach and automatically reached for my phone to call Xander. If I could just hear his voice, I could keep it together long enough to cement this deal and ensure kids like Lucky had the support they needed after I left New York.

The thought of my new family waiting for me to come home was enough to ease some of the tension in my belly. I already had my phone in my hand, so I turned it over to check for any new, dirty messages my man might have sent me.

But the only messages I saw were from Aiden, along with a few missed calls. Panic went through me, but before I could call him, I heard his voice.

"Bennett!"

I looked up to see Aiden and Lucky near a side door, but there was no sign of Xander.

Why would Aiden have Lucky unless something bad had happened?

"Where is he?" I called out as I hurried towards them. "What's wrong? Is he okay?" I asked as I grabbed Aiden's arm.

*Please, God, don't let me lose him. Not now. Not like this.*

"He's okay," Aiden said quickly.

I nearly buckled at the knees as a tidal wave of relief went through me. "Jesus, don't fucking do that to me," I griped. "Where is he?"

"It's his aunt," Lucky said.

"Lolly?" I asked, as anxiety curled through me. "Did something happen to her?"

"She's been in a car accident, B. Some guy phoned Xander about an hour ago to tell him and I guess they took her right into surgery or something. Xander brought Lucky and Bear to my place before heading to the airport."

"Fuck," I said. "I have to go. Which airport?"

"La Guardia."

I hadn't gotten more than a few steps when my father called my name. I turned to see him striding towards me. His eyes settled on Aiden.

"Mr. Vale, what are you doing here?" my father bit out impatiently.

He'd always ignored my friendship with Aiden, but that was mostly because he never saw us together. He may not have approved of Aiden's sexuality, but he sure as hell would have been happy enough to invest Aiden's money for him.

God, I'd been such a fucking fool. Why had I ever thought this man's opinion mattered?

"He came to give me some news... about Xander."

"Xander? Xander Reed?"

"Yes."

My father's eyes went from disinterested to ice cold, just like that. He hadn't even spared Lucky a glance.

Like he wasn't there.

And I knew why. I glanced at Lucky and then stepped forward and grabbed my father's arm to pull him aside. A look at Aiden showed that he knew what I was doing and he went up to Lucky to make sure the young man didn't follow and overhear what I was about to say.

"Do you really not see him, Dad?" I asked angrily as I motioned in Lucky's direction with my chin. "Has your bigotry made you that blind?"

"Son, this is neither the time nor place for you to be bringing one of your... projects," he said as he took several steps back to put some space with us and pasted a false smile on his face as he tried to hide his obvious distaste. He looked around at the men and women who'd gathered for the foundation meeting.

A feeling of calm washed over me as I stared at the man who'd sired me, but hadn't ever been my father. The only father I'd ever even come close to having had died fifteen years ago.

"Lucky's not a project. He's my son. He's been mine in my heart from the moment I met him, and just as soon as I can make it happen, he'll be mine on paper too. Mine and Xander's."

I had the satisfaction of watching my father turn a sickly shade of white. "What are you talking about?

"I'm talking about my life— the one you've been manipulating from day one. I know what you did the night Xander's dad died. His aunt told me you kicked her out of the house and had Xander's scholarship pulled, even though I did exactly what you asked of me."

"That boy wasn't good for you, Bennett. And his father—"

"Don't do it," I warned, raising my voice. "Don't you dare."

I stepped forward, fists clenched, before I even realized it. Aiden appeared at my side and then quickly stepped in front of me. "B," he said softly. "He's not worth it."

I nodded, because he was right. "Can you keep Lucky with you, Aiden? I need to go to the airport."

"Yep, we'll be fine. Go." He handed me a small overnight bag. "I packed some of my clothes for you. They'll be a little big, but—"

"I'll make do," I said as I took the bag and hugged him.

"Bennett, you walk out of this room and it's over. Your career, the foundation," my father warned in a low voice.

"I don't need you in order to help others," I snapped. "So do your worst."

My father stepped forward until he was practically in my face and hissed, "You leave and I'll make sure none of these people throw even a nickel in your direction. What will those charity kids of yours have then?"

"Excuse me."

The feedback from the room's audio system caused me to look over to the stage where Lucky stood in front of a microphone stand that was just a little too high for him. The few people in the crowd still standing slowly sat down, and I saw several of the participants looking around in confusion.

"Young man, that's not a toy," my father stated firmly, but the second he took a step towards the stage, I stepped in front of him.

"Stay the hell away from my kid."

I didn't care that I barely recognized my own voice as I spoke. All I cared about was my father staring at me like he didn't know who I was.

Thank fucking god for that.

"Um, you all should give B… I mean Bennett… the money 'cause he can help a lot of kids with it." As Lucky spoke, he glanced at me. "Kids like me."

My heart swelled with pride as I watched Lucky stand there, confidence on full display, the quiet boy he'd once been, a thing of the past. Even in the few weeks he'd come to live with Xander and me, we'd started to see a change in him. I ignored my father and stepped onto the platform, wrapping my arms around Lucky.

"Thank you, Lucky."

"Love you, B."

"Love you, too." I held him for a moment longer and then ruffled his hair. I put my arm around his shoulder as I addressed the crowd.

"I'm sorry, but I need to go. There's an emergency with my boyfriend's family, and I need to be with him. But I'll leave you in the very capable hands of my associate here." I patted Lucky's shoulder and then gave him another quick hug before whispering in his ear. "Xander and I will call you as soon as we land, okay?"

Lucky nodded. "Don't worry, I'll keep an eye on Bear. And Aiden."

I smiled and said, "I have no doubt."

Aiden had moved up onto the platform at some point, and I exchanged a silent message with him. He nodded.

Yeah, he'd keep my kid safe. "Thank you," I said as I embraced him. "For everything."

He nodded against my neck. "Go take care of your man, Bennett. We're good here."

I stifled the emotion that threatened to consume me. "You're one hell of a man, Aiden," I murmured into his ear. "I hope whatever guy ends up snagging your heart sees that." I kissed his cheek and then I was hurrying off stage. I had to pass by my father who practically simmered with rage, but when he grabbed my arm, I shook it off and didn't slow my pace.

Because at that point, he'd ceased to exist.

The only thing that would keep me from being at Xander's side was goddamned Armageddon.

# CHAPTER 39

## XANDER

The only thing keeping me from yelling at the people filing down the plane's narrow aisle as they searched out their seats was the distraction I'd managed to find just outside the window. I'd spent the last ten minutes counting the various pieces of luggage as they went up the conveyor belt and were loaded into the belly of the jet parked next to ours. After I'd dropped Lucky and Bear off with Aiden, I'd been fortunate enough to catch a plane leaving La Guardia for Denver in less than two hours.

Aiden had told me several times to call Bennett, but I'd adamantly refused. It had taken a lot of begging and pleading on my part to get him to promise me he wouldn't tell Bennett what had happened until after Bennett was done giving his speech. I knew Bennett would be pissed, but he'd understand when he had some time to think about it.

"Okay folks, we're holding the cabin door for one more passenger. It should just be another few minutes before we're on our way. Thank you for your patience."

I wanted to rail at the flight attendant making the announcement to just leave the jackass behind, but I held my tongue. The flight wasn't overly full, and I'd been lucky enough to get the entire row at the back of the plane to myself, a fact I was grateful for since I hadn't been able to stem the occasional tear that slipped unbidden from my eyes.

I forced myself to take deep breaths as I watched rain begin to pelt the window. The plane next to us was all closed up, so I began searching for something else to distract myself with.

"Ladies and gentlemen, we're closing the door now in preparation for takeoff. Please stow your belongings..."

I only half-listened as the flight attendant began going through the rules. I drummed my fingers on the armrest as I watched the rain start to come down in sheets. I hoped the weather wouldn't mean a delay of any kind.

I felt rather than saw someone drop down in the seat next to me. I barely managed to temper myself as I realized it had to be the jackass the plane had been held for. The jerk hadn't even sat down in the aisle seat so we could have the middle one open between us.

I reminded myself to take a deep breath before turning to confront the asshat. But before I could say or do anything, warm fingers closed around mine.

Fingers I knew better than I knew my own.

Fingers that had brought me more pleasure and comfort in the past month than I'd ever known in my entire life.

Before I could stop myself, I began to cry.

He'd come.

My Benny had come.

"Shhh," Bennett whispered as he leaned across the armrest at the same time his hand came out to cup the side of my head so he could tug me against him. I managed to keep my cries quiet as I clung to him. His lips skimmed my temple and he began whispering all sorts of things in my ear.

How much he loved me.

That everything was going to be okay.

That he wasn't going anywhere.

The plane had started heading for the runway by the time I managed to pull myself together. I lifted my head and Bennett brushed his mouth over mine before using his sleeve to wipe at my face. If the people on the other side of the aisle noticed, I didn't care.

Because Bennett was here.

"You're here," I said softly.

He smiled that sweet, gentle, Bennett smile. "Where else would I be?"

"The kids," I said.

"The kids need *me,* not what my father is offering. There are people out there who want to help because it's the right thing to do, not because it looks good on the company brochure or tax returns. I'll find those people, and I'll get them on board and I'll do it all on my own. But not tonight. Tonight, I need to be with my family."

I nodded and wiped at my eyes.

"Have you heard anything about Lolly?"

"Yeah, the hospital called me right before I boarded. She's out of surgery and in intensive care. She's got a broken leg and lots of cuts and bruises, but they said she'll be okay."

"Thank fuck," Bennett said. "Aiden said they had to operate."

"A piece of metal got lodged in her chest, so they needed to perform surgery to remove it. It didn't damage any of her organs, luckily. They said she'll make a full recovery. She should be awake by the time we get there."

"Oh, baby, that's so great," he said, and then he was kissing my temple. "How are you holding up?"

"Better now," I admitted as I clutched his hand.

"You do know you're in deep shit for not calling me, right?" he asked as he tucked my hair behind my ears.

"Those kids mean everything to you, Bennett."

"No, Xander, *you* mean everything to me. You and Lucky—you're my family and you always come first." He covered our joined hands with his other hand and began massaging the skin by my thumb joint. "Promise me you'll never doubt that again."

He was right. There'd been a small part of me that had thought maybe he'd put the kids above me. And it was something I'd been okay with, because the kids needed him more.

But in the hour that I'd had to wait to hear back from the hospital, I'd been as lost as I'd been the night my father had died. And I'd needed Bennett just as badly as I'd needed him back then. I just hadn't had the courage to tell him that. I knew just by looking at him that my lack of trust had hurt him.

I clasped the side of his head and pulled him to me until our foreheads were touching. "Never again, Benny. I promise."

I kissed him and then dropped my head on his shoulder. "How did things go with your father?"

"As predicted," Bennett murmured. "Felt good to finally tell the fucker off." I felt him shift and I lifted my head. "And there's this..."

Bennett unlocked his phone and pulled up a picture. It was of Lucky and an older man with salt and pepper hair. There was something oddly familiar about him. Aiden was in the background, and I chuckled when I realized he was giving Lucky bunny ears.

"What is this?" I asked.

"Turns out our son is quite the charmer," Bennett said. Hearing him refer to Lucky as ours made something inside my belly flip-flop. We hadn't talked about whether or not more kids were in our future, but I knew without a shadow of a doubt they would be.

"Aiden said he had the crowd eating out of his hand after I left. On the cab ride to the airport, I got three emails from potential sponsors saying they were in."

I looked at the picture again. "Wait... is that... the mayor of New York?"

"It is," Bennett said with a laugh.

"Our kid got the mayor to take a selfie with him?" I shook my head. "Man, he's going to be a handful, isn't he?"

Bennett snuggled against me. "He is. I can't fucking wait, either."

"Me neither."

We were both quiet for a few minutes as the flight pulled onto the runway and began rolling forward, quickly picking up speed. I'd never been a great flier, despite having done it so often in my life. I wasn't surprised when Bennett picked up on it and tightened his hold on my hand.

"Hey Xander?"

"Yeah?"

*"Do you wanna build a snowman?"* he suddenly sang, loud enough for the people around us to hear.

I began laughing so hard that I barely noticed as the plane bumped along the runway before finally lifting off the ground. And by the time the plane had leveled off, Bennett had quietly sung all of the songs from *Frozen* in my ear.

Twice.

# EPILOGUE

BENNETT

***Eight Months Later***

"Jesus," I moaned. Xander pressed me against the cool tile wall of the shower as his cock began slowly gliding in and out of me. His hands covered mine where they were pressed against the wall, and he automatically linked our fingers.

"Nope, just me," Xander said right before he closed his teeth over my earlobe. His big body was covering mine from shoulder to ass, keeping the water from hitting me. But it didn't matter because his body heat was warming me in ways no shower or blanket ever could.

"Dork," I said with a laugh. "Hurry up and fuck me or we're going to be late."

His tongue licked the outer shell of my ear as he slowed his strokes even more. "We really need to do something about that bossy mouth of yours," he murmured.

I shivered as I imagined all the things he could do to my mouth. I turned my head so I could look at him over my shoulder. All thoughts of being late fled as I stared into his beautiful blue eyes. "I know how you can start," I said. Lust coiled in my belly as he rolled his hips against my ass, driving his dick deeper inside of me and hitting my gland. His lips closed over mine just as I groaned in pleasure.

"Love you so much, Benny," he whispered against my mouth.

The time for joking fled as he began driving into me in hard, smooth thrusts. With nothing to hold onto for leverage, I was completely reliant on him to keep me upright as he fucked me.

But it was just like with every other struggle we'd faced these past eight months.

We held each other up.

We took care of each other.

We loved each other.

"Love you," I said as I felt my orgasm charging up my spine. Xander's breath was hot and heavy in my ear as he held me in the tightest grip imaginable. His body pummeled mine, but I'd never felt safer or more cherished.

"My Benny," he said softly. The words set off my orgasm and he followed seconds later, his release filling me. I felt boneless as the rush of pleasure began to fade, but Xander kept his arms around me to keep me from falling. He pulled free of me and then maneuvered us so the water was hitting me. By the time he'd finished cleaning me off, my legs no longer felt like jelly, and I managed to turn in his arms so I could give him a proper good morning kiss.

"Morning," I said between soft kisses.

"Morning," he responded drowsily.

I reluctantly pulled free of his hold. "Better hurry it up or Lolly will drive herself," I said. "Remember to knock really loud this time."

Xander groaned in my ear. "Don't remind me," he groaned as he dropped his forehead to my shoulder.

I laughed. Xander had decided to drive up to Bear Trodden Acres the weekend before to surprise Lolly with the fact that we'd arrived in Colorado a few days early. He'd seen her car in the parking lot, so when she hadn't answered the door, he'd started to worry that there was a reason she *couldn't* get to it and he'd let himself into the apartment.

And gotten an eyeful.

Seeing your aunt naked on a frequent basis was bad enough, but seeing her getting pleasured by a sixty-something-year old man on the coffee table was entirely another.

I kissed his cheek and then stepped out of the shower and quickly dried off. I nearly tripped over Bear when I opened the bathroom door. The dog always slept with Lucky, but when it came time for breakfast, he never failed to search me out since I was typically the first one up each morning. The animal sent me a baleful look like he knew what Xander and I had been doing.

"If you still had certain body parts, you'd understand," I said to the dog as I padded to the dresser to slip on my clothes. Bear followed me from the room, so I fed him first before getting the coffee going. Once I'd let him outside, I hurried to Lucky's room.

"Come on, buddy, time to get up," I called as I flipped on the lights and pulled the cover off his bed. I tossed it to the floor before going to the window and drawing back the curtain.

"Too early," he groaned as he covered his head with a pillow.

"I'm leaving in fifteen minutes. If you aren't in the car with me, I'll assume you're going with Xander to pick up Aunt Lolly."

"I'm up," Lucky said as he tossed the pillow aside and sat up.

I chuckled. "Thought so."

"Hey B," Lucky called just before I left the room.

"Yeah?"

I stopped in the doorway. Lucky had turned seventeen a month earlier, and I couldn't get over how much he'd changed. He'd grown taller and filled out, and while he was still lean, the many weekends we'd spent hiking in the Catskills had given him quite a bit of muscle definition. But even though he'd changed physically, he still carried some of the same insecurities that came with the trauma he'd faced as a child.

It hadn't quite been a year since he'd come to live with us, but there were times where he still seemed to worry that we were going to change our minds about him being ours. It wasn't so much that he said anything; it was in the way he behaved. He was always on his best behavior, and if he did something he perceived as bad, like breaking a dish or getting a less than stellar grade on a test or report card, there'd be this silent plea in his eyes as he apologized or told us he could do better.

Xander and I hoped it was something he'd eventually outgrow. In the meantime, we did anything and everything we could to remind Lucky on a daily basis that he was loved unconditionally and here to stay.

Lucky fidgeted for a moment. "You think they'll like me?"

"Who?" I asked as I moved farther into the room.

"Nothing. Never mind... it's stupid."

Deflection was another Lucky trademark. I went to sit down on the bed next to him. "Who?" I repeated, though I suspected who he was talking about.

When he didn't say anything, I asked, "You mean the kids out here?"

He nodded.

Even though school didn't start for a few months, Lucky had been stressing about not making friends long before we'd left New York. While he'd had an okay year at his previous school, he'd continued to feel the sting of losing Calvin. His feelings for the other boy hadn't waned like we'd hoped they would. Our hope was that some distance would help, and if we were really lucky, he'd meet someone else out here who could take his mind off his first crush.

"I think they're going to see the same things Xander and I do. That you're an amazing kid, Lucky. And they'd be damned lucky to be friends with you."

Lucky nodded. "Yeah, I guess."

I leaned my shoulder against his to give him a little bump. "Did you see what I did there? They'd be *lucky* to be friends with you..."

"God, you're such a weirdo, B," he said, his voice sounding a little lighter.

I put my arm around him and gave him a quick kiss on the top of the head. I knew he was probably too old for the displays of affection, but as long as he continued to indulge me, I'd keep on doing it. Anything to make it clear to him how much he was loved.

"Get moving, or the only muffins you'll be seeing this morning aren't the good kind."

"Jesus, gross, B."

I laughed and gave him another gentle shove before I climbed to my feet. After grabbing a cup of coffee from the kitchen, I did my normal routine and went outside to sit on the porch steps so I could enjoy the view. The sight of the morning mist rising over the trees never failed to remind me how drastically my life had changed in the past year. I still cringed whenever I thought of how easily I could have lost Xander forever.

If I'd chosen some other wilderness expedition company to act as our guide for that week.

If I'd lost him to the waters of the raging river.

If I hadn't had the strength to beg him to give me another chance to prove we were meant to be together.

It had all just been too damn close.

But someone or something had been watching out for us. I knew Xander didn't believe in that kind of stuff, but I did. There was just no other way to explain us finding each other again.

Motion to my right drew my attention, and I saw Bear darting into the tree line after something near Jake's cabin. He reappeared a moment later with a large stick and ambled up to where Jake stood on his porch. We hadn't seen Jake since the previous fall when Xander and I had flown to Colorado after Lolly's accident.

Jake's eyes met mine briefly and he nodded at me, but that was it. It would have been easier to ignore him and the entire situation, but I'd learned that nothing good came from pretending. I'd done that my whole life and it had nearly cost me everything.

I climbed to my feet and made my way to Jake's cabin. He continued to throw the stick for Bear, and as I got closer, the dog brought me the stick. I tossed it for him just as I reached the bottom of the steps. Jake's cabin looked almost identical to Xander's, though he'd done some work on his porch to make it larger. The sight of the single chair on the porch saddened me, though I wasn't sure why.

"Morning," I said.

He nodded at me. "You guys back for good?" he asked.

"Yeah, we arrived last weekend. Moving truck hasn't gotten here yet, though. We're actually moving to town. It'll be easier for Lucky to get to school that way... and for us to run the business."

Another nod. The man clearly wasn't in the mood to talk, and I was half-tempted to turn around and go home. This man had feelings for Xander and even though he'd never acted on them, it still made me somewhat uncomfortable. I knew I was it for Xander, but knowing this good-looking guy felt something more than mere attraction every time he looked at my man just weirded me out.

I didn't want it to be that way.

Despite everything, Jake meant a lot to Xander, and I suspected the friendship was important to Jake as well.

"Xander's stopped by a couple of times to talk to you about staying on with the company. And to make sure you were coming to Gary's retirement party today," I said.

We'd completed the purchase of the lodge and wilderness expedition business a few days earlier. Xander and I had spent the past eight months working on everything we'd need to make the business ours. Included in the purchase had been a small house near the lodge which we were set to move into in a couple of days when the movers arrived.

"Been busy," Jake murmured as he tucked his hands in his pockets.

*Fuck, I should just go. He doesn't want me here.*

I ignored the thought and climbed the stairs. No way I was letting Xander lose his friend over this. "I know this must be incredibly hard for you," I began. "To see him with me—"

"It's not," he cut in. "It's... it's good to see him so happy." Jake glanced at our cabin briefly before dropping his eyes to where Bear lay at the foot of the stairs chewing on the stick. "I knew the night he told me about you that there would never be anyone that could hold a candle to you. Even if I'd been in a position to act on my feelings, I wouldn't have... he never would have been okay with settling."

I understood what he was saying. I'd done the same with Aiden when I'd started dating him. I'd tried to make him fit a mold that had been created solely for Xander. It hadn't been fair to Aiden or to me.

"I'm sorry, Jake."

"Nothing to be sorry for," he said. "Things worked out exactly as they were meant to."

"Why didn't you tell him how you felt?" I asked. "Why not take the chance? You couldn't have known I was going to show up one day. He told me what you said to him about life being too short not to say what you mean..."

Jake sighed and then settled his eyes on me. "I don't know the details about what happened between you two when you were kids, but whatever it was, I know it had to hurt like hell."

I nodded because the emotion clogging up my throat prevented me from speaking. Despite putting the past behind us, the memory of that night was still raw. I suspected it would be a good long while before that sensation disappeared altogether.

"Not everyone is as strong as you guys, Bennett. Not everyone is willing to risk their heart again... not even when the perfect opportunity presents itself."

His eyes drifted to our cabin again before shifting back to the view in front of him.

"You lost someone," I said as understanding dawned. He didn't answer and I didn't expect him to. But I did see his body stiffen just a little bit.

An awkward silence fell between us and I knew I should go. I began walking down the steps, but stopped when I reached the bottom. I didn't look at him when I said, "He misses you, Jake."

When he didn't respond, I said to Bear, "Come on, boy." The dog jumped up, grabbed his stick and trotted ahead of me.

"Bennett."

I stopped and looked over my shoulder at Jake.

"Can I bring anything to the party?"

"Yeah," I said. "Some of that weird homemade beer crap that Xander likes so much. He says it's your secret recipe."

Jake chuckled and nodded. "You got it."

I hid my smile long enough so he wouldn't see it and hurried back to the cabin. Just as I reached the bottom step, Lucky came tearing out the front door, clothes askew. "Oh thank god!" he said when he saw me. "I thought I missed you."

I chuckled and climbed the stairs. I slapped him on the back and said, "Go get the keys. You're driving."

"Yes!" he shouted just before he turned and ran back into the house. Lucky still only had his learner's permit, but in a matter of weeks, he'd be taking the test to get his license. Another sign he was growing up too damned fast.

As I followed him into the cabin, I glanced at Jake's cabin one more time. His eyes met mine across the expanse between the two buildings, and I saw him nod before he went back inside.

It wasn't much.

But it was a start.

~

Only a few guests had arrived at the party by the time Xander showed up with Lolly. She had her arm through Xander's as they walked and she was speaking softly to him. After the accident, Xander had spent several weeks in Colorado caring for his aunt until she'd practically ordered him to go home. Lucky and I had flown out once over a weekend, but with Lucky being in school, we hadn't had the option of staying with Xander to help him take care of Lolly.

It had turned out that Lolly had found her very own knight in shining armor in Steve, the director of the nudist colony. He'd been the one to call Xander after the accident, and had been a regular visitor to the hospital, as well as after she'd arrived home. He'd also been the bare-assed guy showing Lolly a good time when Xander had walked into Lolly's apartment the weekend before.

As expected, Lolly had completely healed after a lot of rest and some physical therapy. She'd even made the trip out to New York to spend Christmas with us. I watched her approach for any signs she was favoring the leg she'd broken, but she looked perfectly fit. Better yet, Xander looked completely at peace.

It was something I'd been waiting a long time to see.

I'd known how hard it was for Xander to spend so much time in New York. But he'd done it without complaint.

The adoption had gone off without a hitch within three months of me filing the application, so in theory we could have moved to Colorado shortly after Christmas. But we'd been reluctant to have Lucky start at a new school in the middle of the year. I'd also needed the time to get the new foundation up and running so I could hand it off to the husband and wife team I'd selected to run it. I'd decided to make a clean break from the foundation, since I wanted my sole focus to be on Xander, Lucky and our new business. It had been tough to say goodbye to the kids, but Xander and I had a lot of plans to help kids from all over the country experience the world in a way they wouldn't have the opportunity to otherwise.

It had been much easier to cut ties with my parents. I'd given notice at my father's company, but he'd informed me via a memo that a month's notice wasn't necessary— I was welcome to leave that very day. He'd sent security guards along with the directive to "help me with my things." I hadn't seen him again after that. He hadn't gone through with his threat to encourage potential sponsors to steer clear of my foundation, but I'd suspected that'd had more to do with how that would have made him look rather than doing it for my benefit.

I'd gone to Greenwich to say my goodbyes to my mother a few weeks after I'd gotten back from Colorado, but she'd been predictably disinterested. She'd wished me well, but hadn't asked more than superficial questions about where I was going and what I was going to do. It had been hard to admit to Xander that I'd held out hope that maybe I'd still get my "moment" with her and my father, but it hadn't happened. I'd finally had to accept that some stories just didn't have happy endings.

But Xander and Lucky had given me plenty of "moments" to cherish in the past eight months. Hell, every time I woke up next to Xander, it felt like a moment.

"Hi honey, how are you?" Lolly said once they reached me. I automatically walked into her outstretched arms.

She was the best damn hugger in the world, and despite having seen her private bits more than I cared to admit, I would never get tired of feeling her slim arms hugging me so tight, I was certain she'd never let go.

"I'm good, how are you feeling?" I asked as I led her to one of the chairs we'd set up on the lodge's back patio.

"Great. Margaret and I won our tennis tournament last weekend, so I've been bragging about it to anyone who will listen."

I held up my hand for a high-five. "Way to go, champ. I didn't realize you were already back in top form."

"Well, Margaret has a big rack, so that may have helped. We were playing Hal and Bert. Like shooting fish in a barrel."

I should have known better than to take a sip of my drink when Lolly was around, but as it was, I nearly choked.

As she continued filling me in on the latest and greatest happenings at Bear Trodden Acres, I saw Jake walking across the lawn towards us. Xander had been chatting with one of the lodge employees, but when he saw Jake, he excused himself and went to greet his friend. There was a little bit of awkward tension between the two men at first, but when Jake held up a container of brown liquid, Xander smiled and slapped Jake on the back. I was glad that I didn't even feel a shimmer of jealousy as they walked across the patio to where all the food was laid out on tables. They snagged a couple of glasses, filled them up and began chatting.

Xander sent me a quick look, and I winked at him to let him know I was perfectly fine with him talking to the other man.

The smile that lit up his face had my insides warming. He was so different from the angry, bitter man I'd encountered when I'd stepped off that bus nine months ago. But he wasn't exactly the kid he'd once been, either. It was like he finally felt like he fit into his own skin.

The same way I finally fit into mine.

I liked to think it was something we'd brought out in each other.

Gary's arrival caused the few people milling around to burst into applause. After all, he was the reason for today's celebration. I watched as he, Xander, and Jake talked for a few moments. It wasn't until Gary headed my way that I realized he wasn't alone.

"Bennett," he said as he reached out his hand. I got up to shake it.

"Gary, you remember Xander's Aunt Lolly, right?"

"I do," he said. The pair exchanged small talk before Gary returned his attention to me. "Is Lucky around? I wanted to introduce him to my nephews."

"Yep, he's playing with Bear," I said as I motioned to where Lucky was throwing a ball for Bear in the yard. "Lucky!"

When he looked up, I motioned to him and he jogged over to us. As soon as he saw Lolly, he leaned down to hug her and she gave him an all-in hug like she had me. I loved how he took the time to ask her how she was feeling. He quickly straightened to say his hellos to Gary as well.

"Lucky, I don't think you've met my nephews, right?" Gary said.

Lucky shook his head. I could see a flash of insecurity go through him as his eyes fell on the boys who looked to be about his age. "No, sir."

"This is Tony," he said as he put his hand on the shoulder of one boy. "And this is Will."

"Hi," Lucky said as he nodded his head and shook both guys' hands.

"Hey, man," Tony said.

"Tony will be in your class this fall, and Will is a year behind you."

Lucky nodded awkwardly. Part of me wanted to wrap my arms around him and remind him he was perfect just the way he was, but I refrained. I knew there were some things I couldn't protect him from, and the awkwardness of meeting new kids his own age was just one of them.

"So Will and I are headed to Marmot Falls to meet up with some friends for a swim. You wanna come?" Tony asked.

Lucky's eyes shifted to me. "Um..."

I gave him a quick nod, more as encouragement than to grant him permission.

"Yeah, I'd love to," he said, his body relaxing marginally.

"Cool dog," Will said as he bent down to pet Bear. "You can bring him along."

"Yeah, sure," Lucky said. There were a few more moments of awkward tension as the three said their goodbyes to us and headed off. As Lucky passed Xander, they bumped fists in a way the two other boys wouldn't notice.

"Thanks for that," I said to Gary as I motioned in the direction the boys had disappeared in.

"No problem. I remember that age," he said. He sat down in the chair next to Lolly and continued chatting with the older woman while I went to mingle with the other guests.

Until I spied the one guest I'd been waiting all morning for.

"Hey," I said as I met Aiden halfway across the yard and walked right into his arms. I was surprised when he held me a little longer than expected.

"Hey, B," he said softly.

"You okay?" I asked.

"I am now," was all he said before pulling back. "You look good," he said. "Got you some this morning, did you?"

I punched him in the shoulder. "Pig," I said with a snort. "Come meet people, but behave yourself. A lot of them work for us now, and the last thing Xander and I need are sexual harassment claims," I joked.

"Fair enough," Aiden said. The answer was so *un-Aiden*.

"You sure you're okay?"

"Yeah, I'm good," he said, forcing a smile to his lips. "Where's the kid?"

"Off making friends," I said with a grin.

Aiden nodded. "Good for him. I was hoping to steal him away from you guys tonight for a movie and dinner… tacos preferably, if this hick town even knows what Mexican food is."

I chuckled. Aiden and Lucky had grown close over the past year, and I'd wondered which of them benefited more from the relationship. "I was actually going to ask you if you wouldn't mind hanging out with him tonight. Xander and I are going camping."

He raised his eyebrows at me. "Is that code for getting your slutty ass fucked up against a tree again?"

"Jesus, Aid." I shook my head at him. "But yeah, I fucking hope so. Are you going to take him or not?"

"Yeah, I'll take him… time to show him a few things."

"Don't even think about it," I warned.

"What?"

"Corrupting my kid. I bet you've already googled all the places in Denver that serve your two favorite things. Bourbon and go-go boys."

"Married life has turned you into a prude," Aiden said as he put his arm around my shoulders.

"Shut up," I said. "Stop saying that."

"What, the prude part?"

"No."

"Ah… the married part. Don't worry, B. It'll happen."

"I know," I said.

It wasn't the exact truth, but I didn't want Aiden to know that. After Xander had mentioned marriage the one time last summer when we'd been talking to Lucky about adopting him, he'd never brought it up again. After my adoption of Lucky had been finalized, I'd been certain we'd revisit the topic, but when Xander had asked about starting the process of him adopting Lucky without mentioning anything about marriage, I'd started to wonder if it was something he just wasn't ready for. I'd been hesitant to bring the subject up myself, since so many things in our lives had changed so quickly.

"*You* could ask *him*, you know," Aiden said.

"I will… I just want to let things settle down a bit first."

Aiden tugged me up against his side but didn't say anything else.

Which was exactly what I needed.

~

XANDER

It was after six o'clock by the time Bennett and I made it to my favorite spot on the trail. The Drummond Lake vista was laid out in front of us. The long trail cutting through the grass to the lake, the deep blue of the water sparkling in the late afternoon sun, the verdant greens of the trees stacked on the hills beyond the lake, and the giant snowy peaks of Woodland Rise shooting skyward in the distance.

This was the spot where we'd stood that first full day of the trip the summer before. The spot where I'd wanted to sneak my hand into his and just soak in the moment with him— my favorite mountains with my favorite person. It was as magical as I'd hoped it would be.

Bennett sighed as he took in the view. "So gorgeous," he murmured.

I studied him. "Mm-hm. Absolutely stunning."

I slipped off my pack and then reached around him to unbuckle his waist belt before pulling his pack off. He turned to look at me with furrowed brows.

"What are we doing?"

"Just taking a moment. This is my favorite spot," I explained with a smile.

"Same here. I love it. So glad you brought me back here." He turned to take in the view again and I leaned in to peck his cheek.

"I'm glad you like it as much as I do."

I slipped my hand into his and we stood side by side looking at the wonder laid out before us. After a moment, I stepped around to face him and dropped to one knee.

Bennett's eyes widened at the move and I smiled up at him, trying desperately to keep my eyes dry long enough to get the words out.

"Benny, I have loved you for twenty-five years. Not a day has passed that I haven't known deep down in the center of my soul that you were the best thing that ever happened to me. When I'm with you, I feel whole. Happy, and free, and loved beyond measure."

Bennett's free hand came up to his mouth, and the hand I was holding tightened in mine before I continued.

"When I stood on this spot a year ago, all pissed off and stubborn about you showing up, I didn't realize that my anger was really a stark, all-consuming fear. I was terrified about so many things— me beginning to need you again, you rejecting me again, hell, even the two of us no longer having that special connection.

"What I didn't realize then is that none of those things were even possible. I always needed you. Me needing you couldn't start again because it never stopped. You couldn't reject me again when you never really rejected me in the first place. And it's not possible for the two of us, with what we have and what we've shared, to lose our special connection."

I reached into my pocket for the ring I'd been carrying for a month, just waiting for the perfect time to give it to him.

"I love you so much, Benny. More than these mountains— more than the sun in the sky and the very air around us. I can't imagine my life without you in it."

I took a deep breath. "Bennett Crawford, will you do me the honor of becoming my husband and making all of my dreams come true?"

A sob escaped him as he nodded and collapsed into me, wrapping his arms around my neck and kissing me on the lips. My mouth reveled in the feel of Bennett's lips and tongue against mine, and we kissed for several moments before pulling away and locking eyes.

"That's a yes?" I said with what was surely a stupid grin on my face.

"Of course that's a yes," he said, wiping tears off his face with the heel of his palm. His other arm stayed tight around the back of my neck. "I love you so much, Xander. I never want to be apart from you again as long as I live."

"Then will you wear this ring so Aiden will stop fucking flirting with you?" I held up the band on the tip of my index finger and grinned at him.

Bennett barked out a laugh and took the ring, sliding it reverently onto his finger and staring at it with his own goofy grin on his face.

"Like a little old ring will stop Aiden from flirting with anything that moves," he muttered.

I reached out to tilt his chin up so I could look at his beautiful, happy face before breaking into the Platters song I hadn't been able to get off my mind since buying the ring.

*"With this ring, I promise I'll always love you..."*

"Oh god," Bennett groaned. "Two can play at that game, you know."

"Bring it, sweet cheeks," I said. *"Hit me with your best shot,"* I sang.

*"If you liked it then you shoulda put a ring on it..."* he crooned as we grabbed our packs.

"Dude, I did," I said with a fake pout. "And now I'm *going to the chapel and I'm gonna get maaaarried..."*

Bennett rolled his eyes and grabbed my hand. "Is it too late to change my mind about the marrying thing?"

"Should I say I'm sorry? Because I'm not, really."

"Nah, it's *too late to apologize. It's tooo laaaate."*

"Fuck, okay." I pulled our joined hands up to brush a kiss on the back of his. "Let's stop before you start singing MmmBop."

"Motherfucker. I can't believe you just did that. The joke's on you, asshole. I'm going to be singing MmmBop for a week."

"Serves you right. My job here is done," I said as I squeezed his hand, and we moved forward on the trail.

Together.

The End

~

*Make sure to check out the next page to get a sneak peek of Aiden's story!*

# SNEAK PEEK

## AIDEN

*"Aiden!"*

*I opened my mouth to tell him I was coming, but a crashing wave sent me under the water and I choked as seawater attempted to fill my lungs. Muscles burning, I dove under the wave and fought the current that threatened to return me to shore.*

*"Aiden!" was the first thing I heard the second my head cleared the water. I sucked in a breath and jerked my head in every direction, hoping against hope I could somehow see better in the darkness. It was only by some miracle that I saw the outline of flailing arms in between swells.*

*"I'm coming!" I managed to cry out. "Don't fight the current!"*

*Terror infused my blood, giving me more strength, and I plowed through the water. As another wave tumbled down on me, I dove fast and deep, but when I came up, it wasn't the open sea I was in anymore. And the darkness of night had given way to daylight.*

*"Aiden, help!"*

*I knew that voice.*

*"Bennett?" I yelled in confusion as I whipped my head around to find my best friend. I flailed as I fought against the raging river I was caught in. Muddy water churned and slapped me in the face as I tried to maintain my equilibrium. "Bennett, where are you?!" I shouted.*

God, please let him be on shore. I can't lose him too.

*"Aiden," Bennett called, but his voice was much softer... weaker. I shouldn't have been able to hear it, considering how loud the water was. But it was like Bennett was right next me.*

*Only he wasn't.*

*"I'm coming," I told him, though I knew it wasn't true.*

*I couldn't reach him if I couldn't fucking find him!*

*"I'm sorry, Aiden."*

*"NO!" I screamed at the top of my lungs. Because I knew what those words meant. I'd been hearing them for seventeen fucking years. "You hang on!" I demanded.*

*I would find him. I would save him this time.*

*Energy surged through my blood, and I managed to reach out and grab a branch from a stationary log along the riverbank. I dragged myself up enough to keep from going under and frantically searched for Bennett.*

*And then I saw him. Just a few dozen feet ahead of me. His dark hair was bobbing in the water, disappearing beneath it occasionally as he fought the current.*

*"Bennett, I'm here!" I shouted. I held onto the branch and drifted as far out into the current as I could without letting go. "Grab my hand!"*

*But he floated right past me, his hand just a few feet from my outstretched one. Time slowed down as his green eyes met mine briefly and I saw the words he couldn't say.*

*"NO!" I screamed as I let go of the branch and made a lunge for him. "Stay with me, Bennett!" I begged as a sob caught in my throat. Frustration tore through me as my fingers brushed his, but he didn't try to grab onto them. His blank eyes held mine for a moment before the water took him under.*

*I raged at him, the water, the world, and then surged forward with every last bit of energy I had left. The water clawed at me, but I fought it. A voice in my head told me to just let go... that it would be easier if I did. That there'd be no pain, only peace.*

*I knew that voice.*

*Better than I knew my own.*

*And god, I wanted to go to it. I wanted to feel those arms wrap me in warmth and welcome me home.*

*"No," I whispered. "Bennett... need to save Bennett."*

*I let out one final scream and pushed forward with everything I had. My fingers closed around something cold and firm beneath the water, and I pulled as hard as I could. I fought the water for several long seconds before it gave up its hold on Bennett and his body hit mine. Wrapping my arms around him, I quickly turned him over, mindless of the fact that we were still caught in the river's unforgiving current.*

*It didn't matter. We were together. I'd gotten to him in time. Everything would be okay now.*

*But when I turned his motionless body over, it wasn't Bennett's face I saw.*

*It was my own.*

I jolted awake as I gasped for air, almost as if my lungs really were waterlogged. But instead of being trapped in a raging, swirling river somewhere in the heart of Colorado, I was sitting in my own bed in my posh apartment in Manhattan. My sheets were soaking wet, and I realized it was because I was sweating like crazy. My breath was still coming in ragged spurts as I grabbed my phone off my nightstand. I hit the speed dial button and put the phone to my ear. My fingers were shaking so badly I could barely hang onto the phone.

It was a dream, I reminded myself.

It was just a fucking dream.

The phone rang over and over again, and every second that passed sent my fear higher and higher.

"Pick up," I demanded. "Pick up!"

Just when I was certain it was going to go to voicemail, I heard a sleepy voice say, "Hello?"

"Bennett?" I whispered, even as the relief began to flood my system all at once.

"Aid?" Bennett said. There was a shuffling sound, and I heard another voice in the background.

Xander... Bennett's boyfriend. "It's Aiden," Bennett said. To me, my friend groused, "Dude, it's the middle of the night."

I glanced at the clock and saw that it was just after three in the morning. Fuck, I hadn't even thought about what time it was. All I'd cared about was knowing my friend was okay... that it really had been a fucked-up dream.

"What's wrong?" Bennett asked. "Are you okay?"

"Uh, yeah," I said as I scrambled to think of something to explain the call. "I... I..."

"Jesus, Aid, tell me you're not drunk dialing me again. Who's the guy?"

"No one," I quickly said. "Just that bouncer from *Club Red*," I lied. "He *is* a screamer like we thought," I added.

I could practically see Bennett rolling his eyes at me. "You think you can save the *Who Did Aiden Fuck Last Night* show for another time?"

My chest felt tight as I nodded and murmured, "You bet. Tell Ranger Rick to fuck you back into oblivion."

"Ass," Bennett muttered, but I heard the humor in his voice.

"Night, Bennett."

"Hey, Aid?"

"Yeah?"

"You sure you're okay?"

I felt the backs of my eyes stinging, but I managed to stem the tears. Tears were for the weak. "My ears are still ringing but the screamer can suck cock-"

Bennett hung up on me before I could finish my sentence. My phone buzzed a second later with a text.

*Ass. Night. Talk to you tomorrow.*

I smiled and put the phone down before climbing out of bed. I knew there was no way I was going to be able to get back to sleep, so I took a shower and changed into a pair of sweats and a T-shirt. I grabbed my running shoes, phone, and earbuds and left the building, nodding at my doorman as I went. I spent the next two hours running through Central Park.

Once I got back to my apartment, I worked out for another hour in the building's gym, and only then felt settled enough to try to get on with my day. I took my time showering and getting dressed before going to my computer to pull up the file on the potential client I was meeting with this morning. The guy was an up-and-coming star quarterback for the New York Jets, and signing him would be a coup for the PR firm I ran with my younger brother, Chase. While we were doing relatively well, considering our business was technically still in its infancy, signing a client like Bomber Flynn would put us in a whole new stratosphere, and the potential new business we could garner would be astronomical.

I spent the next hour studying the detailed file I'd put together on the man, and then grabbed my laptop and phone and jammed them into my bag. It took about thirty minutes to fight the morning rush hour traffic and get to my favorite coffee shop. The little specialty cafe was out of my way when it came to getting to my office, but it was worth the extra twenty minutes I had to build into my schedule.

The place was a zoo when I arrived, but that wasn't unusual. As I entered the door, a man bumped my shoulder coming out. He mumbled a soft apology, but before I could respond, he was hurrying down the sidewalk, and all I saw was a head of dark hair and hunched frame as he dug his hands in his pockets.

Once inside the small space, I got in line and waited until I'd caught the eye of the regular barista working the espresso machine. She sent me a bright smile and nodded her head. Although I couldn't cut the line, I knew Emily would have my drink waiting at the register by the time I got up there. I scanned the shop briefly as I began searching my bag for my phone. My eyes fell on one of the few empty tables near the line. A red leather journal was sitting on one of them. As the line slowly moved forward, I waited for the owner to show up to claim it, but when no one did, I reached for it as I passed the table, intending to hand it over to the cashier.

My eyes skimmed over the well-worn journal and caught on the raised initials in the lower right-hand corner.

A.V.

My initials.

The oddity intrigued me and I opened the journal up to skim it for a full name. There was nothing in the front cover so I began flipping to the back cover, but stopped when my eyes caught on a rough sketch. A chill went through my body at the sight of the drawing.

It was of the ocean.

A violent, turbulent ocean with huge waves. I could make out what looked like a small figure drawn into the base of one of the waves. Was it… was it a person, struggling to keep their head above water?

No, it couldn't be. It was probably just how the artist had shaded the water.

*Aiden... I'm sorry.*

My nightmare, which I'd worked so hard all morning to forget, came back with a vengeance. My eyes fell to the words written just below the drawing.

*Ocean tears slide down my face,*
*Instead of my own*
*Which are long gone-*
*Dried up by the sheer number of times*
*I've taken this dive.*
*The truth:*
*It isn't a dive.*
*It never was.*
*It is a push, a shove.*
*A scrambling for purchase.*
*A betrayal.*
*Over and over again,*
*Into the cold bitter depths*
*I plunge.*
*How I forget-*
*I go to the shore in the sunshine.*
*Happy, easy, free.*
*Having forgotten the truth.*
*That when my toes reach the edge -*
*Clouds will hover.*
*Harsh wind will sting.*
*He will bite.*
*Black depths.*

*The fear returns-*
*Reminding me.*

The haunting words rattled me to the core and before I even realized what I was doing, I turned the page and read another entry. My throat closed up as I read about pain and fear that was all too familiar. The world around me ceased to exist as I lost myself in that page, and then the next.

"Morning, Mr. Vale."

I glanced up at the sound of the cashier's perky voice and realized I'd made it to the front of the line without even knowing it. "Morning, Jenny," I said with a nod. I pulled my wallet from my pocket and grabbed some cash. Having the journal in my hand made it awkward, and I was reminded that I needed to turn it over to the smiling young woman so it could be returned to the rightful owner when he or she came back for it. But even as I handed the cash over, I couldn't make myself give her the journal too.

I didn't know why.

Except I did… and I wasn't proud of the reason.

"Have a nice day," Jenny preened as she handed me my drink and change. I dropped the change into the tip jar and tried to force myself one last time to hand the journal over. But then my eyes fell on the initials on the cover.

And I stepped away from the counter.

I just needed a little more time with the thing. I'd return it tomorrow, and the owner would never know I'd read it. So where was the harm?

I wanted to snort at the spin I'd put on the whole thing. I basically lied for a living, so it was pretty pathetic that I'd decided to take work home with me and start lying to myself.

But that didn't stop me from leaving the coffee shop, journal in hand.

One more day.

I just needed one more day to feel that connection with the anonymous soul who'd somehow been able to say the things I'd never had the courage to admit… not even to myself.

# AFTERWORD

Dear Reader,

We hope you enjoyed Xander and Bennett's story! Book 2 in our new series will feature Aiden's story.

As independent authors, we are always grateful for feedback so if you have the time and desire, please leave a review, good or bad, so we can continue to find out what our readers like and don't like. You can also send us feedback via email at skllbooks@gmail.com

# ABOUT LUCY LENNOX

To sign up for Lucy's newsletter, please visit www.LucyLennox.com.

To join Lucy's Fan Group, Lucy's Lair, on Facebook, visit https://www.facebook.com/groups/2017155708550087/

*Connect with me:*
www.lucylennox.com
lucy@lucylennox.com

# ABOUT SLOANE KENNEDY

Join my Facebook Fan group: Sloane's Secret Sinners
https://www.facebook.com/groups/1760064160913779/

*Connect with me:*
www.sloanekennedy.com
sloane@sloanekennedy.com

# ALSO BY LUCY LENNOX

## The Made Marian Series

*(Note: All Made Marian novels are available on Amazon and in Kindle Unlimited and are male/male romances.)*

Borrowing Blue

Taming Teddy

Jumping Jude

Grounding Griffin

Moving Maverick

Delivering Dante

## The Made Marian Shorts

*(Note: All Made Marian short stories are available for free at www.LucyLennox.com)*

Brad

Keller

# ALSO BY SLOANE KENNEDY

*(Note: Not all titles will be available on all retail sites)*

**The Escort Series**

Gabriel's Rule (M/F)

Shane's Fall (M/F)

Logan's Need (M/M)

**Barretti Security Series**

Loving Vin (M/F)

Redeeming Rafe (M/M)

Saving Ren (M/M/M)

Freeing Zane (M/M)

**Finding Series**

Finding Home (M/M/M)

Finding Trust (M/M)

Finding Peace (M/M)

Finding Forgiveness (M/M)

Finding Hope (M/M/M)

**The Protectors**

Absolution (M/M/M)

Salvation (M/M)

Retribution (M/M)

Forsaken (M/M)

Vengeance (M/M/M)

A Protectors Family Christmas

Atonement (M/M)

Revelation (M/M)

Redemption (M/M)

**Non-Series**

Letting Go (M/F)

Printed in Great Britain
by Amazon

35313919R00175